Black Thursday
and Other Lost Australian Bushfire Stories

Edited and introduced by Fiannuala Morgan

Obiter Publishing

Published by Obiter Publishing
PO Box 5133
Braddon ACT 2612
info@obiterpublishing.com.au
www.obiterpublishing.com.au

 A catalogue record for this book is available from the National Library of Australia

ISBN: 978-0-6451063-1-2

Cover design by Karen Downing

Design by Karen Downing

Printed by Ingram Spark

Title page image 'Black Thursday, February, 1881' by F.A. Sleap, engraver, 1888, State Library of Victoria

'To Be Continued ...'

Series editor Katherine Bode

The 'To Be Continued ...' series publishes fiction discovered by literary scholar Katherine Bode and bibliographer Carol Hetherington. They used new digital methods to search the National Library of Australia's *Trove* database to uncover over 21,000 stories published in Australian newspapers between 1828 and 1914. Although fiction is a rarity in newspapers today, prior to World War One Australian newspapers routinely published fictional works, and in the nineteenth century, were the main source of fiction for colonial readers. Some of the stories discovered in this project are short, amounting to only one or two columns on a newspaper page; some are lengthy novels, published over multiple newspaper editions.

Fiction in Australian newspapers came from around the world: from Australia, Britain and America as well as France, Germany, New Zealand, Russia, and beyond. All of the titles discovered – with an interface for readers to interact with *Trove* to discover new stories and correct the newspaper text – are available at http://cdhrdatasys.anu.edu.au/tobecontinued.

The 'To Be Continued ...' series focuses on Australian fiction not previously published beyond the original newspaper pages. It thus uncovers lost pieces of the nation's literary heritage enabling new understandings of the way Australian literature developed and how early Australians understood themselves and their world.

Contents

Introduction

An English Tale for an Emergent Nation: William Howitt's
'Black Thursday' and the Narrativisation of Bushfire i

Lost Australian Bushfire Stories

Black Thursday by William Howitt 1

My Wedding Day: A South Australian Story by Rita 23

How Jack Litton Lost His Christmas Dinner,
and How He Found It by J.A.E. 41

The Other Man by Mary Gaunt 65

'Ria. A West Australian Story by Selburnrigg 107

Through Fire and Water by Wilga 167

The False And The True by J.M. Barr 177

One Night at Gorringe by A.M. 189

Kitty Dunolly, My Schoolmate:
A Victorian Sketch by G.E.C. 201

Rover. A South Australian Story by Sylvia 221

Publisher's note

'Black Thursday' appeared in the *Illawarra Mercury* in 1856; 'My Wedding Day. A South Australian Story' appeared in the *Adelaide Observer* in 1890; 'How Jack Litton Lost His Christmas Dinner, and How He Found It' appeared in the *Bairnsdale Advertiser* in 1890; 'The Other Man' appeared in the *Argus* in 1894 (chapters 17–20 published in this collection); ''Ria. A West Australian Story' appeared in the *Australasian* in 1879; 'Through Fire and Water' appeared in *Australian Town and Country Journal* in 1887; 'The False and the True' appeared in the *Independent* in 1891; 'One Night at Gorringe' appeared in the *Australasian* in 1889; 'Kitty Dunolly, My Schoolmate: A Victorian Sketch' appeared in the *Burra Record* in 1883; and 'Rover. A South Australian Story' appeared in the *Adelaide Observer* in 1893. No changes have been made to the original formatting apart from obvious typographical errors.

An important note on the text

Readers are advised that some stories in this collection contain offensive late nineteenth-century stereotypes, prejudices and words.

An English Tale for an Emergent Nation: William Howitt's 'Black Thursday' and the Narrativisation of Bushfire

Fiannuala Morgan

'Perhaps no such devastation ever fell on any nation and
Black Thursday is an indelible memory in Victoria.' –
Black Thursday by William Howitt

Towards the end of 2019 and across the beginning of 2020, the Australian bushfires now commonly known as the 'Black Summer', wreaked destruction across south-eastern Australia. Three billion animals were killed, 1.8 million hectares destroyed, and hundreds of deaths resulted directly and indirectly from direct contact with the flames and later smoke inhalation. The Black Summer was also an experience of fires mediatised. Those not directly affected, as much as those who were, remained glued to their screens watching as flames crowned trees, engulfed fire trucks, and men, women and children crowded onto beaches and into boats to escape the conflagration. For European colonists in the nineteenth century, bushfires were a strange, but by no means uncommon phenomenon. Rather, they had become part of life in the Antipodes and had also become highly mediatised. Journalistic and, increasingly, fictional accounts, reported the experience of large-scale bushfires not only for those in the colonies but also those back home in England and elsewhere. The focus of this introduction concerns William Howitt's short story 'Black Thursday', first published in 1856, a response to the fire disaster of the same name that took place five years prior. It is through journalistic accounts of Black Thursday that we can identify the emergence and conceptual coherence of the phenomena of bushfire, and it is through early narrativisations of this event that we see the emergence of a literary tradition that moved beyond descriptive accounts to present the phenomenon with associated specific cultural attitudes and beliefs.

Black Thursday on 6 February 1851 was perhaps the first great fire disaster in settler Australian history. Although no official records exist, it is estimated that almost a quarter of the Victorian colony was burned and a million sheep and thousands of cattle lost.[1] Bushfires in summer were an expected element of settler life but the magnitude of Black Thursday exceeded anything colonists had previously experienced. Although there were relatively few reported fatalities, the economic impact was profound. Uninsured, many settlers faced financial ruin and were driven back to the cities. Only six days after Black Thursday, however, gold was discovered in New South Wales, thereby setting in motion a mass emigration to Australia. Five months after Black Thursday, and only two weeks after Victoria had been declared an independent colony, gold was then discovered east of Melbourne on the Yarra River.[2] This timing meant that Black Thursday played a pivotal role in shaping a transformed colony, psychically and physically. The destruction wreaked by Black Thursday ultimately benefited the development of the new colony, as previously impassable land was now opened to pastoralist and prospector alike. For the remainder of the century the event became a reference point for all subsequent fire disasters. It was, William Howitt wrote in his short story 'Black Thursday' (1856), an 'indelible memory in Victoria'.

If bushfires of this magnitude were unprecedented for early colonists, they were certainly novel phenomena for a British public. First reported in British newspapers four months after the disaster, the newspaper

---

[1] Stephen J Pyne, *Burning Bush* (New York: Henry Holt and Company, 1991), 222; Paul Collins, *Burn: The Epic Story of Bushfire in Australia* (Brunswick, Australia: Scribe, 2009), 74.
[2] Tom Griffiths, *Forests of Ash: An Environmental History* (Cambridge: Cambridge University Press, 2001), 64.

article 'Great bushfire in Australia' offers an introductory definition of this category of disaster: 'In a communication to the editor of the *Edinburgh Courant* we find the following fearful account of devastations caused in the Port Philip district of Australia, by what in colonial parlance, are called "Bushfires".'[3] Another account highlighted the natural and locational context in which the phenomenon occurred, reporting, for example, that, 'a great deal of distress has been caused by a conflagration of the grass and trees in the 'bush' or wilderness of…Australia'.[4] In both cases, the use of inverted commas reflects both the semantic and conceptual novelty of the language, while the remainder of the articles offer vivid descriptions of the disaster. Although this was not the first time the terminology of bushfires had appeared in the British press, earlier instances were either more likely to appear in descriptive accounts of colonial life written for prospective emigrants, or to make use of the more general terminology of 'fire in the bush' (1837).[5] It is within the context of Black Thursday, however, that the term moves from the abstract to the definite, marking its emergence as a distinct feature in the reporting of the colonial experience.

In the years succeeding Black Thursday, bushfires also began to take on a greater narrative role in literature set in Australia. Two of the earliest narrativisations of bushfire are Ellen Clacey's vignette 'The Bushfire' (1854), and William Howitt's short story 'Black Thursday' (1856) which directly respond to the events of that day. Even Charles Harpur's poem 'The Bushfire,' although not written as an account of Black Thursday, was published in Australian newspapers just one month after the disaster, thereby, producing for readers an equivalence between poem and event.[6]

---

[3] 'Great bushfire in Australia', *Belfast News-Letter*, 30 June 1851.

[4] 'Destructive fire in the Australian bush,' *North Devon Journal*, 10 July 1851.

[5] 'Distress in Paisley', *Morning Post*, 21 June 1837.

[6] 'Original poetry', *The People's Advocate and New South Wales Vindicator*, 15 March 1851.

More generally, Black Thursday became a recurrent motif in nine-teenth and early twentieth-century serials. In stories of the gold rush, for example, the event acts as a catalyst that drives characters to the diggings. In 'The Mystery of Moore Farm' (1886), when Augustus Skelton's settler inheritance disappears in flames, this adverse event is represented as an op-portunity for reinvention as he takes on the identity of an emigrant digger. In other serials, the event serves to establish the masculine credentials of the bushman and the 'native Australian'. 'Arthur Landon' (1887) by Angus McLean, begins amid the disaster, with Arthur heroically rescuing a lost girl who later goes on to become a love interest when re-acquainted many years later. In 'One Eyed Dick' (1891) a character's proclamation that he witnessed the events of that day, establishes his authority as a 'native Aus-tralian' and a reliable source of bush lore. The event does not confer heroic status on men alone, for example, 'Through Fire and Water' (1887) tells the story of Starbeam, a beloved horse who delivers young lovers 'through the hot flames of a fierce bushfire' and whose hoofs subsequently assume pride of place above the hearth of their home in their English mansion.

Other narratives, particularly those generated decades after the event, focus more fully on the fires' impact on the natural environment: these are more nostalgic in tone and the catastrophe is referenced in relation to the degradation and transformation of the landscape. 'A Tale of Black Thursday' (1894) by Gordon Gerald is a romance that takes place amid the disaster. Much of the narrative, however, is taken up with imagery of the landscape as it existed prior to both disaster and settler expansion, as though they are one and the same. In the wake of the fire it is acknowl-edged that 'the face of the country was completely changed'. 'The Mount Macedon Mystery' (1891) by Ivan Dexter takes place in the same land-scape. Not only is Black Thursday the force that 'ravaged the celebrated forest', but its destruction is also discussed as providing ease of passage for the coming waves of free selectors as they journeyed further inland.

A Recurring Tale

The recurrence of Black Thursday in literature over time suggests its enduring presence in cultural memory. Nevertheless, the event received scant attention in literature across the 1860s and 1870s. It re-emerged as a popular theme decades later with the majority of narrative mentions of the event occurring towards the end of the 1880s and across the 1890s. Accordingly, the event is incorporated into these later narratives with varying degrees of contextual information. For example, in 'The Mystery of Moore Farm' (1886), Black Thursday is a literal historical footnote, and the chapter concludes with the accompanying addendum 'this terrible fire took place, as described on 6th February 1851'. Importantly, earlier narratives of the disaster published contemporaneously also begin to recirculate at this time. Howitt's 'Black Thursday' was republished in full in the *Charleville Times* (Brisbane) in 1896, and appears verbatim incorporated into the adventure serial 'Whose Crime' by Dare Demas in 1894.

'Black Thursday', the narrative, is unusual in its enduring cultural relevance as it re-emerged forty years from its original publication to meld seamlessly into the literary tradition of the 1890s. Accordingly, it raises its own questions about the half-life of certain cultural narratives, such as, under what conditions do they emerge? But also, under what conditions do they re-emerge and endure? For today's reader, 'Black Thursday' seemingly displays many of the characteristics routinely associated with cultural narratives of bushfires: heroism in the moment and community spirit in the aftermath, the successful defence of the settler home and the dissolution of class tension and division in the face of disaster. And while the narrative is ultimately a tale of settler endurance and triumph, it also features an ominous and haunting depiction of the Australian landscape, anticipating in part aspects of the 'bush tradition' where authors such as

Rolf Boldrewood, Henry Lawson and Steele Rudd, depicted the bush-man as a heroic type perpetually engaged in an antagonistic relationship with the bush.

'Black Thursday' first appeared in Charles Dickens' weekly family journal *Household Words* in May 1856 before being republished in Australian newspapers later that year. It is the story of young squatter Robert Patterson, who in the process of herding his cattle through bush in south western Victoria finds himself caught in the inferno of Black Thursday. The narrative sees Robert abandon his livestock in the face of the conflagration as he desperately returns to the homestead to check on the wellbeing of his crippled mother. Anticipating the fire season, Patterson has prudently cleared a firebreak around the perimeter of the property. When he reaches home he not only finds the property accordingly undamaged, but sees it has become a place of refuge and congregation for less fortunate others whose properties have not been spared. Assured that both property and family are safe Patterson sets forth to search for missing neighbours, siblings George and Ellen Maxwell. After saving another family from a burning hut Robert finds Ellen, who advises that although their property is safe her brother George is still missing, and they join forces to continue the search. It is revealed that Robert and Ellen were previously lovers but that some misunderstanding has driven the families apart. After they find a wounded George and take him to the Patterson's homestead to recover, the source of the misunderstanding is revealed. Robert has been the victim of salacious gossip in which he is recounted to have referred to Ellen's recently deceased father as a 'lag,' a derogatory term for convicts. The narrative here makes a strong case for the power of the colonial setting in rehabilitating character and in redressing the wrongs of the Old World, when it says that the father's ex-convict status had no bearing on his character, as 'there was not a man in the penal settlement, who did not honour his political integrity and foresight and who did not reverence his character.' Upon realisation of the misunderstanding the lovers are re-united and their engagement renewed.

The Narrativisation of Fire

Although bushfires had previously appeared in literature, these were mostly superficial accounts of local colour produced for an international audience.[7] Mary Theresa Vidal's *The Cambramatta Store* (1850) is perhaps the first novel to feature a bushfire as a significant narrative event.[8] Despite some vivid imagery of the fire itself, the fact that a character opts to return home and eat supper during the disaster reads only as a thoroughly sanitised understanding of bushfires. It is only in the wake of Black Thursday that literary depictions of bushfire take on more substance. Ellen Clacey's short story 'A Bushfire,' published in her collection *Lights and Shadows of Australian Life* (1854), employs the disaster of Black Thursday as a means of unifying two lovers from distinct class backgrounds, thereby instantiating a literary trope of fire as a social leveller.[9] Howitt's subsequent narrative 'Black Thursday', follows a similar trajectory. However, in addition to a narrative of the dissolution of class division and the unification of estranged lovers, Howitt also re-frames the fire as an event to animate the admirable and virtuous qualities of the young squatter Robert Patterson as he successfully navigates the difficulties of bush-life: defending the homestead, providing refuge for the community and rescuing others. In so doing, 'Black Thursday', is to my knowledge the earliest substantial narrativisation of bushfire.

---

[7] Charles David Harrington, *Landscape in Australian Fiction: The Rendering of a Human Environment* (Bloomington: Indiana University, 1970), 64.

[8] Grace Moore, 'Then came the high unpromising forests, and miles of loneliness': Louisa Atkinson's recasting of the Australian landscape', in Worlding the South: Nineteenth-century *Literary Culture and the Southern Settler Colonies*, ed. Sarah Comyn and Porscha Fermanis (Manchester: Manchester University Press, 2021), 196–214.

[9] Grace Moore, 'Fires, literature, politics and mateship in the bush', *Agora* 48, no. 4 (2013): 53–58.

In order to present this vivid and protracted account of the disaster, Howitt revisits and adapts his earlier journalistic reporting. Howitt reported extensively on the events of Black Thursday for *Cassell's Illustrated Family Paper* (1854) drawing together multiple accounts from different newspapers, to present a sensational report of unprecedented destruction: 'In one day, a whole country of 300 miles in extent, and at least 150 in breadth, was reduced to a desert. It was one blackened and burning waste'. The subsequent fictionalised 'Black Thursday' draws heavily on these journalistic accounts to produce an interesting tension in which this narrative of human survival, love, heroism and triumph is tempered by descriptive elements, particularly in treatments of landscape that border on the gothic. The opening passage for Howitt's tale is drawn directly from his earlier journalistic work, in which the reader is introduced to the pre-disaster landscape surrounding Apollo Bay, 'a vast region of primeval nature … in which the tall white stems of the gum-tees stand thickly side by side like so many hoary columns; and, here and there amongst them descend dark ravines while piles of rocks on the heights, alternate with projecting spars of the mountains and present their solitary masses to the ocean ...' This description only prefigures its imminent destruction, and the narrative quickly moves from the panoramic into the claustrophobic 'solemn, gloomy and soundless woods', where we are introduced to Robert Patterson just prior to the onslaught of the conflagration.

Reading Bushfire Narratives

Literary accounts of bushfire can be read as functional, as they present narratives that consolidate and validate the colonial project by demonstrating settler mastery over the landscape. An out of control fire undermines the legitimacy of the colony by revealing the precocity of settler culture, therefore, narrative became a means of focusing the anxieties of settler Australians and rendering the landscape tractable.[10] Alternatively, these narratives can be read as reflections of cultural attitudes and beliefs. For example, fire historian Paul Collins suggests that Australian identity itself was forged by flames as 'fighting fire became a kind of ritual in which Australian manhood was formed and the ethos of mateship developed in struggle with nature'. Literature then consolidated this understanding in the writings of the nineteenth-century mateship school, much publicised by the *Bulletin,* in which bushfire became the enemy that broke down the 'deadly feud of class, and creed and race; so that selectors, squatters and bush-workers eventually came together to confront the alien threat of nature'.[11] In both instances, bushfire narratives are routinely associated with expressions of national identity.

It can be tempting, therefore, to read 'Black Thursday' as an originary narrative concerning the mythology of bushfires and providing insight into historical settler attitudes and beliefs: not only is it one of the first bushfire narratives, it is also the mythologisation of a historically transformative fire. As argued by Grace Moore, stories such as 'Black Thursday' have become part of the mythology of survival and renewal that continues to sustain Australian country-dwellers to this day.[12] As pointed out by Tanya Dalziell, however, 'fiction … with its tropes and narrative techniques, has a part in determining how the past is conditional and partially known, remembered, distributed and forgotten'.[13] The dominant understanding that Australian national values and beliefs can be found in the so called bush realism of the 1890s, is but one particular his-

---

[10] Grace Moore, 'Home was where the hearth is: Fire, destruction, and displacement in nineteenth-century settler narratives', *Antipodes* 29, no. 1 (2015).

[11] Collins, *Burn: The Epic Story of Bushfire in Australia*, 77, 78.

[12] Grace Moore, 'Surviving Black Thursday: The great bushfire of 1851', in *Victorian Settler Narratives: Emigrants, Cosmopolitans and Returnees in Nineteenth-century Literature*, ed. T.S. Wagner (Abindgon, UK: Routledge, 2016), 129–140.

[13] Tanya Dalziell, 'No place for a book? Fiction in Australia to 1890, in *The Cambridge History of Australian Literature*, ed. Peter Pierce (Cambridge: Cambridge University Press, 2009), 93–117.

toricisation of Australian literary culture advanced in the 1950s. Rather than an interpretation that reads 'Black Thursday' as reflective of national character forged in relation to the land, or as a reimagining of destruction that reinforces the viability of emigration and settler colonial life, consideration of the narrative's original publication context illuminates the complex entanglement of colonial and seemingly proto-nationalistic narratives with mid-century English values and beliefs.

Mediating Bushfire

'Black Thursday' is firmly embedded in the worldview particular to Dickens' *Household Words* (1850–1859), in which Australia is routinely presented as the perceived remedy to England's social distress. Dickens founded the journal with a particular project in mind: to transcend social boundaries with the purpose that each edition, 'amuse, teach, improve and arouse delight'.

Throughout the 1830s and 1840s Dickens depicted Australia as a depository for convicts and overwhelmingly as a place of vice, exile and despair. His attitude shifted, however, around the late 1840s and 1850s. The increased force of industrial labour, coupled with bourgeois apprehension over the poor, the unemployed, and dissident workers combined to inspire – among novelists as well as reformers – a popular advocacy of emigration as an acceptable panacea for social ills.[14] For Dickens, Australia was envisaged as a redemptive space, a position reflected in his establishment of a hostel for fallen women that provided passage to Australia, thereby offering the opportunity for social rehabilitation through the prospect of marriage. Emigration advocate Samuel Sidney was an early contributor on the subject of Australia in *Household Words*, and his writing presented an idealised overview of the social dynamics of the new col-

---

[14] Leon Litvak, 'Dickens, Australia and Magwitch: Part I – The colonial context', *Dickensian* 95, no. 447 (1999): 24.

ony. For example, 'An Australian Ploughman's Story' (1850) describes the passage of the protagonist from convict to squatter, suggesting that industriousness is rewarded with social elevation. A similar sentiment is expressed in 'Three Colonial Epochs' (1850), where good behaviour, liberty and prosperity are depicted as natural progressions for the appropriately reformed convict. Howitt's narratives may be usefully read in conversation with Sidney's work. Where Sidney establishes the foundation for the social dimensions and hierarchy of Australian life, Howitt animates these social distinctions and codes in his more imaginative accounts of the colonist's engagement with the natural world. This is particularly evident in his early *Household Word* contributions, 'New Settler Old Settler' (1856), 'The Land Shark' (1856), as well as 'Black Thursday' (1856).

Howitt's sketches of Australian life were favourably received in Australia. In Frederick Sinnett's article 'Fiction Fields of Australia' (1856), the earliest example of Australian literary criticism,[15] Sinnett isolates Howitt's writing for *Household Words* as some of the few quality representations of 'Australian fiction'. For Sinnett, the dominant literary tradition is but a poor facsimile of Australian life filled with 'embellished caricatures of "Australian-ness" … depictions only of manners and customs, not character. These are not novels, but "books of travels in disguise"…'. Likening writer to painter, Sinnett argues that too often Australia is depicted merely as scenery. What is missing is the animation of narrative setting with 'human feeling and human passions' and 'a picture of universal human life and passion, but represented as modified by Australian externals'.[16]

Howitt's writing is concerned with the virtuous squatter. In 'The Land Shark' and 'New Settler Old Settler' Howitt depicts the squatter in collision with opportunists and capitalists, whose unfavourable depiction hinges on their wholly transactional and instrumental relationship

---

[15] Ken Gelder and Rachael Weaver, *Colonial Australian Fiction: Character Types, Social Formations and the Colonial Economy* (Sydney: Sydney University Press, 2017), 17.
[16] Frederick Sinnett, 'Fiction Fields of Australia', *Journal of Australasia* 1 (Jul–Dec 1856).

with the land. These character types only acquire property, but do not cultivate it, placing them in opposition to Howitt's squatters who work closely with their holdings, often to the sacrifice of health and life. Accordingly, 'Black Thursday' is also the valorisation of two squatter types: the ex-convict Maxwell family, and the emigrant Patterson family. The ultimate unification of Robert Patterson and Ellen Maxwell not only ensures the squatters' consolidation of power vindicated by their virtuous character in the face of disaster, but it also emphasises the egalitarian nature of the new colony. Mr Maxwell's elevation from convict to his rightful place as a man of honour, character and high estimation is possible only in Australia, as 'the injuries of a man of his high talents and noble nature might be comparatively buried in the antipodes; at home they would be a present, a perpetual and a damaging reproach'.

As argued by Sinnett, 'Australia offers fresh scenery, fresh costumes, and fresh machinery … great advantages, to those that know how to use them.' In this case, Howitt moves beyond a previously descriptive account of bushfires to deploy this uniquely Australian phenomenon to animate a narrative of class reconciliation, thereby participating in the journal's broader conception of Australia as a place untrammelled by the rigid social hierarchies of England. *Household Words* often used the device of depicting foreign places to define what it meant to be English. What conflict Dickens saw within England – especially potential class conflicts – was often transposed to colonial relations. Although Australia was imagined as a place where social divisions could be transcended, Howitt's narratives only operate to reify legitimate forms of the squatter type as Australian gentry. As pointed out by Dorice Eliot, while the figure of the roving bushman imbued with the values of independence and loyal mateship is commonly considered the essence of national character, in nineteenth century England it was the figure of the squatter who attracted the most attention. In certain squatter narratives, it is not enough for the squatter to dominate either economic or political systems; it is incumbent that they also cultivate and display signs of gentility, thus, linking them to the traditional English ruling class while simultaneously appearing to share the democratic ideals of the middle class. In 'Black Thursday,' the Maxwells are virtuous not because they are a family of 'unusual affluence', but because they are individuals of elevated taste and education: Mr Maxwell is 'highly-honoured' and the Maxwell children are recipients of first-class British educations. In so doing, these kinds of narrative align with, but do not replicate an English value system. That is, certain narratives about squatters reworked genteel masculinity and femininity in order to unify the squattocracy into a reimagined gentry class, based on, but different, from the English one.[17]

The idea of a value system based on but different from England is significant. Primarily because it displaces the more simplistic idea of the transportation of English values with the botanic-ecological metaphor of transplantation. This shift, as argued by Martin Leer, 'turns our attention to the ineluctable consequences for the present of what has physically happened in the past, to how a process is set moving by the original grafts, certain transplants thrive in the new soil – and become pests – others barely hold out, or die'.[18] Shortly after settlement British observers cited a thickening of scrub on lands they had initially likened to English parks.[19] Without the careful fire management practiced by Indigenous Australians for tens of thousands of years, and the implementation of an entirely different fire regime, the biota of the land radically altered. Just as some weeds took root and spread, we can also conceive of the grafting of certain values onto phenomena. With respect to Howitt's narrative, it

---

[17] Dorice Williams Elliott, 'Unsettled status in Australian settler novels', in *Victorian Settler Narratives: Emigrants, Cosmopolitans and Returnees in Nineteenth-Century Literature*, ed. Tamara S. Wagner (London: Routledge, 2015), 26, 38.

[18] Martin H. Leer, 'Imagined counterpart: outlining a conceptual literary geography of Australia', *Australian Literary Studies* 15, no. 2 (1991): 1–13.

[19] Pyne, *Burning Bush*, 32.

is the grafting of a certain genteel masculinity, and its associations with the dissolution of class tension and division, onto the disaster of fire. Although 'Black Thursday' is originally written for an English audience in the 1850s, its cultural associations shift as it is republished in Australian newspapers across the century. By the 1890s, inflected by the increasing number of 'Black Thursday' narratives, Robert Patterson is no longer an exponent of English values, but rather a bushman, expressive of a developing national identity.

Other narratives in this collection of 'lost' Australian bushfire stories both align and diverge with the themes of 'Black Thursday,' thereby drawing attention to less culturally dominant narratives. In these narratives, the division between the bush and the homestead is clearly articulated: while men move across both with ease, women are relegated to the latter. A number of these stories draw attention to the gendered division of labour involved in firefighting. For example, in 'My Wedding Day: A South Australian Story' (1890), it is the bride who assumes responsibility for providing sustenance for the firefighters as the fire-front approaches. In the 'The Other Man' (1894) by Mary Gaunt, Dolly and Ruth are left alone and defenceless on the homestead. While Dolly is introduced as a competent gardener, she is illiterate in the skills required to manage the environment beyond the reach of the homestead. Unversed in the practical skills required to defend the property, they flee, leaving the homestead to burn.

Across these stories the trope of the woman left alone as she waits for the men to return is recurrent. In 'Kitty Dunnolly, My Schoolmate A Victorian Sketch' and 'One Night at Gorringe', it is not the fire that threatens the safety of the women, but the characters that emerge in the absence of their male protectors. In both instances, a bushfire leaves women exposed to the attack of vagrants and bushrangers. ''Ria, A West Australian Story' (1883) is unusual in its depiction of a women who independently manages her station. 'Ria not only engages in the activity of firefighting, but also leads the men in this effort. Although she is successful in defending her home, the fire only principates her realisation that she cannot both keep a home and defend it and accordingly she resolves to marry. 'Ria's transgression, however, is too significant, and ultimately, she is killed by a scorned man. Though characterised in the gendered and classed terms of the later nineteenth-century, 'Ria and Kitty – and Dolly and Ruth – are also depicted as brave and resilient 'Australians' distinct from their female relatives in England. Other short stories such as 'Rover' (1893) and 'Through Fire and Water' (1887) are tonally distinct, as they present an unqualified celebration of the relationship between man and animal. In these instances bushfires not only serve to highlight masculine heroism, but also the selfless loyalty of domestic animals.

The reimagining of a gentry class in a redemptive, rather than antagonistic, Australian environment that Howitt captured in 'Black Thursday' was lost during the 1890s when the narrative was pressed into the service of an Australian cultural identity being forged in relation to the 'Bush'. The story's continuing relevance, however, was ensured. Unlike 'Black Thursday' many other bushfire narratives did not endure and were never published beyond their initial newspaper serialisations. By bringing these 'lost' bushfire narratives into conversation with 'Black Thursday,' this collection not only presents the opportunity to consider how cultural narratives are deeply historically contingent, but to also move beyond the more dominant narrative of masculine heroism, community spirit and the successful defence of the settler home.[20]

---

[20] The author thanks Kate Mitchell for her assistance in the development of this piece.

Black Thursday

William Howitt

Chapter I

As the voyager approaches the shores of Victoria, the first welcome land which greets him, is the bold promontory of Cape Otway. If it be at night, the blaze from the light-house on its southern point sends him its cheering welcome for many a league across the ocean which he has so long traversed in expectation, and calls forth rapturous hurrahs from the throng of passengers who crowd to the forecastle. If it be day, the eye rests on its lofty forest hills with a quiet and singular delight. These heights fully respond to the ideal of a new land only recently peopled. Clothed with forests from the margin of the sea to their very summits, they realise vividly the approach to a vast region of primaeval nature. The tall white stems of the gum-trees stand thickly side by side like so many hoary columns; and here and there amongst them descend dark ravines; while piles of rocks on the heights, alternating with jagged chines and projecting spurs of the mountains, present their solitary masses to the breeze of ocean.

Amongst the rocks of this wild shore there are sea-caves of vast extent and solemn aspect, which have never yet been thoroughly explored. The forest, extending fifty miles or more in all directions, is one of the most dense and savage in the whole colony. Until lately it was almost impass-able from the density of the scrub, and from the thick masses of vines (that is lianas, or creeping cord-like plants, chiefly parasitical) which, as in the forests of South America, climb from tree to tree, knitting the woods into an obscure and impenetrable shade. Excepting along the track from Mr. Roadknight's station, near the sources of the Barwan, through the heart of the forest to Apollo Bay, a distance of forty miles, you might cut your way with an axe, but would find it difficult to make progress otherwise. The greater part of the promontory – consisting of steep hills covered with gigantic trees intersected by shelving valleys, and dark with congregated fern-trees, beetling precipices, and stony declivities – affords no food for cattle. In one day, however, known to the colonists as Black Thursday, a hurricane of flame opened its rude and impracticable wilderness to the foot of man; but presented him at the same time, with a black and blasted chaos of charred trees, and gigantic fallen trunks and branches.

It was in this forest, in the early morning of this memorable day, the 6th of February, 1851, that a young man opened his eyes and sat up to look about him. He had, the day before, driven a herd of fifty bullocks from the station of Mr. Roadknight thus far on his way towards his own residence in the country, between Lake Corangamite and Mount Gellibrand. He had reached at evening a small grassy valley in the outskirts of the forest watered by a creek falling into the western Barwan, and had there paused for the night. His mob of cattle, tired and hungry, were not inclined to stray from the rich pasturage before them; and, hobbling out his splendid black horse Sorcerer, he prepared to pass the night in the simple fashion of the settler on such journeys. A fallen log supplied him with a convenient seat, a fire was quickly lit from the dead boughs which lay plentifully around, and his quart-pot, replenished at the creek, was thrust into the glowing fire. He had a good store of kangaroo-sandwiches, and there he sat with his cup of strong bush-tea; looking alternately at the grazing cattle, and into the solemn, gloomy, and soundless woods, in which even the laughing jackass failed to shout his clamorous adieu to the falling day. Only the distant monotone of the morepork – the nocturnal cuckoo of the Australian wilds – reached, his ear, making the profound solitude still more solitary. He very soon rolled himself in his travelling rug, and flung himself down before the fire – having previously piled a fresh supply of timber upon it – near where his trusty dogs lay, and where Sorcerer, in the favourite fashion of the bush-horse, slept as he stood.

The morning was hushed and breathless. Instead of that bracing chill with which the Australian lodger out of doors generally wakes up, Robert Patterson found the perspiration standing thick on his face, and he felt a strange longing for a deep breath of fresh air. But motion there was none, except in the little creek which trickled with a fresh and inviting aspect at a few yards from him. He arose, and stripping, plunged into the deepest spot of it that he could find; and thus refreshed, rekindled his fire, and made his solitary breakfast. But all around him hung, as it were, a leaden and death-like heaviness. Not a bough nor a blade of grass was moved by the air. The trees stood inanimately moody and sullen. He cast his eyes through the gloomy shadow beneath them, and a sultry suffocating density seemed to charge the atmosphere. The sky above him was dimmed by a grey haze.

"There is something in the wind to-day old fellow," he said, addressing his horse in his usual way; for he had long looked on him as a companion, and firmly believed that he understood all that he said to him. "There is something in the wind: yet, where is the wind?"

The perspiration streamed from him with the mere exertion of saddling his horse, and as he mounted him to rouse up his cattle. Horse, dogs, and cattle manifested a listlessness that only an extraordinary condition of the atmosphere could produce. If you had seen the tall, handsome young man seated on his tall and noble horse, you would have felt that they were together formed for any exploit of strength and speed. But the whole troop – cattle, man, horse – went slowly and soberly along, as if they were oppressed by a great fatigue or the extreme exhaustion of famine.

The forest closed in upon them again, and they proceeded along a narrow track, flanked on each side by tall and densely-growing trees; the creeping vines making of the whole forest one intricate, impenetrable scene. All was hushed as at midnight. No bird enlivened the solitude by its cries, and they had left the little stream. Suddenly there came a puff of air; but it was like the air from the jaws of a furnace, hot, dry, withering in its very touch. The young settler looked quickly in the direction from which it came, and instantly shouted to the cattle before him, in a wild, abrupt, startling shout, swung aloft the stock-whip which he held in his hand, and brought it down with the report of a pistol, and the sharp cut as with a knife, on the ear of the huge bullock just before him.

Loud and louder, wilder and more fiercely shouted the squatter, and dashed his horse over fallen trees; through crashing thickets, first on one side of the road, and then on the other. Crack, crack went the stinging, slashing whip; loud was the bark of dogs; and the mob of cattle rushed forward at headlong speed. The young man gazed upward; and, through the only narrow opening of the forest saw strange volumes of smoke rolling southward. Hotter, hotter, strongly and more steadily came the wind. He suddenly checked his horse, and listening, grew pale at the sound which reached him. It was a low deep roar, as of a wind in the tree-trops, or of a waterfall, distant, and smothered in a deep ravine.

Chapter II

"God have mercy!" he exclaimed: "a bushfire! and in this thick forest!" Once more he sprang forward, shouting, thundering with his whip. He and the herd were galloping along the narrow wood track. But, as he had turned westward in the direction of his home, the woods – of which he had before seen the boundary – now closed for some miles upon him; and, as he could not turn right or left for the chaos of vines and scrub that obstructed the forest, the idea of being overtaken there by the bushfire was horrible. Such an event would be death, and death only.

Therefore he urged on his flying herd with desperation. Crack upon crack from his long whip resounded through the hollow wood. The cattle themselves seemed to hear the ominous sound, and sniff the now strongly perceptible smell of burning. The roar of the fire came louder, and ever and anon seemed to swell and surge as if urged on by a rough rising blast. The heat was fierce and suffocating. The young squatter's clothes clung to him with streaming perspiration. The horse and cattle steamed and smoked with boiling heat. Yet onward, onward they dashed with lolling tongues. Sorcerer, specked with patches of foam on his dark shining body, seemed to grow furiously impatient of the obstruction offered by the bullocks in his path. As his master's whip exploded on their flanks, he laid back his ears; and with flaming eyeballs and bared teeth, strove to tear them in his rage.

Robert Patterson knew that the extraordinary heat and drought of the summer had scorched up the grass – the very ground; had licked up the water from crab-hole, pool, and many a creek; had withered the herbage into crisp hay, and so withered the foliage that you might crumble it between your fingers. The country seemed thoroughly prepared for a conflagration, and only required this fiery wind to send a blaze of extermination over the whole land. For weeks, nay months, the shepherds and sawyers had spoken of fires burning in the hills; and in the fern-tree breaks of this very forest he had been recently told that flames had been observed in various directions burning redly by night.

If the fire had reached him and his herd before they escaped into the open plains, they must be consumed like stubble. The cattle began to show signs of exhaustion, hanging out their parched tongues, and panting heavily; the perspiration on himself and horse was dried up by the awful heat, and the dogs ran silently, or only whining lowly to themselves, as they hunted every hollow on their way for water. Suddenly they were out in an open plain, yet with the forest on either hand, but at a considerable distance.

What a scene! The woods were flaming and crackling in one illimitable conflagration. The wind, dashing from the north in gusts of inconceivable heat, seemed to sear the very face, and shrivel up the lungs. The fire leaped from tree to tree, flashing and roaring along with the speed and the destructiveness of lightning. The sere foliage seemed to snatch the fire, and to perish in it in a riot of demonical revelry. On it flew, fast as the fleetest horse could gallop; and consuming acres of leaves in a moment, still remained to rage and roar amongst the branches and in the hollow stems of ancient trees. The whole wood on the left was an enormous region of intensest flame; and that on the right sent forth the sounds of the same ravaging fires; but being to windward, the flames could not be seen for the vast clouds of smoke, mingled with fiery sparks, which were rolled on the air. There was a sound as of thunder, mingled with the crash of falling trees, and the wild cries of legions of birds of all kinds, which fell scorched and blackened and dead to the ground.

Once out on this open plain the cattle were speedily lost in the blinding ocean of smoke, and the young settler obliged to abandon them, made a dash onward for his life. Now the flames came racing along the grass with the speed of the wind, and mowing all smooth as a pavement; now it tore furiously through some near point of the forest, and flung burning ashes and tangles of blazing bark upon the galloping rider. But Sorcerer, with an instinct more infallible than human sagacity, sped on, over thicket, and stone, and fallen tree, snorting in the thick masses of smoke, and stretching forward his gaping jaws as to catch every breath of air to sustain impeded respiration.

When the wind veered, the reek driven backward, revealed a most amazing scene. The blazing skirts of the forests; huge isolated trees, glaring red – standing columns of fire: here a vast troop of wild horses with flying manes and tails, rushing with thundering hoofs over the plain; there herds of cattle running with bloodshot eyes and hanging tongues they know not wither, from the fires; troops of kangaroos leaping frantically across the rider's path, their hair singed and giving out strongly the stench of fire; birds of all kinds and colours shrieking piteously as they drove wildly by, and yet saw no spot of safety; thousands of sheep standing huddled in terror on the scorched flats, with singed wool, deserted by their shepherds, who had fled for their lives.

Chapter III

But onward flew the intrepid Sorcerer, onward stretched his rider, thinking lightning-winged thoughts of home, and of his helpless, paralysed mother there.

With a caution inspired by former outbreaks of bushfires, he had made at some distance round his homestead a bare circle. He had felled the forest-trees, leaving only one here and there, at such distances that there was little fear of ignition. As the summer dried the grass, he had set fire to it on days when the wind was gentle enough to leave the flame at command watching, branch in hand, to beat out any blaze that might have travelled into the forest. By this means he had hitherto prevented the fire from reaching his homestead; and he had strongly recommended the same plan to his neighbours, though generally with little effect. Now the fire was so terrible, and sparks flew so wide on the wind, that he feared they might kindle the grass round his homestead, and that he might find everything and every person there consumed.

But, behold! the gleaming, welcome water of Lake Colac. Sorcerer rushed headlong towards it; and wading hastily up to his sides in its cooling flood, thrust his head to the eyes into it, and drank as if he could never be satisfied with less than the whole lake. Englishmen, new to the scene, would have trembled for the horse; but the bush steed knows best what he needs, eats and drinks as likes him best and flourishes on it. Smoking hot, the rider lets him drink his fill and all goes well. The heat produces perspiration, and the evaporation cools and soothes him. Robert Patterson did not lose a moment in following Sorcerer's example. He flung himself headlong from the saddle, dressed as he was, dived and splashed and drank exuberantly. He held again and again his smarting face and singed hands in the delicious water; then threw it over the steed, that now, satiated, stood panting in the flood. He laved and rubbed down the grateful animal with wave after wave, cleaning the dried perspiration from every hair, giving him refreshment at every pore. Then up and away again.

He had not ridden two hundred yards before he saw, lying on the plain, a horse that had fallen in saddle and bridle, and lay with his legs under him, and head stretched stiffly forward, with glaring eyeballs, but dead. Near him was a man, alive, but sunk in exhaustion. His eyes turned wildly on the young squatter, and his parched lips moved, but without a sound. Robert Patterson comprehended his need, and, running to the lake, brought his pannikin full of water, and put it to his mouth. It was the water of life to him. His voice and some degree of strength come quickly back. He had come from the north, and had ridden a race with the fire, till horse and man had dropped here, the horse never to rise again. But Patterson's need was too urgent for delay. He found the man had no lack of provisions; he carried him in his arms to the margin of the lake, mounted and rode on.

As he galloped forward, it was still fire – fire everywhere. He felt convinced that the conflagration – fanned by the strong wind, and acting upon fires in a hundred quarters – extended over the whole sun-dried colony.

It was still early noon, when, with straining eyes, and a heart which seemed almost to stand still with a terrible anxiety, he came near his own home. He darted over the brow of a hill – there it lay safe! The circle within his clear boundary was untouched by the fire. There were his paddocks, his cattle, his huts, and home. With a lightning thought his thanks flew up to Heaven, and he was the next moment at his door, in his house, and in his mother's arms.

Robert's anxiety had been great for the safety of his mother, her anxiety was tripled for him. Terror occasioned by a former conflagration had paralysed her lower extremities; and now, the idea of her only son, her only remaining relative in the colony, being met by this once in a lifetime fire in the dense defiles of the terrible Otway Forest, kept her in a fearful state of anxiety. Mrs. Patterson, though confined to her wheeled chair, was a woman of pre-eminent energy and ability. Left with her boy, a mere infant, she had managed all her affairs with a skill and discretion that had produced great prosperity for them. Though her heart was kind, her word was law; and there was no man on her run who dared in the slightest to disobey her way; nor one within the whole country round who did not respect and revere her. She had been a remarkably handsome woman. The whole of the floors of the station being built upon one level, in her wheeled chair she could be at any moment in any part of her house or premises.

The moment the first joy of mother and son was over, what a scene presented itself! The station was like a fair. From the whole country round people had fled from the fire, and had instinctively fled there. There was a feeling that the Patterson precautions, which they themselves had neglected, were the guarantees of safety. Thither shepherds had driven their flocks, stockmen their herds, and whole families, compelled to fly from their burning houses, had hurried thither with the few effects that they could snatch up, and bear with them. Patterson's paddocks were crowded with horses and cattle, the bush round the station was literally hidden beneath his own and his neighbours' flocks. Stockmen, shepherds, substantial squatters, now houseless men, were there in throngs. Families, with troops of children, had encamped on the open ground near his house, beneath temporary tents of sheets and blankets. His house was crammed with fugitives, and was a scene of crowding, confusion and sorrow. Luckily the Patterson store-room was well stocked with flour, and there could be no want of meat with all those flocks and herds about them. But for the cattle themselves there must soon be a famine; and the moment that the fire abated, scouts must be sent off in all directions – but especially to the high plains around Lake Corangamite – in search of temporary pasture. Meantime fires were lighted in a dozen places; and frying pans and kettles fully employed; for in spite of flight, and loss and grief, hunger, as Homer thousands of years ago asserted, is impudent, and will be fed.

The stories that the people had to tell were most melancholy. Houses burnt down, flocks destroyed, children suffocated in the smoke or lost in the rapid flight; shepherds and bullock drivers consumed with their cattle. Numbers had fled to creeks and pools, and yet had been severely burnt; the flames driving over the surface of the water with devouring force. Some had lain in shallow brooks, turning over and over, till finally forced to get up and fly. Still, as the day went on, numbers came pouring in with fresh tales of horror and devastation. The whole country appeared to be the prey of the flames; and men who were, a few hours before out of the reach of poverty or calamity, were now homeless paupers.

"The Maxwells, mother," Patterson asked – "Is there any news of them?"

"None, my dear Robert, none," replied his mother. "I hope and believe that they are quite safe. They long ago adopted your plan of a clearance ring, and I doubt not are just now as much a centre of refuge as we are."

"But I should like to be sure," said Robert, seriously. "I must ride over and see."

"Must you? I think you must not," said Mrs. Patterson. "But if you cannot be satisfied, let some one of the men go; there are plenty at hand, and you are already worn out with fatigue and excitement."

"No, I am quite well and fresh – I had rather go myself," said Robert; "it is not far." And he strode out, his mother saying –

"If you find they are all right, don't come back tonight."

Robert Patterson was soon mounted on a fresh and powerful horse, and cantered off towards Mount Hesse. It was only seven miles off. The hot north wind had ceased to blow; the air was cooler, and the fires in the forest were burning more tamely. Yet he had to ride over a track which showed him the ravages which the flames had made in his pleasant woods. The whole of the grass was annihilated; the dead timber lying on the ground was still burning; and huge hollow trees stood like great chimneys, with flames issuing from their tops as from a furnace, and a red intense fire burning within their trunks below; and from them burning earthy matter came tumbling out smoking and rolling on the ground. He was about crossing a small creek, when he saw an Irishman – a shepherd of the Maxwell's – sitting on its banks; his clothes were nearly all consumed from his back, his hat was the merest remaining fragment, scorched and shrivelled. The man was rocking himself to and fro and groaning.

"Fehan!" exclaimed Patterson. "What has happened to you?"

Chapter IV

The man turned upon him a visage that startled him with terror. It was, indeed, no longer a human visage; but a scorched and swollen mass of deformity. The beard and hair were burnt away. Eyes were not visible; the whole face being a confused heap of red flesh and hanging blisters. The poor fellow raised a pair of hands that displayed equally the dreadful work of the fire.

The young squatter exclaimed. "How dreadful! Let me help you Fehan – let me take you home."

The man groaned again; and, opening his distorted mouth with difficulty, and with agony, said:

"I have no home – it is burnt."

"And your family?"

"Dead – all dead!"

"But are you sure – are you quite sure?" said Robert, excitedly.

"I saw one – my eldest boy: he was lying burnt near the house. I lifted him, to carry him away, but he said, 'Lay me down, father, – lay me down; I cannot bear it.' I laid him down and asked, 'Where are the rest?' 'They fled into the bush,' he said, then he died. They are all burnt."

Robert Patterson flung the wretched man a linen handkerchief, bidding him dip it in the creek and lay it on his face to keep the air from it, and turned his horse, saying he would look for the family. He soon found the place where the hut had stood. It was burnt to ashes. On the ground, not for from it, lay the body of the dead little boy. Patterson hastened along the track of the old road to the Maxwells' station, tracing it as well as he could in the fire and the fallen, flaming branches. He felt sure the flying family would take that way. In a few minutes it brought him again upon the creek by which the poor man sat, but lower down.

There stood a hut in a damp swamp, which had been used years ago for the sheep washing, but had long been deserted. It was surrounded by thick wattles, still burning. The hut was on fire; but its rotten timbers forcing out far more smoke than flame. As he approached, he heard low cries and lamentations. "The family has fled here," he said to himself," and they are perishing of suffocation." He sprang to the ground and dashed forward through columns of heavy smoke. It was hopeless to breathe in it, for its pungent and stinging strength seemed to close his lungs, and water rushed from his eyes in torrents.

But pushing in, he seized the first living thing that he laid his hands on, and bore it away. It was a child. Again and again he made the desperate essay, and succeeded in bringing out no less than four children and the mother, who was sunk on the floor as dead, but soon gave signs of life as she came into the air.

The young man was now in the utmost perplexity with his charge. It was a heart-rending sight. The whole group were more or less burnt; but, as it seemed to him, not so much burnt as to affect their lives. Their station was three miles distant, and he had no alternative but to leave them here till he rode on and sent a cart for them. With much labour, carrying the children one after another in his arms, he conveyed the woeful group to the father.

As the young man stood bewildered by the cries and lamentations of the family on meeting the father, a horse ridden by a lady approached at a gallop. This apparition contrasted strangely with the lamentable group of sufferers. The young lady was tall and of a most beautiful figure, and was mounted on a fine bay horse. A light skirt, and broad felt hat were all the deviations from her home costume that haste had led her to assume. Her face, fresh and roseate, full of youth, loveliness, and feeling, was at the same time grave and anxious, as she gazed in speechless wonder on the scene.

"Miss Maxwell!" Patterson exclaimed, "in the name of Heaven, what news? How is all at the Mount? Yet, on this dreadful day what but ill can happen?"

"Nothing is amiss, that I know of," said the young lady, "we are safe at home. The fire has not come near us."

"Thank God!" said Robert. "I was going to your house, when I fell in with this unfortunate family. Will you ride back and send us a cart?"

"But I beg you will come with me, for I too, was going to you."

"To me!" cried the young man, in the utmost astonishment. "Then all is not right. Is George well?"

"I hope so," replied Miss Maxwell; but the tears started into her eyes at the same moment and Robert Patterson gave a groan of apprehension.

"I hope so," added the young lady, recovering her self-possession; "but that is the point I want to ascertain. Yesterday, he went with Turcen into the hills to bring in cattle, and this morning the fire surprised them when they had taken two different sweeps along the side of a range. Turcen could not find George again, but made his way home; hoping his master had done the same. George has not yet come, and the fire is raging so fiercely in the hills, that I could think of nothing but coming to you for your advice and assistance."

"Thank you, Ellen!" said Robert with a sad emotion. "I will find him if he be alive." He sprang upon his horse; and telling the unhappy family that he would send them immediate assistance, both he and Miss Maxwell galloped away.

We will not attempt to divulge their conversation on the way; but will let the reader a little into the mutual relations of these two families and these young people. Miss Ellen Maxwell and her brother George were the sole remaining members of their family. As the nearest neighbours of the Pattersons, they had grown into intimate friends. George and Robert had been play-fellows in Van Diemen's Land; and here, where they had come in their boyhood, they were school-fellows. Since then they had gradually grown, from a similarity of tastes and modes of life, the most intimate friends. It was not likely that Robert Patterson and Ellen Maxwell could avoid liking one another. They possessed everything in mind, person, and estate, which made such an attachment the most natural thing in the world. Ellen was extremely attached to Mrs. Patterson, for whom she had the highest veneration; Ellen had received an excellent education in Edinburgh, whither she had been sent to her friends. In her nature she was frank, joyous, and affectionate; but not without a keen sense of womanly pride, which gave a certain dignity to her manner, and a reputation for high spirit.

All had gone well between herself and Robert until some six months ago. But, since then, there had sprung up a misunderstanding. Nobody could tell how it had arisen; nobody except Ellen knew; and whatever was the secret cause, she locked it impenetrably within her own bosom. All at once she had assumed a distant and haughty manner towards Robert Patterson. From him she did not conceal that she felt she had cause for dissatisfaction, but she refused to explain. When, confounded by the circumstance, he sought for an explanation, she bade him search his own memory and his heart, and they would instruct him. She insisted that they should cease to regard themselves as affianced, and only consented that nothing as yet should be said on the subject to her brother or Mrs. Patterson, on the ground that it would most painfully afflict them.

Ellen, who used to be continually riding over to see Mrs. Patterson with her brother, now rarely appeared, and proudly declined to give her reasons for the change in her; adding that she must absent herself altogether, if the subject were renewed. To her brother she was equally reserved, and he attributed her conduct to caprice; bidding Robert take no notice of it. Ellen was not without other admirers, but that was nothing new. One young man, who had lately come into the neighbourhood, paid her assiduous attention, and gossip did not fail to attribute the cause of Robert Patterson's decline of favour to his influence. But Ellen gave no countenance to such a supposition. She was evidently under no desire to pique her old lover by any marked predilection for a new one. Her nature was too noble for the pettiness of coquetry, and any desire to add poignancy to coldness. On the other hand, it was clear to the quietly watchful eye of her brother, that she was herself even more unhappy than Robert. Her eyes often betrayed the effects of secret weeping, and the paleness of her cheek belied the assumed air of cheerfulness that she wore.

Things were in this uncomfortable state at the outbreak of the fire. It was, therefore, a most cheering thought to Patterson that, in her distress, she had flown first, and at once to him. This demonstrated confidence in his friendship. True, on all occasions, she had protested that her sense of his high moral character was not an iota abated; but, in this spontaneous act, Robert's heart persuaded him that there lay something more.

No sooner did he reach the Mount, than, leaving Ellen to send off assistance to the Fehans, he took Turcen the stockman, and rode into the forest hills. It was soon dark, and they had to halt; but not far from the spot where Turcen had lost sight of his master. They tethered their horses in a space clear of trees and fire, and gave them corn that they had brought with them. When the moon rose, they went on to some distance uttering loud cooees to attract the attention of the lost man; but all in vain. The fire had left the ground hot and covered with ashes, and here and there huge trees were still burning like columns of red-hot iron.

Finding all their efforts for the night fruitless, they flung themselves down beside their horses; and, with the earliest peep of dawn they were up and off higher into the hills. Their way presented at every step the most shocking effects of the fire. Ever and anon they came upon bullocks which had perished in it. Here and there, too, they descried the remains of kangaroos, opossums, and hundreds of birds, seared and shrivelled into sable masses of cinder.

Chapter V

They came at length to the spot where Turcen and George Maxwell had parted; and the experienced bushman carefully sought out the tracks of his horses' feet, and followed them. These were either obliterated by the fire, or failed from the rocky hardness of the ground; but, by indefatigable search, they regained them, and were led at length to the edge of a deep and precipitous ravine. In the ravine itself, the trees and grass remained unscathed; the torrent of fire had leapt over it, sweeping away, however, every shrub and blade of herb from the heights.

"God defend us!" exclaimed Robert, "the smoke must have blinded him, and concealed this frightful place. Man and horse are doubtless dashed to pieces."

He raised a loud and clear cooee; instantly answered by the wild and clamorous barking of a dog; which, in the next instant, was seen leaping and springing about in the bottom of the dell, as if frantic with delight.

"That is Snirrup!" exclaimed Turcen; and the two men began to descend the steep side of the ravine. Robert Patterson outstripped his older and heavier companion. He seemed to fly down the sheer and craggy descent. Here he seized a bough, there a point of the rock, and, in the next instant, was as rapidly traversing the bottom of the glen. Snirrup the cattle-dog rushed barking and whining upon him, as if in a fit of ecstatic madness, and then bounded on before him. Robert followed in breathless anxiety; stopped the next moment by the sight of George Maxwell's horse, lying crushed and dead. Robert cast a rapid glance around, expecting every moment to see his friend stretched equally lifeless. But presently he heard the faint sound of a human voice.

There lay George stretched in the midst of a grassy thicket, with a face expressing agony and exhaustion. Robert seized his offered hand, and George called first for water. His friend started up and ran down the valley at full speed. He was soon back with a pannikin of water, which the sufferer drank with avidity.

He now learned that, as had been supposed, in the thick smoke, the horse had gone over the precipice and was killed in an instant. George had escaped, his fall being broken by his steed and he was flung into a thicket, which softened the shock of his descent. But he had a broken leg, and was, besides, extremely bruised and torn. Life, however, was strong within him; and Turcen and Robert lost no time in having a litter of poles bound together with stringy bark made soft with grass and leaves, laid in a sheet of the same bark. They had three miles to bear the shattered patient; to whom every motion produced excruciating agonies. It was not long before they heard people in different parts of the wood loudly cooeeing; and their answers soon brought not only a number of men who had been sent out in quest of them, but also Miss Maxwell, herself.

We shall not attempt to describe the sad and yet rejoicing interview of the brother and sister, nor the rapidity with which the different men were sent off upon the horses tied in the hills for the surgeon; who lived two miles off.

In a few days George Maxwell – his leg having been set and his wounds dressed – had become easy enough to relate all that had happened to him; the dreadful night which he had passed in extreme agony in the glen, and the excitement when the loud, ringing cooees of Robert, which had reached him, but to which he was unable to reply, had occasioned both him and the faithful and sympathising dog, who barked vehemently; but, as it proved, in vain.

From the moment of this tragic occurrence Robert Patterson was constantly in attendance at the Mount with his friend. He slept in the same room with him, and attended with Ellen as his nurse in the daytime. From this moment the cloud which so long hung over the spirit of Ellen Maxwell had vanished. She was herself again; always kind and open, yet with a mournful tone in her bearing towards Robert, which surprised and yet pleased him. It looked like regret for past unkindness. As they sat one evening over their tea, while George was in a profound sleep in the next room, Ellen, looking with emotion at him, said, in a low, tremulous voice, "Robert. I owe much to you."

"To me?" said Robert, hastily. "Isn't George as much a brother to me as to you?"

"It is not that which I mean," added Ellen, colouring deeply, yet speaking more firmly; "it is that I have done you great wrong. I believed that you had said a most ungenerous thing, and I acted upon my belief with too much pride and resentment. I was told that you had jested me as the daughter of a convict."

Robert sprang up. "It is false! I never said it," he exclaimed. "Who could tell you such a malicious falsehood?"

"Calm yourself," added Ellen, taking the young man's hand. "I shall tell you all. Hear me patiently; for I must impress first on you the strange likelihood of what was reported to me. You were driven to a stockman's hut, it was said, by a storm – you and a young friend. You were very merry, and this friend congratulated you in a sportive style on having won what he was pleased to call the richest young woman in the colony. And with a merry laugh you were said to add, 'and the daughter of the most illustrious of lags!'"

Robert Patterson, with a calmness of concentrated wrath, asked, in a low measured tone: "Who said that?"

"The woman who you lately saved with all her family. It was Nelly Fehan."

"Nelly Fehan!" said Robert in amazement; "what have I ever done to her that deserved such a stab?"

"You threatened to send Fehan to prison for bushranging. You reminded him of his former life and unexpired sentence."

"That is true," said Robert, after a pause of astonishment. "And this was the deadly revenge – the serpents! But, oh Ellen! why could you not speak? One word, and all would have been explained."

"I could not speak, Robert. Wounded pride silenced me. But I have suffered severely; have been fearfully punished. I can only say – forgive me."

One long embrace obliterated the past.

The late Mr. Maxwell had been transported for the expression of his liberal political principles in hard and bigoted times. There was not a man in the penal settlement, who did not honour his political integrity and foresight, and who did not reverence his character. But the convicts as a body were proud to claim him as of their class, though sent thither only for a crime of a Hampden or a Sidney. Whenever reproach was thrown on the convict section of society, the insulted party pointed to the venerable exile, and triumphantly hailed him as their chief. No endeavours, though they were many, and conducted by powerful hands, had ever been able to procure a reversal of his sentence. The injuries of a man of his high talents and noble nature might be comparatively buried in the antipodes; at home they would be a present, a perpetual and a damaging reproach. He had lived and died a banished, but a highly-honoured man. Still, as he rose to a higher estimation and an unusual affluence, there were little minds who delighted occasionally to whisper – "After all, he is but a lag." And it was on this tender point that the minds of his children, whose ears such remarks had reached and wounded, had become morbidly sensitive.

Amid the general calamity, this reconciliation was like a song of thanksgiving in the generous heart of Robert Patterson, and quickened it to tenfold exertions in alleviating the sufferings of his neighbours. His joy was made boundless and over-flowing by a circumstance which appeared to be little short of a miracle. When Robert rode up to his own station, he beheld his mother, not seated in her wheeled chair but on foot; light, active, and alert, going to and fro amongst the people whose destitution still kept them near his house. The mass of misery that she saw around her and the exertion which it stimulated burst the paralytic bonds which had enchained her for years. The same cause which had disabled her limbs had restored them.

The conflagration had extended over a space of three hundred miles by a hundred and fifty, and far away beyond the Goulburn, the Broken River, and the Ovens, we have witnessed the remaining traces of its desolation. Over all this space, flocks and herds in thousands had perished. Houses, ricks, fences and bridges had been annihilated. Whole families had been destroyed. Solitary travellers, flying through the boundless woods before the surging flame, had fallen and perished. For weeks and months, till the kindly rains of autumn had renewed the grass, people journeying through the bush, beheld lean and famishing cattle, unable to rise from the ground, and which by faint bellowings seemed to claim the pity and aid of man. Perhaps no such vast devastation ever fell on any nation and Black Thursday is an indelible memory in Victoria.

My Wedding Day:
A South Australian Story

Rita

Chapter I

"Well, Miss Grey, you are going to have a scorcher," said Mr. Green, as he greeted me one summer morning.

I would gladly have doubted his word, for it was Christmas day and, more, my wedding day, as well; but early as it was, the sun was shining from a cloudless sky – shining with all his might; and, though he embrowned the grass and baked the earth, and pumped up every drop of water long ago, leaving nothing but hot stones in the creek beds, he set to work as if he had just taken a contract to dry up the deluge and wanted to get done in time.

"Ah, well," I said, trying to make the best of it, "well, blessed is the bride the sun shines on, you know."

I left the shady verandah and went across to the wool-shed to give a finishing touch to the wedding breakfast, already laid there on a long table improvised for the occasion. Only the decorating part was left to me; and as I arranged such greenery and flowers as I had, the old saw kept running in my head: "Blessed is the bride the sun shines on." Surely the Omen is true, this once, for was there ever such a splendid fellow as Jack or such a lucky girl as I!

Then I thought of my past life, and wondered if I was the same Mary Grey who two years – yes, only two years – ago had been all alone in the world. I remembered my timid, scared feeling at being among strangers when I came as governess to this up-country run. How queer the life had seemed at first, and how home-like it seemed now. It was hard to realise that I could ever be afraid of Mrs. Green, who was like a loving mother to me. I soon got to like my work, too; and then – yes, then came Jack, and had things been ever so bad, life would have seemed *couleur de rose* to me.

So I was dreaming over my work that hot Christmas morning thirty years ago, when I was disturbed by Minnie Green. "Oh, come and see Mr. Stanley (Dick Stanley was to be Jack's best man), and Mr. Brice, and" – with emphasis – "the parson! Such a funny little man, Miss Grey, with yellow hair, and a pink face like a baby's and white hands. Do parsons always have pink faces and white hands?"

I never had an opportunity of answering this question, for just then Jack appeared and Minnie having gone to have another look at the cleric's English complexion and white hands which had so impressed her, we fell into a conversation, interesting enough to ourselves, but of no concern to outsiders till we were interrupted by Mrs. Green.

"Well, upon my word," she said, "what on earth can you two have to talk about? Come Mary; it is time for you to think of dressing. You can't have anything very particular to say to Jack here, and if you have, there is all the rest of your life to say it in." With which profound remark she sent Jack to the dining-room, where a picnic sort of first breakfast was going on; and taking me to my room, she brought me a a cup of tea and told me to rest a little, for I had a thirty-mile ride before me.

Now, though my dress was simple in the extreme, and I could have put it on myself in five minutes, being a bride I must be dressed. Mrs. Green and Minnie, who was to be my bridesmaid, undertook this office and hindered me sadly. My dress was plain white muslin, simply made, and I had not intended wearing a veil; but Mrs. Green said that as they seldom saw a wedding, and she did not suppose I would be married again in a hurry, I might as well do the thing in style while I was about it; so to please her I shrouded myself in a length of plain tulle that covered me almost from head to foot, really the effect was rather good.

At last I was dressed; but somehow we managed to be late and it was a quarter of an hour behind time when I went across to the wool-shed on Mr. Green's arm; while Biddy held an umbrella over my head, and Mrs. Green followed sticking in utterly unnecessary pins to the very last moment. Everyone was waiting; and the shed decorated with such greenery as was available, looked quite festive. At one end stood the breakfast table with the cake, homemade but imposing, a towering monument to Mrs. Green's housewifely skill. By a small table stood the clergyman in his surplice, looking a trifle out of place; while round about were arranged all available seats from chairs to milking-stools and slab benches, with stick legs. They were all occupied, for as I have already said, a wedding was not an every day occurrence, and people had turned out in full force.

We advanced with all possible decorum, and the ceremony proceeded as usual till the ring had been put on and the blessing given, when someone, breathless and dusty, dashed in at the door and cried, "Fire! Bushfire! Close here." Instantly most of the forms were upset and there was a rush for the door.

"Hi! Stop a minute," cried Jack, as he collared his two friends and dragged them back, "we will get this over now."

The clergyman hesitated, then, skipping a good deal, he began the exhortation on which wives get so much good advice and husbands so little.

"Oh, never mind all that," cried Jack, stamping with impatience: "we will have the 'amazement' and all the rest of it some other time. What have we to sign? Be quick."

Jack's friends made the poor clergyman show where he had to sign, and we all did it in a desperate hurry, the two witnesses scrawling something when their turn came and bolting at once. Jack just took me in his arms and gave me a hurried kiss. "Good by, dear little wife," he whispered, "good bye"; and he was gone, leaving me and the clergyman alone together.

He – the clergyman – was a young man just out from home. He had a clear complexion and fair hair parted down the middle and was altogether the mildest-looking little man imaginable; his little round face just now displaying the blankest possible astonishment. "Ye husbands – loveth himself – ye wives – subject – plaiting of hair and wearing of gold – amazement," he muttered incoherently, looking from me, standing alone in my white veil and dress, to the deserted and upturned forms, and the cake towering in solemn grandeur, to the end of the room. I believe he manfully intended to do his duty, if no one else did, and finish that ceremony to the bitter end; but to read that exhortation at one poor woman left all alone would have been, to say the least of it, personal; so he gave it up and shook hands, as is the practice of clergymen.

"I – I wish you every happiness, Mrs. Rushton," he stammered; then, remembering that I had just been unceremoniously deserted by my bridegroom, and not being sure whether such was the custom of the country or not, he muttered something about "sympathy"; and then, gathering his wits together with a violent effort, he burst out like Mr. Wilkie; "Where are they? What is the meaning of this most indecorous behaviour?"

I did not answer, but ran to the door to look out.

"What does this mean?" he repeated following me.

"Can't you see? Can't you smell?" I answered impatiently. "It is a bushfire."

The head station was built in a valley at the foot of a range of hills that formed a sort of semi-circle behind it. They were thickly wooded with "stringy bark," and covered with fern and grass trees, and from among them now rose, through air already quivering with heat, a column of thick white smoke, that floated upward in billowy clouds. The fire was near, that one could tell by the burning gum-leaves; and though it could not have been burning long, it promised to be a large fire, and a fierce one, for, as we watched, puffs of reddish-brown rose before the white smoke, showing that the flames were getting stronger.

The first set of men had disappeared over the ridge already, but Jack and his friends were only half-way up, and had stopped to cut boughs from some young saplings. They looked back, and I snatched off my veil and waved it to Jack; they returned the salute with a flourish of their branches, and then resumed their climb; while I twisted that unfortunate veil into a turban and went to the house with the bewildered parson.

We found Mr. Green giving orders for the boughs with which the verandah posts were decorated in honour of Christmas to be pulled down, and all inflammable things to be put away.

"Will the fire come here?" asked the Rev. Augustus Smith anxiously.

"Not if we can help it," said Mr. Green "but it will be hard work stopping it on a day like this, and it is well to be ready for it."

"If the fire don't come, the sparks will," said Biddy, whose experience of bushfires was extensive, "and them branches is just the things to ketch."

"Yes; get them down at once," said Mr. Green, and he hurried off, calling back to his wife, "Send up some tea to the men as soon as possible."

I went to my room to change my dress, and there on my bed was my habit laid out for my homeward ride with Jack. "Dear me! how differently the day was turning out from what we expected," I thought. If it had not been for that fire I would have been putting on my habit, instead of this print morning dress. No. On second thoughts, I decided things had happened so fast that, supposing the ceremony to have been finished properly, we would have just sat down to breakfast and I would be cutting the cake, instead of which I went to the kitchen and cut large hunks of bread with cheese to match.

It really was a disappointing wedding-day. What was the good of getting married only to lose sight of my bridegroom at once, and have to work away as if nothing had happened. And Jack, poor fellow, what a day he must be having, hard at work in the heat and dust and smoke. I felt half-inclined to give in and have a real good cry, but laughed instead, for through the window I saw the Rev. Augustus working hard under Biddy's directions, taking down and carrying away the decorations put up with so much care an hour or so before.

Mrs. Green and I set to work at once on woman's work in time of fire – boiling kettles and getting tea and provisions ready for the men – no light task in this instance, for there were thirty or forty men, and no other station near enough to share in the providing. When the first batch was ready it was taken up the hill by two of the men's wives.

Mr. Smith and I next busied ourselves in taking out and filling all the tubs in the establishment, and placing in them bags and branches to be used in beating, should the fire come near the house.

We paused, Mr. Smith and I, when we had done all we could, and gazing upward, wondered what it most feel like to be before that awful fire. Even where we were, the air quivered and danced with the heat and smoke, and the baked air almost hurt our feet. What must it be up there? we wondered. The wind had strengthened, driving the smoke across the sky; and the sunlight coming through it, shed a lurid yellow glare on all around. Behind the hill the smoke rose thicker, faster and darker, and the deep sullen roar of the fire could be heard. As we watched, a figure appeared on the top of the hill, then another and another, till quite a dozen were in sight. I could just make out Mr. Green, with Jack and his friends beside him. They seemed to be consulting about something. More men kept coming up by twos and threes, dragging or carrying scorched branches: some flung themselves down in the nearest shade, with the characteristic impulse of old-hands at bushfires to take a rest when they could get it. The rest stood or lolled in groups, evidently waiting for orders. At last the council of war on the hilltop came to an end. Mr. Green pointed along the ridge, and shook hands with Jack, who, with ten or a dozen men started in the direction indicated.

We had not noticed – or, at least, I had not, for, of course, I had eyes for no one else while Jack was in sight – that all this time the two women had been scrambling down the hill, accompanied by a man, who turned off to the stables, while the women came down to the house, whither we followed.

"Mr. Green says will you give Jackson tea and tucker for ten men; Mr. Rushton is going over to the big range," Mrs. Brown, one of the women, was saying as we came in.

We all fell to work at once. Mr. Smith cut beef and sliced plum-pudding, while Mrs. Green and I made substantial sandwiches; Biddy hurried up the kettles, and Mrs. Brown and Mrs. Jones packed things up as soon as they were ready. As we worked we asked brief questions, and got them answered still more briefly with most aggravating interruptions at interesting points.

"Is it a big fire?"

"Yes."

"Where were they when you got up?"

"Just coming off the steep range. They had stopped the fire all along, but it got into the stringy bark and came along over their heads. Are these the bags, Mrs. Green? Yes, they had to run. It got behind Mr. Rushton and a lot of 'em. Where do you keep the clean towels?"

Imagine my feelings when at this point she dived head first into a cupboard and became deaf to questions. I can see it now, that country kitchen, fresh whitewashed in honour of Christmas, with a bunch of gum-boughs hung from the ceiling by way of a fly-catcher. A good-sized room, with a roughly flagged floor, just now intolerably hot, for we had a roaring fire in the large fireplace, on which two large kettles and a foun-tain were singing and spluttering. The window-panes were hot to the touch; plates taken from the shelves were ready warmed, and the butter was clear transparent oil. It certainly was warm work.

At the end of the long table stood Mr. Smith, just now with knife and fork suspended, as he gazed at Mrs. Brown, who was now intent on sorting towels.

"But – but, Mrs. Brown –" he gasped.

"What's that?" she said, emerging from the cupboard.

"How did they escape?"

"Oh, they came through it, of course. Here's a towel to wrap that pudding in."

I suppose, if I had had time to think of it I would have been wretched about Jack's danger – I was anxious as it was; but we were all so busy that I had no time to fret; beside, I knew he was safe. If he had been killed or badly hurt, nothing would have hindered Mrs. Brown from telling me every detail.

I suppose we all looked hot; but poor Mr. Smith was the picture of misery, as he stood in his hot black clothes slicing beef in a temperature considerably above 100 degrees.

"Why don't you take off your coat?" said Biddy, noticing his distress.

Poor little man; I believe he blushed furiously, but can't be sure, for it was a simple impossibility for his face to get any redder than it already was.

"Do, Mr. Smith," said Mrs. Green. "I wouldn't work in a hot thing like that for anything; besides, it's real good cloth, and it's sure to get spoiled. Here, Biddy; take Mr. Smith's coat and hang it up somewhere out of the way."

"Look sharp, sir," said Biddy, holding out her hand; "I've no time to lose."

So he had to give it up. And I think that after a while he was glad, though just at first he looked hotter and more uncomfortable than ever.

When we had packed up the provisions and seen Jackson start we all went into the back verandah and looked up at the hill. The fire was nearer now and the smoke was thicker; ashes and bits of burnt fern and gum leaves were falling all around; the sun shone hotter and the parched air seemed to scorch one's face. On the hill-top the men were cutting down branches and evidently getting ready for a struggle.

"They are going to burn a track," said Mrs. Brown. "I expect they'd like their tucker now; they won't have time to eat when the fire comes."

"Where is it now?" I asked.

"About half a mile off; but it won't take long to come," said Mrs. Brown.

"But," said Mr. Smith, looking puzzled, "why don't they extinguish it farther off?"

"Because they can't," said Mrs. Brown. "It's in a grass-tree gully. If they were fools enough to try to stand against it, they would be shrivelled up like so much brown paper." And she went into the kitchen, where Mrs. Green and Biddy were already preparing more tea and provisions.

All this time I had been longing to hear more about Jack; but every one had been too busy to answer questions; now I tried again.

"What?" said Mrs. Brown. "Oh, Mr. Rushton? He isn't hurt; not that I know on at least. Someone got his arm burnt, but I don't think it was him" – in an aggravating, doubtful tone – "Mrs. Jones here saw it all; I only saw them afterwards. They did look like sweeps, and no mistake."

"I didn't see much," said Mrs. Jones modestly; "I only see half-a-dozen men beating like mad; and all at once the fire got into the trees and come along over their heads and they never took no notice till the sparks and things had lighted the fern behind them. Where's the sugar Mrs. Green? Yes, they had to run for it, they did! But it was all so smoky you couldn't make out which was which. The fern was blazing and burning bark was coming down like rain. If it had been up-hill they had to go, not down, wouldn't have got away, no, not one of 'em. Oh, no Mr. Rushton isn't hurt; he got his eyebrows singed and lost the ends of his moustaches, that's all. My husband has lost half his beard, and got a hole the size of your two hands in the back of his waist coat."

Chapter II

"What time is it?" asked Mrs. Green, when the two women had started up the hill once more. "Two o'clock? You don't say so! Well, we may as well have a bit of something ourselves. The fire will be on the top of that hill in half an hour at the rate it is coming. If they can't stop it, it will come down here, and we'll have to turn to and fight with the rest of them."

"We'll have to look out anyways," said Biddy. "The sparks will be all over the place with this wind, and it's not much time we'll have then to be thinking of dinner."

The children were called in, and we sat down to a picnic sort of meal, consisting of cold beef and plum pudding, and a tart or two from the unfortunate wedding breakfast. These tarts reminded me of a fact that I found hard to realise – that I was really married, and that this was my wedding day; yes, actually my wedding day! and here was I, the bride, sitting down to a demoralised sort of Christmas dinner in a hot kitchen, with a half roasted clergyman in his shirt sleeves and Mrs. Green in a voluminous cooking apron. And Jack? where was he? Over a mile away, fighting the fire in heat and dust and smoke. In danger, perhaps! Oh Jack, dear Jack! And I lost myself in loving, anxious thought, till I was roused by Biddy's "My word!" she said, coming to the back door. "It's near now, roaring like anything and they're beating like mad."

We jumped up at once and went outside. There was a fierce deep roaring, rushing sound like a big bushfire, and nothing else. The smoke hung over us thicker than ever and like a lurid cloud kept off the sunlight, the sun itself showing through it as a dull deep crimson disc, and through the roaring and crackling of the flames we heard the sound of the branch-es as the men fought with all their might.

While we watched, Mrs. Brown and Mrs. Jones came hurrying down again bringing with them some of the eatables they had just taken up.

"They've no time to eat," said Mrs. Brown "but they're just dried up with thirst. They want some more tea just as soon as you can send it up."

"I will take it," I said.

"Pray, allow me," said Mr. Smith.

"Well," said Mrs. Green, "I expect Mrs. Brown and Mrs. Jones are tired; and beside they want their dinner."

I went in search of my shadiest hat, and the parson donned his coat – a great mistake, as it proved – and we started off, he with two buckets of tea and I with one. Now, full buckets are awkward things to carry up a hillside at the best of times, and when they are full of tea, every drop of which you know will be precious to the thirsty men above, you get nervous and consequently spill more. Mr. Smith started with a light heart to carry those buckets up that hill, and if his heart was heavier when he reached the top the buckets were considerable lighter. We got on well enough at first, but soon came to a steep place where, though our arms were aching furiously, there was no place flat enough to set the buckets down. Then we had to sidle along the hill, and Mr. Smith had to hold one bucket higher than the other to keep it off the ground; and in spite of all his care, the up-hill bucket would keep catching on sticks and stones, and sending cataracts of streaming tea over his legs. He did not complain; but it must have been too hot to be comfortable. At last we got on a cattle track, which made the walking easier, though it had its drawbacks too, being six inches deep in soft well trodden dust. The condition of the par-son's moist legs after two minutes' walk through this may be imagined. He sailed benignly on, however, with one long coat-tail in each bucket of tea, till I could stand it no longer.

"Mr. Smith," I said, "I am afraid the tea will spoil your coat."

"Dear me! dear me!" he said, "what shall I do? They will go in, and I can't put the buckets down, and the tea will be spoilt. Dear me! what shall I do?"

"Shall I pin them up for you?" I asked.

"Thank you, thank you, Mrs. Rushton; if you would," he answered gratefully.

I managed to set my bucket down and steady it with my foot, while I pinned the tails of his coat together behind, so that it looked like a demented swallow-tail.

"Thank you, thank you, very much indeed," was all he said just then; but when we came to a place where we could set down our loads and rest, he observed, as he mournfully gazed at his muddy legs: "Really Mrs. Rushton, I am afraid this kind of work is detrimental to my cloth."

At last we reached the top and found the men hard at work. The fire had come upon them before they expected. Where a track was already burnt, they stopped it easily enough; but just here they were having a hard fight. So much we learned from one another as they stopped to swallow a pannikin of tea and then rush back to their work again. How hot they looked; hot and tired with faces scorched and grimy and eyes red with the stinging smoke. I had seen thirst before, though not quite so bad as this. Mr. Smith had not, I think, and his face grew very grave as he watched them.

"Well, parson," said one, as he drank the tea, in a voice husky and weak from exhaustion, "you're a Christian for this if you never said a prayer."

The clergyman looked distressed; he was a little shocked at first, I think, then I heard him murmur to himself: "A cup of cold water? I never knew what that meant until to-day."

When we got down again, he insisted on making another trip at once. I could not help admiring him as he started up the hill again with a bucket in each hand, this time without his coat.

"Well," said Biddy, looking after him, "he's got some pluck in spite of his coat."

"He's a brick!" said the children, and I quite agreed with them.

The fire was stopped on the hill behind the house, and the men had gone along the ridge to stop it farther on. We had dismantled the neglected breakfast table, and rearranged it with more regard for compactness than elegance, ready for the men's supper, and at last the long hot day was nearly over. Having nothing particular to do, I went and sat under the back verandah to rest. Mrs. Jones did likewise, and leaning her elbows on her knees and her chin on her hands, gazed silently upward at the smoke that told of the fight still going on. Mrs. Brown seized a broom and proceeded to sweep up the leaves scattered about by our decorations, talking meanwhile about other bushfires she had seen. Now that the fight was no longer in sight, the sense of excitement and conflict we had felt all day in some degree abated. Peaceful home sounds – the crying of a calf, the musical sound of milking from the bailyard close by, and the cheerful tinkling of teaspoons in the kitchen – contrasted strangely with a lurid glare of a smoky sunlight and the distant roaring of the flames. In a gum tree close by were a crowd of magpies that had flown screaming away from the fire, and were watching it intently, now and then bursting into a flood of angry song; while once or twice a flock of paroquets whizzed shrieking overhead.

I paid little attention to Mrs. Brown's conversation; but fell to thinking – of Jack, of course – till Biddy came across to the dairy with her buckets of milk and Mrs. Green came out and called the children in to tea. They came scampering in, discussing the day's events with a vivacity which put day dreaming out of the question for the time being.

During tea the talk was still bushfires; no one ever talks of anything else while one is burning. Afterward, when Mrs. Brown and Mrs. Jones had departed to their respective homes – cottages a little distance off – and Mrs. Green and Biddy were busy preparing for the men, whom they expected soon, I sat on a verandah and tried to talk the children into a calm enough state of mind for bed time. It had been a wildly exciting day for them and a "continual feast" as well, for they had made raids on the kitchen every now and then, carrying off their booty to be devoured in some place where there was a good view of the fire. They implored me not to speak of bed at first; but in spite of themselves they grew drowsy as they calmed down, and were soon ready to say "good night."

When they had gone I lost myself in my own thoughts again. How long I sat there dreaming I do not know. The sun had set, the short twilight was over and the smouldering logs shone out like large red stars from the blackened hillside above, when I noticed a strange light to my left. Going to the end of the house I saw a line of fire coming toward us along the flat. A smouldering log must have rolled down from above and lighted the grass. "Fire ! Fire! just here!" I shouted.

Mrs. Green and Biddy rushed out and took in the situation at a glance. Biddy just threw back her head, put her hands to her mouth and "coo-eed" loud and long.

"Get a can and wet the grass at the end of the house, Mary!" Mrs. Green called to me as she ran round the house shutting the windows, to keep the sparks out.

"Biddy," she continued, "throw water on the roof! it's as dry as tinder."

Biddy gave one more long "coo-o-ee!", and, seizing a bucket, fell to work; while Mrs. Green disappeared into the house, returning with the children, blinking and bewildered. Rolling them in blankets, she deposited them in the bed of a dried up creek near the house. Meanwhile, I had been running backward and forward with two large watering-cans from the tubs we had filled in the morning, trying to soak a strip of grass to check the fire in its advances on the house. My task was only half finished, however, when the fire came up. I caught up a branch and called to the others for help. We beat and beat with all our might; but the wind was high and the grass long, and it seemed as if we could not keep it back. The heat was intense and the smoke choked and blinded us; but we kept on till I felt as if each blow would be the last, and dimly wondered what would happen when I gave in, as I must do soon.

I do not know how long we worked; it seemed hours; but I suppose it was not many minutes. All at once we heard men's voices and running feet, and a dozen strong arms were beating beside us. It was a sharp tussle, but they got it under, and were just congratulating themselves on arriving in the nick of time, when a voice – Jack's voice – was heard calling for help, and they saw that the fire, though turned away from the house, was making straight for the wool-shed, which stood on a slight rise a little beyond. Jack was fighting it single-handed. It seemed to be getting the better of him; then while I watched, I saw him fall, and the fire rushed onward. And then I suppose I fainted, for I remember nothing till I felt myself slowly and painfully coming back to life in my own little room. At first I was only conscious of a deathly sick feeling; then I remembered that something had happened, something dreadful. What was it? Ah! Jack, I believe I called his name aloud; and then – could it be true? I heard his dear voice answering me, and felt his strong arms and his kisses on my face. It was no dream but Jack himself! I hid my face on his shoulder and sobbed. I have a dim recollection of hearing someone say, "She'll do now," then the the door was shut and we were alone. I had my arms around his neck and clung closely to him unwilling to loose my hold even to look up at his face.

"Hush, Mary," he said – "hush, my darling. I am here, safe and sound. Look up dear, and see for yourself."

At last I did look up. Could that be Jack? It looked more like a badly blacked Christy minstrel. "Why, Jack?" I cried, "you are as black as a – –" and I paused for want of a simile.

"A kettle?" he suggested. "Come, little woman, don't call names. I fancy there's a pair of us," he added, looking laughingly at me.

Of course I sat up at once and looked toward the glass to see what was the matter, and this is what I saw – Jack kneeling by the side of the coach, looking like a sadly dishevelled sweep, for one of his shirt-sleeves was burned off to the shoulder, and he was more or less black all over; while his eyes were red, and his teeth, displayed now by a broad grin, shone like a negro's from beneath the singed and stubby ends of what had once been his moustache. As for me, my light cotton dress was ornamented by sundry prints of a human hand in black, while round my waist was a broad band of the same hue. My left cheek was one dark smear; while on the other as well as on my forehead and lips, were numerous rough but unmistakable impressions of Jack's moustache.

It was no use trying to be sentimental under the circumstances; so I laughed instead, to Jack's relief, for he had a man's hatred of scenes.

"How did you escape?" I asked. "I thought I saw the fire go over you."

"Why, so it did," he answered. "When I found I could not stop it, I lay down and let it go over me."

"Oh, Jack! you must have been hurt."

"Well, I found it rather warm, certainly, and I am afraid my clothes have suffered. There, there, little wife; don't cry like that." The thought of his danger had been too much for me. "I am quite safe, thank God. I don't think I am seriously damaged, though my complexion is a little spoiled for the present."

He staid talking a little while, and then had to rush back to his task. They had just managed to save the wool-shed, but a good deal of fencing had gone. The worst of the fire was over, but it needed watching.

Next morning a rather dilapidated but very happy bride and bride-groom started on their homeward way, after saying good-bye to a still more dilapidated parson and being honoured with three very husky cheers from all hands.

How Jack Litton Lost His Christmas Dinner, and How He Found It

J.A.E.

Chapter I

Christmas Eve, and a hot and sultry one; a crowd of men, young, middle-aged and old, all mounted, and most of them leading pack horses, are trooping round at the door of the Travellers' Rest – the one inn of the little township of Never, far away up in the Gippsland hills. They are shearers who have that morning received their cheques at Ponji-wonji station, the last shed they have worked at on a long round and are now bound for their respective homes. Of course the horses are hastily hung up, and a rush for the bar takes place, for a longish ride in a blazing sun on a dusty road has made all thirsty. The younger portion mostly affect soft stuff – hop beer, shandygaff, etc. – while the seniors prefer hard tack i.e., whisky, brandy and rum. The question (when the first drought is appeased) is, who is going on? And the party is a good deal divided in opinion on the subject. One tall, handsome young fellow, the beau ideal of Gippsland native, who has been uncommonly irritable and fidgety for the past two days, starts up and declares that go who will he means to be at Myrtle Flat for dinner on the morrow.

"Nonsense! Impossible! Absurd! Why, its ninety miles! You're mad!" are the exclamations uttered by his companions; and even steady-going Harry Benson, to whom Jack Litton has more particularly addressed himself, pooh-poohed the notion.

"It can't be done, Jack, my boy, though I know how anxious you are to get home tomorrow, and I should like very well to do so, too, but we must both be content to get in in time for the Boxing Day sports, and that will be good work for the horses."

"I tell you it can and shall be done," said Jack Litton impatiently. "Tom Hirst, the boundary rider at Ponjiwonji, told me of a track by which I can save more than thirty miles, and old Aunt Sally is as fit as a fiddle, and I mean to try it. You turn up Caroline Creek to the old reef, then up a spur on to the main divide, and follow that all the way till you drop down at the head of Myrtle Flat, about fifteen miles from home. Won't you come with me, old fellow?"

Harry Benson shook his head. "I don't like parting company, Jack, but I couldn't do it. Aunt Sally may pull through in the time, though it will be hard work for her, but my horses couldn't stand it, and that New England colt of yours will knock up. I've heard of that track. It's terribly rough, and not a drop of water from the Caroline till you get on the Flat, fully thirty miles, and it's nearly 4 o'clock now. I wish you would give up the notion, and come round with me. It will be a beastly ride, and what does a day matter?"

"A good deal to me," replied Jack. "You ought to know – it's mother's birthday as well as being Christmas and I've never been from home on that day since I was born. I wrote and told her I'd be hone in time, and she'd fret her heart out if I didn't keep my word. So go I will."

While this colloquy took place between the friends the rest of the party were making their own arrangements. The majority decided to go on to Harris's, twenty miles further on their road, while a few of the older hands, who had rapidly made up for their enforced abstinence while at the shed, determined to stop where they were for the night.

"Harry," said Jack, "I'll get you to take the chestnut colt with my swag round with you, and I'll fill my water bag and take some biscuits and cheese, and I'll do first rate."

Jack proceeded to make the preparations he spoke of, and ate a hasty snack before starting on his arduous journey, and his friend quietly placed a small bottle into the pouch that held the provisions.

"You may be glad of it before you get through," observed Harry, when the other remonstrated. "I only wish you'd let it alone, this mad notion of yours, or that I could keep with you."

Harry and Jack had been friends and companions from childhood, their parents being near neighbours, but the former was the senior by about five years. A square built, powerful young man, with close cropped hair and bushy beard of dark brown, he had a somewhat grave and thoughtful look, and, though fairly handsome, was at a disadvantage beside his younger mate. Jack's 6 feet 1 inch in height took the actual breadth off his shoulders and the muscular development of his lithe limbs, while his curly black hair, dark blue eyes and fresh complexion, with a saucy, devil-may-care expression, made him very attractive in appearance. He was only twenty, and this had been his first shearing tour, while it was Harry Benson's fourth.

"Come, lads, have a glass with me, and then I'm off," cried Litton gaily. "I'll be home to the Flat and tell them you're all along the road."

And with hearty handshakes, and mutual good wishes, he mounted Aunt Sally, and followed by a ringing cheer Jack Litton cantered briskly away down the hot, dusty road.

Though he left the inn with a dash, Jack Litton had far too much judgment to travel far at such a pace, and very soon pulled his mare into a steady walk, turning up the Caroline Creek where the main road crossed it. For some fifteen miles he followed an old worn track that at one time had had a good deal of traffic upon it, but was now but little used. Now on one side of the creek, now on the other, crossing backwards and forwards, now keeping close to the water's edge, and again going over some steep spur, upwards and still upwards the road went. Here and there were traces of recent fossicking, and a hut now and then showed that a few miners still lingered on it, but practically the Caroline had been abandoned, when the reef so named had burst up. The afternoon was close and hot, and for the most part shut in among high and steep hills, there was but little air stirring. But still he pushed briskly forward.

A word now as to Aunt Sally, as she plays an important part in our history. Barely 15 hands high, at the first glance she appears unequal to the task of carrying so tall and muscular a rider. But mark the grand set of the shoulders, the deep girth and powerful quarters, supported on short, flat, clean legs and unexceptionable hoofs, and there is plenty of evidence of her weight-carrying abilities, while the game head, with its full bright eyes, well carried on a muscular neck, tells of the good blood that flows in her veins, though her pedigree cannot be traced for more than two generations with any certainty. Dark brown, almost black in colour, with tan muzzle and a small star, she was as good a specimen of the Gippsland stock horse as her master was of the youth of the district. She had been foaled at Litton's home twelve years before, and for the last six had carried Jack over every kind of country without a mistake.

At last, as the shadows of evening were closing round them, Jack and his mare reached the deserted workings of the once popular Caroline; the buildings fallen to decay, and the larger pieces of timber standing up, gaunt and grim as skeletons. Wheeling round the back of the old claim, Jack faced Aunt Sally at the last and steepest spur yet encountered. The gallant little mare mounted the pinch with quick, eager steps and occasional snorts, and emerged from the gloom of the creek into the full light of the setting sun. The general direction our hero was pursuing was to the south-west, and though there were abrupt turns to all points of the compass, the main course had been well preserved. Arrived on the main ridge, or divide, between two distinct watersheds, Jack pulled up for a few minutes to give Aunt Sally her wind, and to take note of the country before him.

Like the backbone of some gigantic snake, the divide stretched before him for miles, while spurs, answering to ribs, shot down on either side, with deep precipitous gullies between them, and as far as the eye could reach the timbered hills lay like the dark green billows of a troubled sea. No sign of human occupation was visible anywhere; no track even could be distinguished on that bare and rocky ridge, though a half-obliterated blaze might be discerned here and there on the trees. As he had ascended from the twilight of the north-eastern side of the divide into the light of the setting sun, so now also he met a south-west wind blowing short, sharp gusts, but not cool and refreshing; hot and tainted with smoke, it seemed to blow from the mouth of the furnace, and the dull red haze in which the sun was sinking told of distant bushfires.

"A bad look out for us, old girl," said Jack, as he re-mounted his mare. "I didn't think of this when I started. We're going into an ugly country to be caught in a bushfire, but we can't turn back now, so go along my pet, and get through it as fast as you can."

Aunt Sally tossed her pretty head and stepped gaily on, picking her way with cat-like activity over rocks and fallen timber, now jumping a log that crossed the track, and now scrambling round the head or butt of some fallen giant, but still making good progress. The sun faded and a young moon threw a faint light over the scene, and mile after mile was covered, and still, as they advanced, the smoke-laden wind blew stronger, and the dull red glow on the horizon increased.

"This fire's a boomer," thought Jack. "I shall have to look out pretty sharp to get through it safe. But it can't be helped now."

A peak rising up above the rest of the hills on his route now loomed large against the red background, and he recognised it by the description given him as the Night Cap, a land mark on his course, about half-way between the little township of Never and Myrtle Flat, and he pushed on to gain its summit and survey the country beyond. A good deal of very rough ground had to be traversed, for the gullies bit deep into the ridge at that part, and its crest zigzagged about, doubling the distance to his point of observation, and the smoke came more heavily on the increasing wind, and the light became brighter, and a sound like distant surf could be distinguished as he advanced. Jack and the fire were rapidly nearing each other.

At last the panting mare gained the top of the peak, and Jack again halted to look around and see what course he should take. The fire was raging along the southern side of the divide, and advancing rapidly, spreading from spur to gully and gully to spur, with fresh bursts of flame, as grass and scrub flared suddenly, with sharp crackling sounds, and then burnt more steadily in the heavy dead timber that encumbered the ground, or roared up the hollow trunk of some dead, standing tree. It was a terrible prospect. A regular sea of fire lay before him and to his left. He turned his gaze back on the road he had come, and calculated how long it would take him to retrace his steps, and whether he could outstrip the advancing fire, and felt that the chances were decidedly against his doing so, the narrowness of the road giving the flames, which overleaped all obstacles, a dreadful advantage. Even as he stared wildly around he noted that the fire had taken hold in the gullies leading up to the ridge behind him, and that his retreat was virtually cut off. There only remained the northern side of the divide to turn to, and that was an unknown and almost untrodden wilderness, a tangle of spurs and gullies, from, which it would be difficult to extricate himself, even if the fire did not follow him into its recesses. However, it was the only course open to him to escape the terrible peril that threatened him, and observing one spur that seemed clearer of scrub and timber, and a little less precipitous than the rest, he turned his willing beast towards it, with but faint hopes of escaping the impending danger.

Chapter II

Christmas Day on Myrtle Flat. Bright, sunny and very hot, even for an Australian Christmas. The south westerly wind that has been blowing all the previous night and early morning is dying away, and indications of an approaching thunderstorm are perceptible, as Mrs. Litton busies herself preparing the dinner for her expected son, often glancing anxiously down the road to see if there are any signs of his coming. A fresh and still comely matron, a little over forty, she is active and bustling, preferring to do her own housework, though in very comfortable circumstances. People at one time wondered how so pretty a girl as Mary Gibson, with a bit of property, too, could think of marrying a crabbed, lame, ugly man, old enough to be her father; but she did, and for love, too, and the love yet remained, and was only equalled by that for her only son – our friend Jack. To extenuate her want of taste, we must tell our readers that Andrew Litton was not a commonplace man. The younger son of a substantial farmer in the north of England, he had had a fair education, besides learning his father's business; but having been jilted when quite young, he had enlisted in a distinguished Highland regiment, and served with it through the Crimean war, and subsequently in India, during the mutiny, where, having attained the rank of Sergeant Major, and gained the Victoria Cross, he had to retire on a pension, with one leg shortened by nearly two inches. His strongly marked features, bronzed and roughened by campaigning, looked harsh and stern, and the gruff abrupt manner acquired in the same school were not generally prepossessing, but a kind heart and well-informed mind were hidden under the hard outer crust, which his wife was one of the few who could penetrate. Though dearly loving his son, his habits of discipline and grim manner and appearance had rendered him more an object of awe and reverence than affection, on Jack's part, while his mother gained his fondest love.

Myrtle Flat, is an extensive stretch of rich land on the bank of one of the finest rivers in Gippsland, and is dotted over with thriving farms, and of all these, though there were some larger, there were none more fertile or better kept than Andrew Litton's. His savings during his military career and his share of his father's property, amounted to a tidy little sum, with which he emigrated to Australia, where he met, wooed and won his bride, an orphan, who had been brought up by an aunt, a farmer's wife, who had carefully nursed the girl's small inheritance as well as herself, so that she found herself at one and twenty mistress of a nice little head of dairy cattle, and three or four hundred pounds in the bank. Coming into Gippsland on their marriage they had selected a capital piece of land on Myrtle Fat, which, with their stock and capital, and their early experience in farming, enabled them to make the best use of. They had a small but comfortable house, standing in a well stocked orchard and garden, which they had occupied for several years, their first residence, a few hundred yards away, being turned over to the men's use. The out buildings stood between the two, and were ample, and in good order, and the whole establishment showed the signs of comfort and plenty, and care and good management. Andrew Litton limped into the kitchen with a basket of fresh gathered fruit to find his wife putting the finishing touches to a fat goose, before putting it into the oven.

"No sign of Jack yet, father," she said with a sigh. "Whatever's keeping the boy? All last night I've been looking for him and he's not come yet. I wish we'd never let him go round the country shearing – that he isn't here today, of all days in the year."

"Tut, tut, woman, what's fretting ye? The lad can't be tied to your apron strings all his life. He must learn to rough it a bit, and work his way, and know what 'dooty' means."

"Isn't it his duty to be hero today, when he promised?"

"Maybe, maybe, but he may have other 'dooties' which come first.

Never fear, he'll be home soon. I just saw Mrs. Benson, and her lad's not home either, and you know Harry would come as soon as Jack."

"True," said Mrs. Litton, "but I can't help missing him so much today. He's never been away from us before on this day. Something must have happened to him. The sky over the ranges was all red last night with bushfires."

"Don't worry about that old girl," Andrew replied, laying his hand kindly on her shoulder, "that's out of his road altogether. I saw that, too, last night, and was glad the wind was taking the fire away from the flat, and think we'll have a thunderstorm soon, and that will put it out and cool the air a bit."

Poor Mrs. Litton kept delaying her dinner as long as possible, in the vain hope of her son's arrival, and at last, when the goose was dried to a chip and the vegetables spoilt, she and her husband sat down to it with but sorry appetites, and made a pretence of feasting. The storm came on in the evening, and added to the mother's uneasiness, and Andrew smoked an extra pipe and drank two or three glasses of toddy in grim silence. Night came at last, and the couple went to bed, after the dullest Christmas Day they had spent since their marriage.

Boxing Day morning was lovely. The storm had passed and left the air clear and fresh, while the sun shone in a cloudless sky over Myrtle Flat. On a piece of common land in front of the public house, store, blacksmith's and butcher's shops that constituted the township, preparations were being made for the sports usually held on that day, and by noon nearly all the residents had assembled there. Spring carts, buggies and drays, crowded with children, drew up on the green. Young men and women, dressed in their best, come cantering along from all directions, while many, who lived near the scene of action, came on foot.

Among those were Mr. and Mrs. Litton and their near neighbour, Mrs. Benson. The latter, a faded, careworn woman of fifty, was accompanied by her daughter, a rather plain, awkward girl of fourteen. Her lines had not been cast in such pleasant places as the Littons. Left a widow with a baby girl and a son of twelve years old, she had had a hard struggle to keep her little bit of land, and clear off the debts with which her thriftless husband had encumbered it, and though she and her boy had worked bravely, they would never have succeeded but for the quiet, unostentatious help of her gruff but kind neighbour. As Harry had grown up, things had improved, and his yearly shearing tour always brought in a very serviceable sum, so that she was now almost out of her difficulties, but the years of toil and anxiety had told upon her, and she was already an aged woman. Andrew Litton, leaning on a stout crutch-handled stick, limped through the crowd with head erect and chest thrown out, like the ancient warrior he was, giving short nods and brief greetings to his acquaintances, while his wife smiled and spoke pleasantly to all, and Mrs. Benson answered her friends in her usual weary, subdued manner. The absence of their sons, who would, if there, have been active competitors in the various games, had a disturbing effect upon all three, and as a commencement was made with some of the children's races, their eyes were anxiously turned towards the road from town by which they might to expected to come.

At last, when some of the minor events had been concluded, a cry was heard, "There's Harry Benson at last, and with two packhorses."

"Yes, that's Harry's old grey and the big bay, but where's the chestnut? And where's Jack Litton?"

Driving the two loose horses before him at a smart canter, Harry was soon it the midst of the throng, who welcomed him warmly, but he pushed on to where his mother and the Littons were standing. "How d'ye do, mother. How d'ye do, Mrs. Litton. How d'ye do Andrew," he cried, with hearty handshakes, "but where's Jack?"

"Jack!" exclaimed Mrs. Litton. "Isn't he with you?"

"No!"

"Isn't he here?" cried Harry, in some alarm. "Hasn't he come home yet?"

"No," said Andrew, "he has not come home. Why is he not with you?"

Harry turned pale as he replied, "He left me on Christmas Eve to take the short track along the divide, so as to be home to dinner yesterday. Can he have lost his way?"

"Heavens," exclaimed the poor mother, "and there were bushfires burning on the range all last night and yesterday. My boy's lost, lost," and she cried bitterly.

Old Andrew stood erect, stern and silent, but his twitching fingers, his face pale to the lips, and the heaving of his chest, told how deeply he was affected.

"Come, mother," he said, gently, touching her arm, "let us get home, and I'll go and find him."

"Not you, sir," said Harry eagerly, "I will go, and I am sure others will, too."

A score of the young men were rushing to their horses, when old Steve Goodall, the oldest bushman in the assemblage, reared his gaunt form, and in his strident voice, cried "Steady boys, steady, don't be in too great a hurry. I'll make one if you'll listen to reason, an do as I tell'e, an we'll be off in 'arf an 'our."

While old Steve, whose professed occupation was hunting kangaroos or wallaby, but who was strongly suspected of cattle duffing and illicit distillation, but also was admitted to be better acquainted with the intricacies of the ranges than any other man in the country, was speaking, Andrew Litton had led his weeping wife home, and kissing her tenderly at the door, had called up one of his men to bring up Major, the horse he usually drove in his waggonette, and put a saddle on him at once, and in a few minutes he was galloping towards the ranges, as if charging an enemy.

Steve Goodall had in the meantime issued his orders. "Twelve on ye with the best horses will do. One of yeas take a tommyhawk, a strong sheet or two, a piece o' line an' things, in case one has, which Lord forbid," he whispered, "to make a stretcher. Take some tucker too an' summat to drink, and then git away an' quick all quiet as you can. You Harry git a bite quick an take my roan mare; she's fresh an' strong, an' yours is tired an' foot sore. Look sharp now, lad, while I saddle old Ginger."

His orders were promptly attended to, and in half an hour a dozen well-mounted young men, including our friend, Harry, fully equipped with ambulance requisites, were cantering away from the scene of the sports now neglected by everyone.

As they came to Litton's slip pannel Steve's sharp eye caught sight of the fresh hoof prints. "Hullo," he shouted, "Master Litton's gone off before us on that big cart 'oss of his'n, an' the way he's ridin' him they'll both be cooked afore he gits to Jones's; we mun push on and look arter him," and with that the whole party quickened their pace, but still keeping a rate that the horses could last at for some distance. At the end of six or seven miles they overtook the poor veteran, exhausted by the emotion and the unwonted exertion, which caused great pain to his crippled leg. His horse, too, unused to such work, was blown and staggering with fatigue, and would very likely have fallen if pushed much further. With much persuasion they got the old man to remain at Jones's farm, now near at hand, where he was laid upon a sofa and attended to by the good wife, while her husband joined the search party.

Under Steve's guidance, the party resumed their journey, and when they reached the region where the fire had raged they searched diligently in every direction, but without avail. The heavy rain that had fallen had so washed the ground that no tracks could have been seen, had there been any, and at last, wearied and dispirited, they turned their horses' heads homewards. Harry and Steve determined to renew the search on the morrow, though with but faint hopes of finding poor Jack alive, and some of the others offered to accompany them, and they were arranging their plans as they slowly returned to Jones's. At Jones's they found poor Andrew Litton, ill in body and mind, though trying to bear up with soldierly fortitude. As he was quite unfit to mount his horse again Mr. Jones's buggy was brought out, and old Major harnessed to it, and Harry Benson undertook to drive the suffering old man home, and thus, in melancholy fashion, the cavalcade slowly returned to Myrtle Flat.

Chapter III

We left our friend Jack, threatened on three sides by the advancing bushfire, and turning down a spur on the only one that seemed open to him. It was now a good deal after midnight, was, in fact, Christmas Day, and hailed as such all over the colonies, but was not ushered in very merrily to him. The moon was down, and though the lurid light of the flames reddened, the sky, they shed little or no light on the shadowed track he was pursuing down into far away and unknown gullies. Poor Aunt Sally, good and game as she was, began to show symptoms of distress, the heat and stifling smoke being more the cause than either the length of the journey or the pace she had come. Still, when Jack patted her steaming neck, and spoke encouragingly to her, she stepped stoutly on, and though her progress in the darkness was necessarily slow, yet it was sure.

The spur was not particularly steep in grade, nor very much blocked with fallen timber, but though in the darkness Jack did not notice it, it bent sharply to the westward, and ran parallel to the course of the divide at that point. Just as he was beginning to congratulate himself on his escape from danger, a red glare again faced him; the angry crackling of flames was heard, and he found to his horror that the fire had crossed the divide, at a spur lower down, and was eating its way up towards him. It had already taken possession of the gully on his left and he would soon be face to face with it. Which way could he turn? Stout-hearted young follow as he was, he shuddered at the thought of being enclosed in a ring of fire, and memories of the day, of his loved and loving mother, of his just, though rather stern father, crowded upon him, and almost unmanned him.

As the scene around was lit brightly up, he saw something – he could not tell whether man or beast, leaping and scrambling through the undergrowth in the gully, nearly in the direction in which he stood. Glancing beyond the point the form was last visible at, he noted that across the gully, which at that part was tolerably clear and open, was a stretch of bare naked earth without bush or tree upon it, reaching to the base of a precipitous cliff that at part seemed to be pierced by a cavern of some sort. There perhaps he might find a shelter, and towards it he urged the tired and terrified mare. They were just in time, and reached the cliff before the flames had spread so far up the gully. The bare ground he crossed was covered with hillocks of earth, with pits between them, but this he scarcely noted at the time, and Sally's instinct led her safely through. But she shied, and snorted with alarm, as she was directed to the entrance to the cave. Looking down, Jack saw what had startled her. The figure of a man, lying face downwards, and apparently either insensible or dead.

Jumping to the ground at once, Jack, with the bridle on his arm, advanced to the prostrate form, and bending over it discovered that it still breathed, but was quite unconscious. Fortunately, he had made but very moderate use of his water bag on the journey, so there was a good drop still left in it, and filling his pannikin he sprinkled some in the man's face, and put the vessel to his lips. This slightly revived him, and he opened his eyes, and uttered some unintelligible sounds. Litton raised him, and placed him in a half-sitting position against a mound of earth. Then remembering what Harry Benson had placed in his saddle bag, he reached for it, and found a soda water bottle filled with whisky. A small dose of this still further revived the stranger, and Jack succeeded in getting him within the opening in the cliff, and also, leading in the reluctant Aunt Sally.

Short as the delay was, had it happened a little further from the refuge, it must have proved fatal to one, or both, for they had scarcely reached its shelter when the fire swept past. The upturned ground, not more than a hundred yards in diameter, offering nothing to feed it, it circled round it, but so great was the heat, so dense the smoke, that poor Jack crouched down by the side of the man he had assisted, in almost as helpless a condition, and the poor mare cowered against the rock, with her nose to the ground and trembling in every limb. How long this lasted Jack could never tell. At last, by a great effort, he roused himself, and mixed and drank a little of the spirits and water, giving another dose to the man thus strangely thrown on his protection. There was but little water now left, but Jack wetted his handkerchief and wiped poor Sally's parched nostrils with it, and soothed her, when not too busy with his human charge. Thus the short remainder of the midsummer night passed, seeming long enough however to our hero.

When the light broke through the veil of smoke, Jack stepped out on to the bare open space to look about him. The fire had burnt itself out among the grass and scrub, but many logs and dead trees were still blazing fiercely. All immediate danger was past, and the sooner he could make a start for home the better, but what to do with the helpless man, now dozing in the cave, troubled him. Looking about him, he saw now that the ground he stood upon had been worked for gold. Though he had never followed mining as an occupation, he had occasionally visited diggings and came to the conclusion that this man, who had run here for safety, was the owner of the claim. Looking down the gully, a well worn foot path, showing distinctly on the bare and blackened ground, could be traced for some distance, and he at once came to the conclusion that the man's habitation was there, and that where he lived, there must be water. He led Aunt Sally down the track for nearly half a mile, when he found the smouldering ruins of a log and bark hut. The roof had fallen in, some of the logs were still alight, and not a particle of bedding, food or clothing, was left. A little way off, as he anticipated, he found a pool of clear water, at which both he and poor Sally refreshed themselves, and refilling the precious water bag he returned to the cave. Up to this time the anxiety he had undergone had prevented his thinking of food, but he now began to feel the want of it, and was glad to find a good parcel of biscuits and cheese in his saddle bag. With some difficulty he roused up the man and urged him to share his meal. In the daylight he saw that he was an old man, with long, grey beard and hair, large framed, and probably once very powerful, but now wasted and pinched by disease or privation. When he spoke his accent proclaimed him a German, and in his own way he expressed himself.

"Vat you here come for? To spy my claims? You tell dem beeples out dere and you I kill."

Jack was rather surprised at such a return for all his kindness, but concluding he was slightly crazed, hastened to assure him that he would not betray his secret, and asked his name, and where his friends lived, that he might help him to reach them. Then in a moment his mood changed, and he moaned and cried pitifully.

"Ah, Hans Bobardt will die, and never his little girl Mina shall see. The fortune that for her he save, she never get, dat littel girl."

"Where does she live?" asked Jack.

"At Hardscrape," replied Hans, between his moans. "Mien goot beeples dere live, and my littel Mina – but dare I get never – I been ill dese two week, and I no more can walk dere."

"How far is it from here?" asked Jack, who had heard of the little mining village of that name, as being nearly forty miles from Myrtle Flat.

"Six, eight, nine miles," replied Hans. "I dere cannot come."

"Oh yes you can," replied Jack, cheerfully. "Get on my horse, and show me the road, and I will get you there safe enough." With much trouble he persuaded the old digger, who was a marvel of rags and dirt, to mount Aunt Sally to whom he clung in a helpless fashion. The road he indicated led down the gully, and as they passed the burnt hut Han's lamentations broke forth again.

"I vas ruined. All mien broperty is gone. I will go too."

Jack led his mare, who, with drooping head, followed patiently in his footsteps, the old man, from time to time, indicating the road to take. Many steep spurs and deep gullies had to be crossed, and many times they stopped to rest where there was a little shade, for the old digger was evidently very ill, and could with difficulty keep his seat over the bad pinches. They had got out of the burnt country and the poor mare, whose hollow flanks showed how badly she had fared, managed to pick a few mouthfuls of grass from time to time, and thus they crept along till well on in the afternoon they reached the little hamlet of Hardscrape.

One quartz reef and a few alluvial claims were all it could boast. The miners' houses were scattered about as fancy or convenience dictated. A solitary store, bearing the name of Dougal Cameron, was the most conspicuous building, and a small white state schoolhouse stood a little way beyond it.

"Dose is mien beeples, and mien little girl Mina dere she live," cried the old German, with tears running down his dirty cheeks. "Vonce more I dem see."

Jack halted and rapped at the closed door of the store, and helped the exhausted old digger to slide to the ground, where he half sat, half lay, till the door was opened by a tall, bony, old man, who asked rather roughly, "Who are ye, an' what dy'e want?" Catching sight of the limp bundle of rags on the ground, he shouted to someone inside the house. "Meestress, here's auld Hans come hame, and either drunk or deeing. Make haste woman."

"Where did ye fin' him, lad an' what ails him?"

Jack briefly told him, as a plump, kindly looking old woman came out and took the digger's hand.

"Mina! Mina!" he cried, "I will die, and her not see."

"There's a bit children's feast an' lecture at the school room yon', and the lassie's there," said the storekeeper. "Rin over an' ask for her while we get t'auld mon inside."

Jack crossed over to the little school building, from which a hum of voices sounded, and knocked at the door. It was quickly opened, and a tall, finely formed young lady, whose pretty blue muslin dress set off her blonde beauty to perfection, stood there, and looked him all over in a manner that recalled to his mind that his neat riding garb was now dirty and disordered, his face flushed and streaked with soot and dust, and that his appearance was decidedly against him.

"Your pleasure, sir?"

And Jack timidly asked, "Is there a little girl called Nina Bobardt here?"

"Nina Bobardt? What do you mean, sir? There is no such person."

"Nina Cameron, perhaps I should have said. The old man said his little girl Nina."

"I cannot understand your meaning, sir," replied the girl, with raised head, flashing eyes, and heightened colour. "My name is Mina Cameron. If you have any business with me, say so. You see I am engaged at present."

"I beg your pardon, Miss," said poor Jack, humbly. "I'm sure I meant no offence. The old man – Hans Bobardt, he calls himself – that I have just brought in from the ranges, kept talking of his little girl Nina all the time, and wanting to see her before he died, so I came across from the store to fetch her, but never dreamt you was she."

"What!" exclaimed Miss Cameron, with a sudden change of manner, "Poor old Uncle Hans ill – dying! and you have come for me. I'll follow you in a moment." And re-entering the school house, she quickly came out with a broad-brimmed, straw hat on her fair hair, and crossed the road like a young fawn. Jack stared. He thought he had never seen a prettier creature, and felt woefully ashamed of his untidy appearance and awkward blunders. However, he followed her into the store, where he was accosted by Mr. Cameron.

"Come here, laddie, an' tell me aboot it – how ye faund the puir ould fellow. 'Deed an' I'm sure we're much beholden to ye. The meestress is looking after him, an by guid luck, Dr. Bolus came up yestreen, to the mine manager's wife, an' I have sent roun' to ask him to call befores he goes awa'. But come here, an' get a bite an' sup, for ye seem to ha' had a sair job wi' him."

Jack followed his kindly host into the living room, at the back of the store, and, while he refreshed himself with a substantial meal, related his recent adventure.

"An' sae y'ere Andrew Litton's son, at Myrtle Flat. I've heard o' him, though we've only lived three years in these pairts. An' ye brought that puir, feckless body along, an' you sae keen to get to ye're ain hame! An' ye canna wil get there the night. It's too far, an' you, an' your beast are baith too weary, an' n thunner storm is coming on, an' sae ye'll just bide here. Your mares in the stable, an' weel cared for by this, sae bide easy."

In the course of the conversation that followed, Jack learnt that Mr. and Mrs. Cameron, with old Bobardt, who was uncle to Mrs. Cameron, had come to Hardscrape from the western gold fields, about three years before; that the old man who was possessed with the idea that he would make a fortune in the ranges was away prospecting there nearly all the time, only coming in for a supply of necessaries, but never having more than a few pennyweights of gold on those occasions.

"He likes a drap when he can get it, an' then he brags less, an' ye canna believe a word he says. When he's sober, ye canna get a bawbee, or a word oot o' him. But he aye talks of my Jean – Mina he an' the mither ca' her; she's teacher at' the schule over yonder – an' the great things he'll do for her. But I fear his most spent noo, puir auld body. Jean!" he continued, as his daughter now came into the room, "this laddie, whae's been sae kind to yuur're guid uncle, is a freen of a freen of yours. This is Jack Litton. Ye may ha heard Harry Benson tell of."

It was now Miss Cameron's turn to look a little foolish, as Jack, washed and brushed, and looking very saucy and handsome, rose with extended hand.

Jack had heard his friend talk of Jean Cameron as the one he had always hoped to win for a wife, when he should be able to provide a comfortable home for her, free from debts and mortgages, and Jean had often heard of him, from Harry, so that her treatment of him at their first meeting seemed rather ungracious. However, they soon became excellent friends. Meantime the thunder storm raged without, and the old prospector, who seemed sinking fast, was visited by the doctor, who could give no hope of his recovery. The shock caused by the fire, acting on a frame enfeebled by age and privations, was past remedy, and he could live but a few hours more.

Jack Litton, thoroughly worn out, was only only too glad to turn into the bed improvised for him, where he slept, unheeding the storm, while the Camerons attended to their dying relative. The morning was well advanced when Mr. Cameron visited his sleeping place, and disturbed his slumbers.

"Rouse up, laddie. You puir auld fellow is going fast, and is speering for ye, or I wadna ha wakened ye sae airly."

Jack dressed himself and followed his host to the room where old Bobardt lay, with his niece and grand niece in attendance on him, and two strapping lads of seventeen or eighteen, who were introduced as young Dougal and Alick respectively, were also in the small apartment.

"Dot is de young mans vot know. I schwear him to not tell, or I him kill. But he may speak now. Gif me dot tin box you keep for me."

Jean went out and soon returned, bearing a battered cash box. With trembling hands, he opened it, with a key hanging from his neck by a string, and from among some old papers it contained, he selected one.

"See dot, it is mien vill. I leafs every ting to mien little girl, Mina. You see me poor. I am rich — dot quartz reef in de rock, wat dot young man know, is tousands, millions, pounds. I gifs it her. Den from mien chimney to de door, I much gold bury. I plant him — ounces, pounds, fine gold, you dig him up for her. She be von great lady. Ah! I very poor you know. I make her rich."

The old digger sank back, and closed his eyes, and babbling in faint and incoherent tones, he gradually fell into his last sleep, and our hero retired from the death chamber.

Shortly after old Cameron called him to breakfast, apologising for the absence of his wife and daughter, but furnishing him with a substantial meal, which he would need before his long ride. The young Camerons brought out Aunt Sally, looking fresh and lively, after her abundant feed and rest, and with mutual good wishes he took his leave.

"Ye'll be sure an' come after New Year, you an' Harry an' the lads, an' I will gang wi ye and we'll see what puir auld Hans has left you."

Jack's forty-mile ride from Hardscrape to Myrtle Flat was as rough, monotonous and uneventful as possible and towards evening he reached his home a little surprised at not seeing his father sitting in the verandah as usual. He hurried indoors, and found his mother sitting mournfully with Mrs. Benson, trying to console her.

It is needless to picture their meeting, and before he had half related his adventures the tramp of horse's feet was heard, and the search party appeared in sight of the house. Jack went out to meet them, and a shout of delight went up, when the missing one was seen. Grim, old Andrew, for the first time, to the knowledge of any one, hugged his recovered son while tears shone in his eyes for the first time.

Jack fully realised how deep was his father's love for him. The searchers were all invited in to hear what had caused Jack's protracted absence, and partake of much needed refreshments, while the farm hands provided for the weary horses. And the tale was told, and commented upon till far into the night before the happy party broke up.

Jack home, safe and sound, there is but little more to tell, but as a postscript is said to contain the pith of a lady's letter, so ours contains what Jack found. Harry Benson blushed like a girl when Jack extolled the charms of Miss Cameron, and readily agreed to accompany Jack on his visit to Hardscrape, and early in the New Year they went there, and all being equipped for a couple of days' camping out, and some picks and shovels provided, our friends, with Mr. Cameron and his two sons, started into the ranges. Jack led the way on Aunt Sally, and retraced without much trouble the road he had travelled on that terrible Christmas Day. And the party arrived at last in front of the memorable cave. Seen under a clear light and by practical miners, as the Camerons were, it proved to be partly a natural cavity formed by fallen rock, and partly a tunnel driven on the course of a quartz reef of considerable width. This, on being carefully examined, was pronounced by the experts to be a buck reef of the most decided kind, and not worth wasting a charge of powder upon, and they then proceeded to look for the deposits in the hut.

"Old Hans had a bit of surfacing up near his reef," said Alick Cameron "but I don't think it could have been very rich, but we'll see his fortune now."

Commencing, by clearing away the logs and rubbish where the old hut had stood, the young men started with pick and shovel to turn up the earthen floor, and in a short time produced a piece of old rag tied with rotting twine, and containing about two ounces of gold.

"Is that the great fortune, I wonder," said the finder.

"No, not all of it," answered his brother, unearthing a similar parcel.

"Mind how ye handle it," said their father. "Ye hae burst yin clout, an' the gouds gaen in the earth again. Ye'll hae to pan it out, but we'll hae supper now and finish the work in the morn."

The party camped in the gully that night, and at daybreak resumed the search, which resulted in the finding of several more small packages, amounting in all to about twenty ounces.

"Try it a bit deeper lads, there's no telling where he may ha pit it, an' look well as ye gang."

The young fellows plied their tools vigorously, but no more plants could they discover, and both pronounced it new, unbroken ground, and they were just about leaving it when one of them was attracted by the appearance of a piece of stone just turned up.

"Something here at last, dad; there's a real quartz reef here, I think," and he went a little deeper still.

A few hours' work served to show that a gold bearing reef had lain unsuspected beneath the hut of the poor fossicker, whose boasted hoard did not amount to a hundred pounds in all, and whose jealously guarded reef was absolutely valueless. Prospects and specimens were obtained from the newly found reef, and all hands returned to Hardscrape, where they proceeded in due form to apply for a lease, and subsequently worked it, obtaining several rich crushings, and with every probability of many more.

Before Christmas Day came round again Jack Litton was again called upon to ride to Hardscrape, in the capacity of best man, on the occasion of Harry Benson wedding the fair Jean Wilhemina Cameron.

The Other Man

Mary Gaunt

Chapter XVII. Telling Dolly the News[1]

Dolly's home in the Forest was a very humble one, only a weather-board cottage with a shingle roof and a broad verandah in front. It was high on the side of a hill facing the south, so that they got refreshing sea breezes sometimes in the middle of the summer, but there was no view. The dense close forest shut them in on every side; only just round the house was a small cleared space, part of which was laid out a garden, where Roger cultivated vegetables in his spare time, and Dolly managed to grow a few flowers. Not that there was much difficulty about it. In the rich vegetable soil, once the land was cleared, the flowers grew like weeds, and the only trouble was water. Pumping it up from the well took time and labour, and often neither Roger nor the man who helped him on the little selection had time to spare, but even then Dolly herself would pump sometimes rather than her precious garden should suffer.

And she had her reward. The little house nestling among the hills was a charming little home, as different as well could be from the weather-board cottages surrounded by unlovely potato plots which as a rule are the homes of the selectors in the Heytesbury Forest. In years to come the southern lands of Victoria may be all smiling cornfields, where the fierce heat of an Australian summer is always tempered by the cool breezes from the Southern Ocean, but at present the ranges between Geelong and Warrnambool are densely wooded, covered with immense trees and a scrub so thick that the work of clearing the land and making it fit for the

---

[1] 'The Other Man' was serialised in the *Argus* between 13 October 1894 and 12 January 1895. This is an excerpt.

use of man is worthy of Hercules himself. And yet there are many settlers there, for the land, once cleared, is rich and valuable.

The summer of '85-86 was exceptionally hot even in the south of Victoria, and Dolly bemoaned that her garden was being ruined.

"It'll be all dead with the heat, Roger," she said. "Ruth won't admire it at all."

"Oh, yes, she will. She'll understand. Besides, think what the Kooringa garden must be like this summer."

And Roger was right. To Ruth, coming from the turmoil and discomfort of Kooringa, the little cottage on the hill was a very haven of rest.

"Burnt up, Dolly? Indeed, no. You should just see Kooringa garden. And how well the passion flower has grown over the verandah! It makes quite a little bower. And those gladioli, how fine they are!"

"I do think it's rather nice," said Dolly, pleased. "I water that creeper well, though, for it's so close to the house and no trouble. But, oh dear, there really is a good deal to do about the house. I wonder if you see any falling off. You see baby wants such a lot of attention now he's beginning to walk, and with only one servant there's really a good deal to do."

"You manage wonderfully, Dolly, I think," said her sister, ready as of old to admire anything Dolly did. "It must be such hard work."

"Why, no," said Dolly. "You see, it's all for Roger and myself and baby, so it makes such a difference. You know, you really don't seem to care how hard you work when it's to make your home nice, do you?"

"No," said Ruth, and Dolly went on.

"It's so nice to work for Roger. He's so pleased with everything I do. Oh, Ruth, I'm such a happy woman."

"Dolly, I'm so thankful."

"If only you were happily married too, Ruth, if only –"

"Come wife, come," Roger's voice broke in on their *tete-a-tete*.

"Come out and show Ruth round the estate. It's a little cooler now, and you might open the windows."

Ruth rose up thankfully. She had not yet told her sister of her engagement to Dr. Finlayson, and somehow she was glad to put it off for a space. She must tell her soon, she knew, but the engagement seemed to have been almost forced upon her by circumstances, and she could hardly yet decide whether she was glad or sorry to throw in her lot with the doctor. At least tomorrow would be soon enough to tell Dolly, she thought, as they wandered round the little farmyard in the cool of the evening inspecting the cocks and the hens, and stirring up the pigs to make them show off their good points.

"They're real Berkshire pigs," said Dolly proudly, "and it was my idea entirely having them, wasn't it, Roger. You see, I'm sure pigs pay best of all, and we grow vegetables so easily it seems a shame not to have them. Roger was afraid they'd be a bother, because he and Davis sometimes when they're clearing on the other side of the place aren't in till after dark. But I knew I could feed them. Gretchen and I – she takes as much interest in them as I do – and then they make such a difference. Why, our last pigs we bought when they were tiny little things at 3s. each, and after we'd had them three months we sold them at about £2 each. Wasn't that good?"

"She's a capital little farmer, this wife of mine," said Marsden laughing, but evidently very proud of his wife. "Look at all her cocks and hens there. They're all to be turned into solid cash I'm told."

"Now, Roger, you're laughing. Look here, Ruth. I made £30 clear out of my poultry and eggs last year. Wasn't that a good lot? Pigs go into the general funds, you know, but the poultry is my very own."

"Married woman's property," said Roger. "She's got a stocking somewhere, and she's hoarding, Ruth. She won't let me touch any of that money."

"No, of course not. Don't you think I'm right, Ruth. That's a reserve fund. If we ever want money very, very badly there'll be that, and if we don't I shall save it for the boy. He must go to the grammar school, like his father, and he must have a university education if we can only afford it. So you see it's best to begin saving now."

"Wise Dolly," said Roger, patting her hand, and Ruth, smiling assent, wondered if she could ever be so happy. If ever to her would come the peace and joy of loving and being loved.

To many such a life would have seemed sordid and hard and narrow, but Dolly standing there in the evening sunlight in her neat blue print with her baby in her arms and her husband by her side was a person to be envied by her elder sister.

She called herself ungrateful when next day brought her a long letter from Dr. Finlayson, so tender and so loving – so full of her and her only – surely not Dolly herself had more wealth of love lavished on her. Surely she could be a happy woman too, if only she would take the love which was offered so freely instead of looking vainly backwards at what could never be.

She read her letter in the short Australian twilight; in the next room she could hear Dolly singing softly as she hushed her boy to sleep, and out on the verandah her brother-in-law, his labours over for the day, was puffing away at his pipe.

"A penny, Ruth," he said, coming to the window, "a penny for your thoughts. You haven't spoken a single solitary word since I brought you that letter, and I want to be entertained now my work's done."

"A penny for yours then, I'm sure you leant against that post so long I thought you were never going to move again. Come now, what were yours?"

"I was thinking I ought to get another pig. I could easily put in a few more vegetables, and Dolly manages so splendidly there's always plenty of milk. Then I might put something away towards the boy's education, too."

"Dolly would be so pleased," said Ruth; and then added with a little laugh, "Dear me, the care of matrimony."

"It has its compensations," said Marsden, sitting down himself in a garden seat close to the window, so that he had his sister-in-law in full view. "You haven't embarked on its troubled waters yet, Ruth; why's that."

"Nobody asked me, sir," she laughed.

"Now, what's the good of telling me fibs. As if I didn't see with my own eyes Maitland was awfully gone on you two years ago. I never could make out why that never came to anything, for I used to think you rather liked him, too."

"Just like a man," she said, looking him bravely in the face, though she felt the blood mounting to her cheeks. "Just like a man. We took compassion on one another because you and Dolly were so absorbed in one another that if we had not got up a rival flirtation, we'd have been dreadfully dull and out in the cold."

"Oh, yes; it's all very well to put it that way, but if ever I saw a man in love it was Maitland. You have not met for two years, have you? I wonder if he's got over it. I suppose you know he's at Tamba now."

"Is he?" she managed to ask.

"Oh, yes, Waterworks or something. Shall I ask him over?"

"No, no; what nonsense – not for me."

"What," he asked in astonishment, "you mean to say you wouldn't care to meet Maitland after being such chums. Well, I –"

"Well, you what?" asked Dolly, coming into the sittingroom, and putting her arm round her sister's neck. "Well, you what?"

"Don't understand women."

"Pooh, my beloved husband; whoever supposed you did."

"Well, but Ruth says she wouldn't care to see Maitland. Aren't women fickle. We were thinking of asking him down for Christmas, weren't we, Dolly?"

Dolly, with her hand on her sister's shoulder, could not fail to see she was somewhat more agitated than the occasion seemed to warrant. She had always thought there was something between her sister and Dick Maitland, and now that she had the chance determined to put the matter straight.

"Yes, of course, we'll ask him," she said. "I expect he'll be awfully glad to come. Tamba's a dull place to spend Christmas in."

"It's so far," objected Ruth.

"Well, I like that, considering Maitland used to ride over ten miles just to spend an afternoon with you. Do you remember the cold afternoon I was skinning sheep, and you two girls came down, and then Maitland and Finlayson rode up. That was the beginning of it, wasn't it? Weren't they jolly times. Poor old Finlayson, though, he was always a bit out of it. And he's such a good sterling chap, too, is Alick, I suspect he's really the best at bottom, though one couldn't help taking to Dick Maitland. Poor old Alick! He's doing very well, I hear; making his fortune in fact. I hope some designing woman doesn't catch him for his cash."

"What would you say?" began Ruth, feeling that she must tell them of her engagement. "What would you say – if – if – I told you that – that –"

"Not that you're engaged to Dr. Finlayson?" asked Dolly impetuously-ly, and, seeing confirmation in her sister's face, flung her arms round her, and kissed her in the old warm-hearted loving style.

"Oh, Ruth, I'm delighted – delighted! Roger, isn't it good news?"

"You're a lucky young woman," he said, "a very lucky young woman. So that's why you didn't want to see Maitland. Poor old Dick, it will be a blow to him; but, after all, I believe you've chosen wisely."

Dolly could talk of nothing else. Not only that evening, but all the long hot days when Roger and his man went away to their work on the other side of the selection, and the two women were left to their household duties, assisted by one maid servant – a solemn young woman, who, though she was English to all intents and purposes, yet retained enough of the characteristics of her German parentage to make her an invaluable servant.

"It's delightful, isn't it? You mothered me when I was married, and now I must look after you. I suppose you have not fixed the day yet?"

"Oh, yes," said Ruth, bending her blushing face down over the plums she was stoning for the Christmas pudding – for a Christmas pudding is a necessity in Australia, even though the thermometer be at 105 deg. in the shade – "oh yes, we have – at least I thought about the middle of February, but Dr. Finlayson wants it at the end of January."

"What!" Dolly spilt all the flour she was weighing out in her surprise. "February! My goodness, you are in a hurry. I'll just write to Melbourne tonight to Moubray's and tell them to send us a roll of longcloth and another of muslin. We'll begin on your trousseau at once. But my dear child, you can't possibly be married before June at the very least. We might manage by May, but then May's unlucky."

"But I shan't want much," protested Ruth. "It isn't as if I were going to have a grand wedding. Not even as mildly grand as yours was. You see I can't be married from Kooringa."

"Indeed no, you must be married from here, and Roger and I'll do our very best for you. The little church is only five miles away. Really not so far as Mullin's Hill, you know. But have you quarrelled altogether with the Kooringa people? Aunt used to be kind in her way."

"So she is still. Only they were so awfully angry about Polly, you know. And then when I told them next morning I was going to marry Dr. Finlayson, it was worse than ever. I really don't think anybody but the children spoke to me afterwards, and they were all in disgrace for tumbling into the water. So, Dolly, you see I really must be married soon, and if you'll only keep me till the wedding, I'll –"

"Keep you, dear? You know I'm only too delighted to have you for as long as ever you'll stay, and you mustn't be married before June, for goodness knows when we'll ever be together again. Do you hear, Ruth?"

Ruth nodded, and her sister went on.

"I wonder what has become of Polly? Will Ned Clegg marry her, do you think?"

"Oh, it's all right. I was going to tell you, only you've talked so persistently of my engagement I haven't had a chance. In Dr. Finlayson's letter – well, Alick, then – in his last night's letter he says he thought I wouldn't be happy unless I knew what had become of them. So he asked every creature he came across, till at last Arthur King confessed he knew they were going to Geelong, and then he traced them easily enough. They had been married somehow or other, I don't quite understand how, and were having a mild little honeymoon on the £38 he'd saved with a view to matrimony. Alick said he found them in very poor lodgings, and they looked such a boy and girl, in spite of the dignity of the married state, that he gave them a good talking to, and asked them what they intended to do next."

"Go back to Kooringa and be forgiven, I suppose. Fancy Polly married! I can only think of her as a fat, over-grown girl in dresses much too short for her."

"Well, her dresses are still too short for her. I helped her make two new ones just before she ran away, and that's all the trousseau she had, poor girl. No, they won't forgive her at Kooringa though. Alick says both he and Lily tried their very best. He says he thinks though that James Wilson doesn't want another son-in-law on the station, and I can't make him see that he's about the very worst advocate poor Polly could have had, at least with Ann and aunt."

"Poor Ann, it is hard on her, when she thought she'd made an impression, too. But what's to become of the newly-married couple? Thirty-eight pounds won't last for ever."

"That's what Alick said to the young man. He was full of all sorts of wild notions, but Alick recommended him to get a place at once and stick to it, and not to build any hopes on the old folks relenting. However, he says he was able to settle them before he left, for that night at the club he met Lowe, of Bandelowie – you know, on the Darling, not far from Wilcannia. He was growling about his men, so Alick recommended him to try young Clegg. He didn't much like the idea of a wife, but finally agreed to take him. Alick sent for him, and he just jumped at it. Mr. Lowe'll pay their expenses up, give him 30s. a week and a hut to themselves. Poor Polly!"

"Lucky Polly! After all it's not bad. She's got the man she wants – she's never been accustomed to any luxury – and she'll do very well if only she doesn't have too many children. But how good of Alick Finlayson, wasn't it?"

"He is good, you don't know how good he is," said Ruth looking at her sister with flushed cheeks and tearful eyes.

"And are you as much in love with him as he is with you, Ruth?" asked Dolly.

"I – I don't know," faltered Ruth, "we have been such friends since you went away, and till last week I never thought – I – I mean I was so surprised."

"Well so was I," assented Dolly frankly, "but that doesn't prevent me being delighted all the same. Roger thinks you're a very lucky girl, and he'll be the best husband that ever was seen. If he's half as good as Roger – oh Ruth – you ought to be happy."

"So I am."

"No, you're not – not wildly – not as happy as he deserves. I don't think you're even content to sit still and allow yourself to be loved. What is it, Ruth? Once I used to think you were in love with Dick Maitland; but, then, he was so evidently head over ears in love with you that –"

"Oh, nonsense, Dolly, I've told you before."

"I don't care what you told me before, dear. Women always tell lies about their love affairs one way or the other, and I believe the evidence of my own eyes. Roger was always in love with me, I know, in a cheerful sort of way; but, Dick Maitland well, Dick Maitland – I have often thought of it since – was just heart-brokenly in love with you."

"Oh, Dolly, don't."

"What, crying? Don't cry, dear, don't cry; there wipe your eyes. You're not bound to marry a man however in love he is with you if you don't want to, and both Roger and I would much rather you married Alick Finlayson. You don't love him. Ah, but you like him, and esteem him so much that you will be sure to love him in time. I don't see how a woman can help loving a good husband, and he will be the best husband in the world to you. There – there's my naughty boy waking up and crying for his mother. Ruth, as soon as you're done, write to Moubray's for that longcloth."

Chapter XVIII. The Forest Fire

Ruth wrote for the longcloth, and immediately the two young women set to work. Roger smiled at his wife's energy, and used to ask her if she was sure the farm did not suffer, but she only laughed, and declared she hadn't a sister to marry every day, and everything must give place to the all-important trousseau if Ruth adhered to her plans and insisted on being married in the second week in February. Christmas passed, and the New Year came ushered in by a heat greater even than usual in an Australian summer. Marsden's man, after the manner of his kind, had taken a fortnight's holiday, but his employer went every day to work clearing on the other side of the selection, and the two women were left at their work undisturbed.

Marsden used to read to them every evening as they sewed, and all Christmas Day and New Year's Day he spent playing with his boy and lolling on the sofa watching them.

"It's quite refreshing to see your industry," he said.

"It's rather hard on you, I think though," said Ruth. "Two of your holidays have been completely spoiled by our energy."

"Oh, Roger doesn't mind, do you Roger? He likes reading to us in the evenings, and I only worked on New Year's Day because I intend to have a real holiday on the 6th. We shan't do a thing that we can help that day – and Roger, you must stop at home from work, won't you, all day long?"

"Waste a whole day?" he asked.

"Our wedding day and baby's birthday?" she said with a little anxious quiver in her voice.

"Why, of course, my darling," he hastened to reassure her, "I never dreamt of doing anything else. That is the feast of St. Dolly, you know Ruth, and must be kept with all due reverence."

But Dolly did not have her husband on her wedding day after all.

On the evening of the 5th he rode over to the little post-office five miles away as usual, and came back with a rather vexed look on his face.

"I'm so vexed, wife," he said, "so sorry, but I'm afraid I'll have to go over to Crafer's tomorrow. Here's old Atkinson writes to say he's got a buyer for the wood, a man who buys to sell again in the Melbourne market. He thinks he'll take it all off my hands at a fair price. It'll bring about £40 he thinks, but he's arranged for me to meet this man at his place tomorrow."

"Oh dear," sighed Dolly, "oh dear, that is hard, and we can't afford to miss such a chance, can we? Of course, you must go. Ruth and I will think of you all the same, and we'll get on with our sewing better than ever, because we've been so careful not to leave anything we could help to be done tomorrow."

"And I wanted to stay, but we can't afford to lose this chance."

Nevertheless next morning at 6 o'clock when Roger ought to have started on his journey he felt himself very unwilling to go. Both Ruth and Dolly were up to give him his breakfast and see him off, and Dolly in honour of her *fête* day had put on a new dress.

The breakfast was dainty and the table was prettily decorated with flowers freshly gathered, even though it was so early.

"By Jove," said Marsden, "I don't expect there's another man in all the district round has such a pretty home and such a charming wife and sister to wait on him." And he threw an appreciative glance round the table as he helped himself to some more salad.

"And you're going to have such a day," sighed his wife. "Just hark to the wind."

Indeed it was a fierce hot-wind day, as they found when they came out together a few minutes later – he to saddle his horse, she to look on and see as much of him as she could. Though it was barely 6 o'clock the sun was like a ball of fire in a copper-coloured sky, and the mighty north wind came raging through the gum-trees, tearing at their branches, tossing up their bark as it rushed roaring away to the sea.

"Now, you two girls, be good, and don't got into any mischief while I'm away. I'll be back by 7 or 8," and he mounted his horse, and waving his hand to them, rode away, and was soon lost to sight amongst the surrounding trees' trunks.

"Poor Dolly," said Ruth, sympathetically.

Dolly laughed.

"If I never have any greater trouble I'll be lucky, shan't I? Come along, Ruth. We ought to make rapid strides in your *trousseau* – why, its only just after 6. Let's have a cup of tea, and then set to work."

Dolly felt rather low-spirited, so they worked on in silence till about 7, when Roger junior wakened, and his mother bathed him and dressed him in his little white shirt only for coolness sake, and after giving him his breakfast, set him on the floor to amuse himself. But baby, usually so good, was cross and fretful, and again and again his mother had to put down her work and take him in her arms and soothe him.

"Poor little chap, it's the heat," said his aunt. "Give him another bath. Here Gretchen, bring in a bucket of water will you, please."

The girl brought in a pail of water a minute or two later, cool and fresh from the well, and, pouring it into the baby's bath, stopped a moment and looked at the boy splashing about in it.

"There is smoke outside," she remarked solemnly.

"Smoke, is there?" said Dolly, "I hope to goodness the brushwood won't take fire and burn the fences like it did last year."

"I think it will," observed her handmaid, and her mistress sighed.

"What a nuisance! Well, we couldn't do anything against a wind like this. The fences will have to go," and she went on playing with her baby, who had stopped crying, and was thoroughly enjoying himself.

"Don't you think there's any danger," asked Ruth, when Gretchen had gone back to the kitchen.

"What of? Of the house catching? Oh, no, there's a clearing all round. Last year all the scrub was burnt, and a lot of the fencing, too, but it didn't come near the house. It's hard luck, though – 30s. a week for a fencer, and as soon as the fences are up they get burnt down again. Look at baby; he's good enough now. I expect he'll go to sleep again when I take him out."

But Baby Roger was by no means disposed to be amiable when his mother did take him out of his bath, and he cried and protested still more vehemently when she tried to lay him down to sleep. So she lay down on her own bed beside him and took him on her arm, and when Ruth peeped in softly half an hour after both mother and child were sound asleep.

The blinds were down both in the sitting room and in the bedroom, and it was comparatively cool and dark, and Ruth, taking her sister's seat in the rocking-chair, sewed on contentedly for some time. Then the door opened, and Gretchen stood there, looking rather frightened.

"Oh, Miss Grant," she said, "do look here a minute, please."

"Hush," said Ruth. "Mrs. Marsden and baby are both asleep." And she followed her softly into the kitchen. "What's the matter?" she asked.

For all answer the girl pointed to the window, and Ruth saw thick clouds of smoke, driven by the fierce hot wind, rushing past, hiding from sight even the fence that surrounded the garden.

"Good gracious," she cried, rubbing her eyes, as it they might have deceived her, "why Gretchen, is it smoke?"

"Smell it," said the girl laconically, and indeed the air was redolent of the strong aromatic smell of the burning gum leaves. "Oh miss," she added, "it's an awful fire."

Ruth opened the door, and the two women peered out. The little yard was thick with smoke, and the wind was roaring through the tree-tops so that they could hardly hear one another speak. Snatching up a tea cloth from the dresser, Ruth put it over her head and, followed by Gretchen, made her way across the yard to the slip panels. The sky was heavy and overcast, whether by the clouds or by the smoke they could not tell, the air was thick and heavy with it, and, leaning over the slip-rails they could see nothing but smoke like a fog, shutting out even the tree trunks. Two or three wallaby rushed past seemingly too terrified to notice their proximity, and a tiny bandicoot leapt under the rails and took refuge in Gretchen's dress.

"Oh, Miss," she cried, "that's the worst sign, I've heard my father say.

We'll be burnt up if we don't run," and she made as if she would have started off there and then.

Ruth laid her hand on her arm.

"Wait a minute. We must tell Mrs. Marsden," and she rushed into the bedroom where mother and child were still sleeping peacefully.

"Dolly! Dolly! darling!" she cried, snatching up the boy. "Oh, Dolly!"

Dolly sat up rubbing her eyes. "Why, Ruth, what is it?"

"Fire, dear! The whole forest is on fire!"

Dolly was on her feet, and at the door in a moment. They knew little enough about it any one of the three, but a glance was sufficient to show Dolly her sister was right. This was no ordinary brush fire, but a raging conflagration, sweeping all before it. The house, the outbuildings – all were of wood with shingle roofs, now dry as tinder – a spark would set them alight, and the fire would be roaring on them in less than half an hour.

She wrung her hands. "Oh, Ruth, Ruth."

"Dear, you know the country best, which –"

"Down to Mitchell's," put in Gretchen; "quick, get baby and let's run."

"But the animals, we can't leave them," sobbed Dolly, "Oh, Roger, Roger."

"Hush, dear. There, I've opened the hen-house door. You let the old hen out of the coop. Now the pigs – we'll leave the stye open – and, Gretchen, Gretchen, catch Maggie."

They rushed about in hopes of giving every living thing a chance of life, and Dolly opened the cage door and let her canary go free. It fluttered round helplessly, and finally perched on the verandah just out of reach.

"It's no good," panted Dolly, "we must save ourselves. We'd better put on our ulsters, or the sparks may catch our dresses."

In the bedroom little Roger was sitting on the floor just where his aunt had left him, crying quietly to himself. His mother, after putting on a heavy winter cloak, wrapped a blanket round him. Then she found that a heavy boy of twelve months old wrapped in a blanket was as much as she could manage, and returned to the sittingroom, where her sister and maid, also in their ulsters, were putting anything that seemed to them valuable into their pockets and into two pillow cases in hasty preparation for departure, while on the doorstep the household magpie, still uncaught, was dancing up and down calling shrilly –

"What's the matter? What's the matter? What the devil's the matter?"

"Oh, poor Mag," cried Dolly, and Gretchen made a sudden dart and caught the bird, and, evading a vicious peck, put him in her ulster pocket and buttoned it down over him, where he relieved his feelings by crowing like the farmyard cock and using up all his voluminous and somewhat profane vocabulary in unavailing protest against his cramped quarters.

It was not ten minutes since Gretchen had called Ruth, but the smoke was growing thicker, and thicker, and breathing was absolutely difficult.

"We must start," said Ruth, and Dolly sobbed –

"Oh dear, I do hope there's nothing left alive and shut up that I've forgotten."

"The fire's quite close," cried Ruth, as another gust of wind threatened to lift the roof from the house, and the three women rushed out and fled before the north wind, down the garden and through the forest, the magpie in Gretchen's pocket shrieking wildly, and the boy in his mother's arms sobbing with fright. Straight before the wind they ran, right through the forest; there was not even a track to guide them, and the smoke was blinding now. Round this great tree, under that heavy branch, across these rough logs, and always it seemed to their excited imaginations that the fire was close behind them.

About a mile and half from the homestead, just after they had left the boundary fence, they came to a creek, which cut right across their path; the banks were rather steep, and its bed was broad, though the heat had reduced the water to the merest trickle, and in no place did it come higher than their ankles. They scrambled down the banks, walked through the water, which was cool and refreshing to their hot feet, and struggled up the opposite side. Then they paused a moment to take breath, and looked back the way they had come. There was nothing much to see; the wind was as high and the smoke as thick as ever, but still, though the smell of the burning gum leaves was so strong, there was no sign as yet of the fire.

Dolly sat down for a moment on a log to rest. The boy was heavy, the heat stifling, and they had come the mile and a half in less than five-and-twenty minutes.

"The creek will stop the fire, Ruth," she panted. "Surely we're safe enough now."

But even as she spoke a small flock of sheep, with one or two wallabies among them, dashed out of the forest, crossed the creek, and were soon lost amidst the fern and undergrowth.

"They don't think so," said Ruth. "Let me carry Baby, dear, just for a little."

Dolly pushed her hands aside and rose to her feet.

"No, no, I can manage," and Gretchen, as if struck with fresh terror at the sight of the frightened animals, resumed her headlong flight through the bush, and the two others followed her as best they might, their only guide, the wind behind them.

Chapter XIX. A Struggle For Life

Another half-hours' scramble and they emerged on a tiny clearing about an acre in extent, surrounded by a post-and-rail fence, with a weatherboard cottage in the middle. On the verandah a woman and half-a-dozen children were standing anxiously looking out, but so dense was the smoke the newcomers had come half way across the clearing before they were seen by those on the verandah.

"Hey, honey," called out the good woman as they approached, "but who are yer? What, Mrs. Marsden, from Bolwarra. I was afeard ye might be along, but hey, whaur's your man?"

The tears came into Dolly's eyes as she thought of Roger. What would she not have given to have had him by her side.

"He – He went over to Crafer's," she answered.

"To Crafers? Why, but I seed him my-self last night."

"He went this morning," said Ruth.

"This morning! Lord sakes! He never leaved ye this morning. Why, the wind were blowin' such a hurricane as never was."

"It wasn't so bad when he left," protested Dolly, "and I never dreamt of such a fire as this. Last year the brushwood was burnt, but it didn't do much harm else. He said he'd be home at 7 tonight, and now," fairly breaking down, "there won't be any home for him to come to."

"Lord sakes! Lord sakes!" muttered Mrs. Mitchell, looking at Ruth, "The innocents ye are – to leave ye with a north wind a blowing like this. Ye'll be Mrs. Marsden's sister now? Ay, I've heard till of ye. But come in, come in, an' give the babby a sup o' milk. He's greetin', poor thing. God knows how long we can stop here."

"But Mrs. Mitchell, where's your husband?"

"Down Warrnambool way hoein' 'taters. Last week he went. We can no live by the selection alone yo see – but adeary me" – going to the door and looking out at the drifting smoke, "I dunno can we save the house wi'out 'im. Johnny ha' ye filled everything wi' watter – the pig bar'el an' all?"

"Yes, Mammy," said a bright little lad of twelve, setting down a heavy bucket full of water and leaning against the doorpost while he wiped the heat drops from his forehead; "yes, Mammy, there ain't nothen left 'cept the cups, and them ain't no good. What shall we do now?"

Ruth glanced round her quickly.

Some sheds at short distances one from the other stretched from the house to very nearly the edge of the clearing. They were used evidently as stables, cow-byres, and pig-sties.

"Do you think we can stay here Mrs. Mitchell?" Ruth asked. "Hadn't we better go while we can?"

"Well, I dunno," said the good woman "it's the only home we's got. I'd like well to save it if I could, an' we're four full grown women, not to count the children. The clearin's all planted wi' 'taters, too," she went on, looking round at the neat furrows. "Green 'taters can't burn. We's stop as long as we can."

"Very well; we'll help all we can. But the children; they are such mites."

"Oh, they're helpful,' said the mother. "Clary's thirteen, and Johnny he's handy, an' Sam he's good, but he's hurted his foot, an' maun just mind the little ones. The babby – she's but three months old. But what can we do, though?"

"Let's pull down those sheds; the bark roofs will burn like anything if we leave them standing. But what shall we do with the little ones, Dolly?"

Dolly had been sitting with her baby on her lap, watching her sister with eager eyes.

"Yes, yes," she said, "I'll put baby among the potatoes."

The two mothers ran out of the house, and Dolly folding the blanket close around her boy laid him down in a potato furrow so that the bending green leaves might shelter him somewhat. Mrs. Mitchell put her three-months old baby beside him, and a tiny girl of two years, who had no shoes on and who clung terrified to her mother's skirts, was sat down and told to "be good now and mind baby," while Sam, a pretty, delicate boy of eight or nine, who had hurt his foot and could hardly walk, was told to mind the lot.

Then the women and the rest of the children set to work with might and main to pull down the outbuildings; even a little boy of five, who had lost his hat and who only had on a shirt and a pair of trousers, helped with the rest. It was hard work – work they were none of them accustomed to – and in their hurry they had no time to look for tools, and though all worked with a will there was no method in it, and they did not progress very fast. The smoke, too, was thicker than ever, and made their eyes smart and water. Just overhead, close at hand almost, it seemed, hung the sun, a round blood red ball, which they could look at easily with the naked eye, and the children kept crying –

"The moon, the funny moon, mammy, do look at the moon."

They worked on steadily for what seemed like hours till the first shed was level with the ground, and then Ruth suddenly raising her eyes saw the lurid glow of the flames through the smoke and brushwood. They would be right down on the little clearing in a very few minutes. She dropped the axe she had been using and pointing with her finger called –

"Mrs. Mitchell, Mrs. Mitchell, look! look!"

"Children, children," called the good woman, wringing her hands, "leave the sheds. We mun save the house," and they all made for the house, which was very nearly in the centre of the clearing.

"Johnny," cried his mother, "you get on the roof, and we's hand you up wet blankets an' sacks."

Like all Australian cottages, the house was one-story and the roof very low, so that the boy had no difficulty in obeying his mother, who, having dragged out the kitchen table, stood on it, handing him up buckets of water and blankets, while the other three women with the children went backwards and forwards to the waterhole bringing water in every available vessel, from the biggest wash-tub to the tin dipper.

The forest behind them was in flames now, the smoke was stifling, and the heat unbearable, while the strong north wind bore before it great burning branches and sheets of bark.

The outhouses were on fire, and the fence was a ring of flame; still the little band worked on. Mrs. Mitchell was a stern, hard-featured woman of five-and-thirty, who looked considerably older than her years, and her children evidently believed in her, and worked well under her guidance.

"Johnny, my lad," she said, "it's wet the roof ain't it?"

"Fine an' wet," he answered. "I think we'll save it yet, but the sheds is all afire, an' it's comin' quite close."

"Never heed the sheds if we can save the house," she said. "An' we'll do it, we'll do it."

The workers themselves were wet through, and safe therefore from the flying sparks and Ruth was just beginning to think they might really succeed, when a cry from the eldest girl startled her.

"Mammy! Mammy! it's aglow on the other side. The lean-to's caught."

"No, no," cried the poor woman sharply. "No, no. Oh, God! oh, God! It's the third time I've been burnt out. Not this time, Lord. Not this time."

The boy slid down off the roof just as the flames burst out on the other side, and above the roaring of the bushfire they could plainly distinguish the crackling of the weather-boards, and knew their efforts had been in vain.

Clara called out again that it was "aglow inside," and the poor woman threw one more despairing look at her home.

"We's run now for our lives," she said, and they turned and ran to where they had left the children. The babies were crying in the furrow, while the two elder ones were crouching under the potato plants for shelter from the fierce heat, which was almost unbearable.

"We can't stay here," said Dolly, snatching up her child: "the waterhole – let's get into the waterhole."

Mrs. Mitchell shook her head.

"It's five-foot," she said, "wez'd be drowned. We mun run through the forest."

"But – but it's all on fire."

"No matter, we can't stan' here to be roasted alive. We's wet oursels in the watter, an' there's a clearin' four times this size about a mile away. Here, Sam, you get on Mammy's back," and she stooped to let the lame boy climb up. "Clary, you carry the babby – an' – an'–"

"Gretchen, you must carry the little girl," said Ruth, "I'll take Billy, here," and she caught the bare-footed boy of five and dipped him in the waterhole, "and Johnny must take his brother's hand, and keep close with us, else he'll be lost in the smoke."

"God bless you, Miss," said the woman gratefully as she saw her children disposed of among them, "what should I ha' done wi'out ye this day?"

They fairly raced across the little paddock, and in less than three minutes after the house had caught they were ready to start on their perilous journey through the forest, and Ruth called on Mrs. Mitchell to lead the way. The house was now one mass of flames. It seemed certain death to stay where they were, for even the potato plants were shrivelling up fast, while behind them the forest was one lurid mass of flames from the scrub and undergrowth to the tops of the tallest trees, but ahead as yet only the tops of the trees were on fire, and their hope lay in reaching the clearing before the scrub was impassable. There was not a moment to be lost, as they slipped over the charred and smouldering remains of the post-and-rail fence. Billy, Ruth picked up in her arms, but poor little Tom, clinging tight hold of his elder brother's hand, and being dragged on despairingly cried out pitifully as the burning coals touched his bare feet.

"Keep close, Johnny," implored Ruth, fearing lest the children should get lost in the smoke, "Tom, take hold of my dress."

Bravely Mrs. Mitchell led the way; straight on she went, heedless of the dense smoke and the burning leaves and pieces of bark that every now and then fell on her. Luckily the little lad on her back had his wits about him, and swept them off or extinguished them in his hard little hands. Next to her came Gretchen plodding on as stolidly and as calmly as if running for her life with a heavy child on her back was an everyday occurrence with her; and behind her came Clara, frightened, but quiet, and guarding her little charge with the tenderest care; Dolly followed and last of all came Ruth, sometimes carrying Billy, and then when her strength gave out setting him down to run beside her while she gave a helping hand to poor little Tommy, who, very little older than the other child, found his way impeded by the sharp stones and rough logs. If she had had time she would have torn up her skirt or a piece of blanket to bind up the poor little bare feet; but there was no time for now every dry twig and piece of bark kept bursting into flame, so she could only help on first one and then the other and implore Johnny to hold tight to his brother's hand. Once or twice Dolly in her anxiety looked round, but her sister waved her on.

"Go on, go on," she cried. "You can't help us. We're all right; go on. There's no time to spare."

And, indeed, there was not, for already the fire was roaring overhead – already her ulster was full of smouldering holes, and the boys shirts were nearly burnt off their backs, and she kept putting the fire out and dragging them on with encouraging words. It was barely a twenty minutes' run to the little clearing, but to her it seemed hours and hours. She thought they never could reach it. All her life passed before her. She thought of herself and her sister, two lonely little girls clinging to one another; of their life at Kooringa; of Dolly's marriage; of Maitland; of her engagement; of her perplexities and sorrows, and wondered if after all she would not be better dead, and out of it all. But not – oh, not such a cruel death as this. She must get out of it, she would; and she picked up again the smallest boy, who was beginning to flag, and implored the other two not to give up yet.

"Such a little way now, boys; such a little way."

Yes, such a little way, but could they do it? All the birds seemed to have left the forest long ago, but lizards and snakes glided past them, rabbits scuttered away through the fern, and dingoes and wallabies fled before the advancing flames, and paid no heed to their human companions in the race for life. At last, just as she begun to feel that she could stand no more, that the smoke was overpowering her and the heavy weight dragging her down, the whole party emerged on a little plain covered with long yellow grass dry as tinder now in the middle of summer. It was nearly two acres in extent, and they made for the centre so as to be as far away as possible from burning branches and falling trees and Ruth, gathering up the last remnants of her strength, put her arms round both little boys, and more than half carried them up to their brothers and sisters. Then she sank exhausted beside them, feeling that not to save her own life, no, nor her sister's, which was twenty times dearer, could she have gone a step farther.

"Mrs. Mitchell," asked Dolly, vainly trying to hush her child, who was crying pitifully, "are we safe here do you think?"

"I dunno," said the woman, raising her head and looking round. "I dunno. The wind's that high an' the smoke's smotherin'."

The fire was making headway fast now; the ground felt scorching beneath their feet, and the air was filled with burning leaves and great sheets of bark which were borne aloft on the fierce wind, and which, falling all around them, set alight not only to the crisp grass, but to their clothes as well.

"The grass'll be alight in a minute all over," said Mrs. Mitchell hopelessly. "God help us! – we mun die."

Ruth looked up hopelessly. Dolly had flung herself on the ground with her baby fast clasped to her breast and her head on her sister's knee.

"Oh Roger, Roger," she heard her moaning. "My Roger, you'll never see your baby again. Oh, my Roger –"

"Hush! hush!"

The howling of the wind and the roaring of the flames made an infernal din, and every now and then, through the smothering smoke, they could see the great trees, veritable pillars of flame, falling with a terrible crash. The grass on the plain was luckily scanty, but it was burning in patches already.

"Surely we're safe now," said Ruth, grasping her sister's hand, "surely?"

"The grass is catchin'."

"But – but – couldn't we burn it in front of us like people do?"

"I dunno," said the woman wearily. "I reckon if we had a man amongst us we might. But we're done – Eh! my man, my man! but I'll never see ye more;" and Ruth, looking up, saw the tears streaming down her hard face as she rocked herself to and fro with the two youngest children clasped close in her arms.

The others seeing their mother give way, raised a pitiful wail, and the girl felt that now indeed was her last hope gone. Closer she bent over her sister, put her lips down to the dear face she had loved so tenderly all her life, and prayed with all her heart that the smoke might be merciful, and they feel no pain. It was such a terrible death – such a terrible death, such a ghastly horrible death.

"God help us," she sobbed, "God help us! God be merciful to us! If only –"

Chapter XX. Saved!

What was that? Surely it was a man's voice shouting, and surely that was the galloping of a horse, heard even above the crackling of the flames and the roar of the tempest.

Ruth started to her feet.

"We're saved! We're saved! They're coming to help us!" she cried wildly, as bursting through the ring of flame at the southernmost end of the plain came two men urging forward their frightened horses with whip and spur. They saw the women and children at once in spite of the dense smoke and made straight for them. A moment more they were beside them, and Ruth could hardly repress a cry, for the man who sprang from his horse close beside her, put his hand on her arm, and peered down anxiously into her face was the man she had thought never to see again; the man she had parted from with such bitterness and heart-breaking on Dolly's wedding day – this very day two years ago.

"Is it you? – is it you?" she cried, "or am I dead? Or dreaming?"

"My darling," he muttered, "I have come in time."

But Dolly knew him at once. She had no doubts as to his identity.

"Mr. Maitland, Mr. Maitland," she sobbed, "you will help us, you will save us now!"

"Yes, yes. Come on, Hardy," he said to the other man whom they did not know; "we haven't a moment to lose."

It was all done so quickly. The women held the horses, and the two men proceeded to set alight to the grass south of where they stood. Systematically they did it, as the women might easily have done if they had not been so frightened and worn out, and soon all the southern end of the plain was one mass of flame, driven before the high north wind, while the smoke was more stifling than ever.

Help had not come a moment too soon, for the northern end was now alight and swept down on them rapidly, and they retreated on to the patch they themselves had burned, which though hot and black and smoking, had by then burned itself out. The grass fire swept on till it met the burnt patch and then died out for want of fuel to feed it, and the rescued party found they had the little blackened plain for a refuge and were saved.

The hot black ground burnt their feet, the smoke nearly stifled them, but this little patch was an ark of refuge, and they were safe if the forest burned, as it promised to do all night. The fierce wind blew sheets of burning bark, branches, and leaves on to them, and it was only with care they kept the children's light clothes from catching. The men huddled them all together as far from the fire as possible, and Maitland, gently seating Ruth beside her sister, drew the blanket Dolly had round her boy over both their heads, while the little lads Ruth had brought through the burning bush crouched down beside them and buried their faces in their skirts. The others huddled up to them hiding their faces as best they might, and Ruth felt Maitland close beside her, and his presence gave her courage to bear the cruel heat and the deadly weariness that was creeping over her. Hardy's horse had escaped, and was racing round and round the ring of fire like a thing demented, and Maitland at first had a desperate struggle to keep his own mare quiet, but at last he managed to soothe her, and stooped over Ruth. Dolly was crying quietly, her head on her sister's shoulder, and Maitland, handing over his horse to the other man, knelt down beside them to make his voice heard. His face was burnt and blackened by the nearness of the flames, and Ruth felt her own eyes fill with tears as she met his anxious gaze.

"You are not hurt?" he asked, anxiously.

She shook her head. "Sure?"

"Indeed no. Are we safe now?"

"Quite safe."

"But – but – you were only just in time."

"Oh, my God," he muttered; "only just in time."

"You came through the fire for us?"

"No, no. We started, Hardy and I, because I heard Marsden had gone to Crafer's and I knew you'd be alone; but we were too late. The fire was on us; we couldn't push through and Hardy knew of this place, so we made for it. I thought – I have been thinking –"

His voice failed, and Dolly raised her head.

"Oh, Mr. Maitland, you're making light of your share. Mr. Hardy told me you would go on till he said he knew we must be dead if we were at Bolwarra or Mrs. Mitchell's. Why your face is all burned –"

"Only scorched –"

"Roger? Do you know – Will he be safe? He will, won't he?"

"Certainly – quite safe. Don't cry, Mrs. Marsden. Oh, don't cry, there's a good girl."

"I – I – can't help it I'm the selfish one, I know. I haven't been able to think of anything but baby and not seeing Roger anymore – and Ruth – she has worked for me and these children – and you – and you – and Mr. Hardy – to whom we are just nothing at all, have risked your lives to save us. Ruth, why don't you thank him? I can't."

Ruth put her hand in his for a moment, and her heart beat so madly she thought Dolly must hear.

He had risked his life for her – he would have given it willingly – she read it in the anxious passionate face bent over her, and she forgot everything in the one glad thought that he loved her still – after all these long weary months – he loved her still, and the pressure of her hand, the gladness in her eyes were all the thanks he needed.

The other man broke in on them.

"I think it's going to rain," he said.

Maitland rose to his feet and stamped out a piece of burning bark that had fallen close beside them.

"I am sure I wish it would," he said. "We're nearly roasted alive here."

"Oh, the worst is over now," said Hardy.

"'Tis hot, to be sure, but the brushwood's burnin' itself out, and once the rain comes we'll be all right. We must just be patient; and, indeed, it's a miracle we're alive to tell the tale. Be good now, children, be good; 't ain't no good to cry. You'll come down to my place and get your teas as soon as the rain comes."

They were wonderfully good and patient, those little bush children, as they sat there on the ground leaning one against the other extinguishing the sparks which fell on them, and which as time went on grew fewer and fewer. Dolly's boy raised a pitiful wail every now and then that went to his mother's heart, and Mrs. Mitchell, hugging her baby close, was silently wiping the tears away.

Poor thing, her husband was away, she had seven children, and had lost everything she possessed in the world.

"Don't cry, ma'am," said Hardy, with rough kindness. "'t might have been worse. See, the kids are all right, and the fire'll clear the land for you fine. We'll start off for my place soon as we can – it's not above three miles off, an' my old woman'll look after you."

"But are you sure it's all right?" asked Ruth. "Look at the fire. What could stop it?"

"Forty acres of 'taters, Miss," he said, "and the house right in the centre. Oh, we're all right. To be sure the fences have all gone, and that means a pot o' money; but Lord! I'm in luck compared to the rest."

"Is everyone burnt out?"

"Lord! yes. They've been runnin' in ever since seven this morning, mostly women an' children, for the men's all away harvestin'. We're not above a mile from the township, you know, and it's pretty well clear there, but there's not a house standing in the forest for miles round. I saw t'wasn't a bit of good trying to stop the fire. It'll burn on till it reaches the sea."

"It was brave of you to come for us," said Ruth. "It was the bravest thing I ever heard of."

She dared not trust herself to speak to Maitland, but to this man she might safely pour out her gratitude.

"Woa, mare, woa then. The devil fly away with you! 'T'was only a spark, an' you've seen plenty of them today. Indeed, Miss, you haven't much to thank me for. I was just dodgin' about helpin' the women an' kids, when one comes along wringin' hands and sayin' the Mitchells was farthest out and 'ud be burnt, and then Mr. Maitland come and says quite sharp like, 'What about Marsden, of Bolwarra – anyone seen anything of them!' I remembered then I'd seen your man ridin' through the township quite early before things began to look bad, and –"

"Like a jolly good fellow, Miss Grant," said Maitland; "he just turned and rode with me to your help."

"Well, I don't know," said the man, "I would n't ha' been any good much by mysel', I'd ha' turned back long ago. But Mr. Maitland, he kep on till his hair an' his clothes was afire an' then it was too late. I'm mighty dry I know. I wish that storm'd hurry up."

"It's coming, it's coming," said Maitland, "but it's weary work waiting."

It was weary work waiting, only the knowledge that they were safe kept them up. Maitland stooped over them now and again, and his touch and his presence brought Ruth such comfort and such happiness she could have sat there quietly supporting her sister for hours, wilfully shutting her eyes to the future. Why should she want the time to pass? Today the man she loved was close beside her, tenderly guarding her, her more than friend, her saviour – the old barrier was still between them – tomorrow – tonight even – they must part. Why should she wish the time to pass?

And so the afternoon stole slowly on – the hot burning afternoon – the heavy smoke lightened a little, and the furious wind gradually subsided. Four o'clock – five o'clock – six o'clock – the clouds had been gathering steadily, and now there came a vivid flash of lightning and a deafening clap of thunder – another and another – and then there followed a perfect deluge of tropical rain which hissed as it fell on the red-hot forest. The two men raised a shout they might hope to get away now – and Dolly awakening Ruth tried to raise her to her feet. But she was stiff and cramped, and would have fallen but for Maitland's sustaining arm.

"You are tired," he said gently, "and cramped. You must let me help you. We shall get away now. Mrs. Marsden," he added, "you must come down to my house. I left word for Marsden I'd bring you there. Hardy says he and Cuningham, the blacksmith, can manage for Mrs. Mitchell between them."

"Thank you," said Dolly, wearily, trying to hush her fretful child. "When can we go? The fire must be out now. I'm wet through already."

"Is it far?" asked Ruth.

"A little over three miles. And you are worn out," he added.

"No, no. I was thinking of the little children. That poor little chap's feet are so terribly cut and burnt."

"He shall ride, shan't you, old man? Hallo Hardy, where's your horse? I saw him a moment ago."

"Made clean tracks the brute, at the first flash. He's gone in the direction of home, though. You put up Tommy and the little girl. Oh, no, by Jove! that won't do. Here's Sam here with a bad foot too. Put them two up an' we must hump the little ones amongst us somehow. Here, I'll take the little chap, and lead the way. And, I say, look out for falling branches an' trees. 'T'aint no joke, I can tell you."

The storm still continued and the rain was pelting down when they started on their journey. All round them the trees were falling and branches were snapping off, but they felt they could wait no longer, they must risk something. Weary as they were, their progress was necessarily slow, but they had hardly gone a mile in the pouring rain when they heard a loud cooey ringing through the forest. Hardy put his fingers in his mouth and sent back a shrill reply, and there came bursting through the blackened forest Marsden and Cuningham, the blacksmith, who, it appeared, was some distant connection of Mrs. Mitchell.

The latter was loud in his congratulations, but Roger said hardly a word. He put his arm round his tired wife and lifted the heavy boy from her arms, while the blacksmith undertook to lead the horse, and thus set Maitland free to help Ruth, who was drooping under the weight of Mrs. Mitchell's little girl.

He took the child, and drew the girl's hand through his arm.

"You must let me help you, just this once," he said, "only this once."

"You are tired," she said, "and Polly is so heavy."

"I am not tired, and Polly is not heavy. Won't you let me help you?"

And they walked on silently through the blackened forest, and the rain poured down in torrents. The little girl put her arms round his neck and rested her cheek against his.

"I does love you," she said. "You putted out the fire, an' didn't let it burn Polly."

He laughed a little.

"There," he said, "there, you see I have my reward."

Ruth would have said something, but a sob choked her, and Maitland drew her a little closer to him.

"Hush, dear," he might have been speaking to the child, "my reward is very great – all I would ask. Bear up a little longer. Brave little girl – only another mile now."

Every now and again they heard the trees falling, and once or twice one fell just in front of Hardy, who was leading, but he just turned aside a little and went steadily on. The sooner they were out of it the better. Cuningham volubly related how Marsden had come riding back from

"Crafter's" "like mad," and wanted to push his way through the fire, and how he, Cuningham, and Wilson, of the Shearers' Arms had stopped him and assured him that Hardy and Mr. Maitland had gone already – and if they couldn't help them mortal man couldn't, and now when the storm gathered he would wait no longer, and he (Cuningham) had come with him because he really never had thought to see any of them alive again.

They were plainly visible now, the glimmering lights of the town that seemed to stretch out friendly arms to welcome them. Was it the rain or the tears in her own eyes that made those lights so unsteady? Strangely her thoughts went back to that winter's night, her first night at Kooringa, when she had looked out on the lights through the pouring rain. It had been her first step in the unknown world. Would she go back and wipe out all those months with their few joys and their great sorrow – would she if she could – and be again the innocent girl who had looked out drearily at the light gleaming through the winter's rain? Would she? And then with a great rush of pride and gladness she knew she would not – she knew she was proud and glad because the man beside her had risked his life for them – wildly glad when she thought that this had been done for love of her. Wrong, very wrong, cruelly wrong; but she thought not of that, as they emerged on the main road and the glimmering lights were close at hand.

The blacksmith put his hands close to his mouth and raised another loud cooey, which was answered by shouts and the sound of many hurrying feet. Men and women rushed out into the rain – questioning, pitying, congratulating – and offers of shelter came from all sides.

"It's all right, it's all right," cried Maitland, raising his voice. "Mr. Marsden's people are all coming down to my house. But will any of you help Mrs. Mitchell and her little children?"

"That's all right," said Hardy, "we've arranged all that. Hand over the little girl to Fred here – he'll carry her down to my place, and you let us have your mare for the boys and I'll send her up by an' by. Good night, Mr. Maitland, we've done a hard day's work together, haven't we?"

"Good night mate," said Maitland, handing over the sleeping child to a lad of sixteen, Hardy's eldest son. "We've succeeded too, that's best, and I'll never forget how you stood by me."

"Cheer up, Mrs. Marsden. It's only a step now. Where's your servant? Come along. My housekeeper'll look after you."

"Mag'll be pretty glad to get out," said Gretchen stolidly; "he's been in my pocket all day. I wonder he ain't smothered."

The magpie gave an assenting croak so opportunely that it made Dolly laugh – a laugh that ended in a sob, and Marsden turned and put his hand on Maitland's arm.

"I owe you more than ever I can pay," he said. "How can I thank you?"

"You needn't, old man! you needn't. I assure you I went because – because Hardy went. Any one of the men here would have done the same. Come on, old chap, your wife is worn out and there's my house over there. See the lights in the window to welcome you. I told my housekeeper to expect you, but I thought we'd be here hours ago. And it's getting quite chilly with all this rain."

Chapter XXI. Poor Alick Finlayson

Maitland's housekeeper, a decent-looking old body, opened the door at the sound of their voices.

The house was small, only a weather-board cottage like the one they had left that morning, and very plainly furnished; but to the two tired, weary women the little white-curtained bedroom seemed a very haven of rest.

Mrs. Baker showed them into the room and then disappeared, and returned again bearing two glasses of wine.

"Mr. Maitland sent it," she said. "It'll do ye a world of good. Ye can have some tea after."

"Thank you," said Ruth.

"Oh, Ruth, Ruth," sighed Dolly, when the woman had gone, "what are we to do?"

"We must be brave, dear; we have been so fortunate."

"But we have no clothes?"

It certainly was a problem that had to be faced. Their hats were fit only for the dust-heap, their boots were so much charred leather; their heavy ulsters, burnt into holes as they were, had protected in some measure their light cotton dresses; but everything they had on was blackened from contact with the blackened ground; and as for their faces, not even the pouring rain had cooled them after their long exposure to the heat.

"Oh, I'm more thankful than I can say," said Dolly. "It's a little thing to make a fuss over, but what shall we do?"

Then just as they were ruefully contemplating their dilapidated garments there was a knock at the door, and Mrs. Baker reappeared with a bundle under her arm.

"Mr. Maitland went over to Mrs. Scott, the banker's wife," she said, "an' she's sent you over some things with her love, an' she's so sorry. She'd like to come over, but Mr. Maitland said best not, ye was that tired. An' now, as soon as ye're ready, there's supper in the diningroom."

"How good, how kind everybody is!" murmured Dolly, "and oh, Ruth, what should we have done without Mr. Maitland? And he thought of everything, too. Just fancy his thinking about clothes!"

Dolly was quite cheerful again, and a warm bath quite revived her. She had her husband and her child, and though her home was gone and everything in it, that was a misfortune she shared with half the dwellers in the forest. Indeed, she was a thousand times better off than they, for

Marsden had some little money, and there was a small insurance on the house and furniture, besides Dolly's savings.

"How good of her," said Dolly, as she unpacked the bundle; "isn't she kind? She's sent us everything we could possibly want."

"Everyone is kind, I think," murmured Ruth faintly.

"Why, Ruth, how tired you look! You're much more done than I am. Go to bed, dear, and I'll bring you something to eat."

"No, no. I'll be all right. I'd rather sit up."

Dolly, looking at her anxiously, thought that the day's events had indeed shaken her sister. For herself, she was so relieved and happy it seemed only natural to talk, and she chattered on, content with mono-syllabic replies, till they were both dressed. The dresses were somewhat loose, but they were very plainly made, hardly more than wrappers, and with the Indian scarves Mrs. Scott had thoughtfully sent tied round their waists, they looked rather picturesque when they entered the sitting-room where Maitland and Marsden were awaiting them. Their faces were still hot and burning, scorched with the fierce heat, but altogether they looked so different from the two sodden and bedraggled women who had entered the house that Maitland could not repress an exclamation.

Dolly smiled.

"Yes, rather a difference, isn't it, Mr. Maitland?" And then, changing her tone and laying both her hands on his arm, "Oh, Roger, Roger, how are you going to thank this man? If it hadn't been for him you'd have had no wife and child to come home to."

"I know," said Marsden, " I – I –"

"Nonsense," said Maitland, gently pushing Dolly into a chair and drawing up another for Ruth. "Mrs. Marsden, I've been trying to explain ever since you left that it's nothing. I have only done what any other man in the place would have done – what other men have been doing all round. Hardy, for instance. He left wife and children to help – left his fences to burn – while I – if I had died there isn't a soul to whom it could matter."

"Hardy told me himself, though God knows I don't make light of his share, he never would have gone if it hadn't been for you."

"And how close it was," said Dolly, with a shudder. "Why, your eye-brows and eye-lashes are all burnt off."

"Yes, I expect I am something of a show, but one breath of flame did that without really hurting me at all. And Marsden, after all, as I've told you again and again, it was all the merest chance. We only made for Hankey's clearing, when we'd given up all hope. Come now, here's Mrs. Baker with some dinner. It's nothing much, I'm afraid. The township has been in such a fever of excitement; it's difficult to get anything."

It was a very quiet meal. Ruth, though she had touched nothing since breakfast, felt as if each morsel would choke her, and neither could Maitland eat. Marsden had been so wild with anxiety all day long that he was content to sit and listen to his wife, who, having rung the changes from deepest despair to wildest happiness, was now graphically talking over again the story of the day from the time when Ruth had awakened her to the moment when Maitland had ridden to the rescue, and again she overwhelmed him with praises and thanks.

After they had finished Maitland asked them if they could manage for the night.

"It's only a humble little house, you know," he said. "I took the furni-ture from my predecessor just as it stood, and was somewhat astonished to find how largely it was made up of packing cases."

"The room we were in was very nice," said Dolly, "wasn't it, Ruth? Such dainty white dimity everywhere."

"Uh, that's Mrs. Baker; she's a great believer in the virtues of white curtains and covers up everything in them. Look at my chairs! – they've all got petticoats on."

"A delicate hint," said Dolly. "Mrs. Baker means you should get the house a mistress!" and then seeing with a woman's quickness she had said something wrong, she hastened to add, "and a piano too. Fancy an unmusical man like you with a piano!"

"Old Acheson, poor beggar, was, I believe, very musical. He drank, unluckily, and was stone broke when he left, so he begged me to take the piano at about a quarter its value. They tell me it's a very good one. I hope you'll feel equal to trying it tomorrow."

"Yes, indeed, we will," said Dolly, "and now, if you don't mind, I really think we ought to go to bed. Look at Ruth, she looks as if she really couldn't hold up her head."

Indeed she did look weary, but she did not at once agree with her sister.

"I – I must write a note first, please," she said to Maitland. She had remembered now, she had been remembering all the evening, her engagement to Finlayson, and the thought was a pain to her. She could not think of it calmly as she had done yesterday, with the man she had loved so passionately standing before her.

"A note," echoed Dolly, "why Ruth – oh, of course, Alick Finlayson, to be sure. Yes, do write, Ruth. He'll be wild with anxiety when he hears of the fire," and yet she looked curiously at Ruth. There was something wrong, she felt. Maitland was most evidently in love with her; she had noticed that with a woman's keen perception, even in the midst of the bushfire; and Ruth – he had risked his life to save hers – what would Ruth do?

With trembling hands Ruth scribbled a note to Finlayson, which Maitland stamped and promised to post before he went to bed.

"I hope you will be comfortable," he said. "Mrs. Baker has done her best."

Then he wished Dolly good night. Ruth came last, and he held her hand a moment without saying a word.

She tried to say "Good night," but the words would not come, and the tears would force their way between her down-dropt eyelids.

Dolly had drawn Roger away, so for the moment they were alone, and he bent down and kissed her hand.

But Mrs. Baker came up.

"I'll take care of Miss Grant, sir. Mrs. Marsden's got her husband and her baby, an' she's that thankful she don't want nothin' else; but this young lady's just wore out,' ain't you, Miss?"

Once safe in their room Dolly turned to her husband –

"Oh, Roger, Roger, what is to be the end? Dick Maitland's awfully in love with Ruth?"

"Yes, of course, he always was; I told you that long ago. They tell me he rode off like one demented this morning. However, she's engaged to Alick Finlayson, and he's a jolly good fellow, too; so Maitland's clean out of it."

"Well, but Roger – I must tell someone – I believe she's in love with Dick Maitland."

"What the –. Phew, poor old Alick! He wouldn't have a chance against him, and after he's saved her life too. In love with him? By Jove, I never thought of that, and more unlikely things have happened."

In love with him! Once she had got rid of Mrs. Baker, which was not till that good woman had seen her safe tucked up in bed, Ruth sat up again and tried to think it out calmly. In love with him – the very sound of his voice, the touch of his hand set her heart beating. And Alick Finlayson had never done that – Alick – so good – so kind – who trusted her so entirely – who had been her friend and companion for the last two years – her comforter in her loneliness. She pitied him with the pity that is not akin to love – she was sorry – but another face stood between them – the love she thought she had banished rose up stronger, more passionate than ever. He was hers, hers, hers – and she rejoiced over it. What though he was the husband of another woman – his wife was nothing to him – he never even saw her. Surely there was little harm in loving him. He had kept away bravely, and not till her utmost need did he come to her, and then he had come at the risk of his own life. What should she do? Before her the outlook looked cruelly hopeless. How could she marry Alick Finlayson when her heart was full of another man – when his face, his eyes, his very tones haunted her – when she could even rejoice over the hardships and dangers that had brought them together again? Marry Alick! No, no, a thousand times, no: it would be doing him a cruel wrong. Whatever her life might be she must not marry Alick Finlayson, and she almost hated him that he had bound her to him. She tried vainly to plan out her life anew – to remember that save for a bare pittance she had nothing but the few trinkets she had put in her pocket as they left the doomed house. She could not marry the man who loved her. She could not go back to Kooringa. Between her and the man she loved was a barrier stern and inexorable. What should she do? What could she do?

She tried to decide something – the sooner it was decided the better – but her head ached; every bone in her body ached with weariness, and her mind could grasp nothing beyond the one glad fact she loved and was beloved. Toss and turn she did, but no sleep came to her tired eyes. Over and over again she thought out the incidents of the day, and she longed for the morning – the morning when she might make her plans afresh – might break her engagement, and be once more a free woman. The ring Alick Finlayson had given her was still on her finger, and she drew it off and laid it on the little table beside her bed. Why should she wear his ring? What right had he to expect it of her? How she longed for the morning. She had written briefly enough telling him of the fire, but tomorrow she would write a very different letter. Tomorrow she would see Dick Maitland again – she wanted nothing more – she did not want to look beyond. How slowly the time went. One – two – three – the clock in the sitting-room tolled the hours and yet she could not sleep. She would be ill she felt if this went on, and then at last, just as the early summer's dawn began to peep through Mrs. Baker's clean white dimity curtains, she fell into a troubled sleep, and dreamt that she was running away from a devouring fire, toiling through the bush with heavy leaden feet. She felt the hot breath of the flames on her cheek. She tried to cry out, and then, lo, it had overtaken her, and it was not a fire, but Dick Maitland holding her in his arms as he had done on Dolly's wedding day, and whispering "My darling, my darling, my darling."

'Ria. A West Australian Story

Selburnrigg

Chapter I

"He'll be dead soon, missis; what are we going to do with 'im?" The speaker, a short, stout, common-looking young fellow, was holding down on the bed the body of a man passing through his last agony – a fearful agony it had been for the young wife to witness, who was thus addressed. She was wiping his distorted face with a damp cloth, her wide-opened eyes were fixed on him in terror, and every breath she drew was a sort of sobbing moan of fear and horror.

"What are we to do with 'im?" the young man repeated. "They'll want a cor'ner's inquest, and if we have to wait till the doctor gets out here it'll be unpleasant. Better fetch him in to town!"

"Oh, we'll take him in. We'll take him in!" she said. "We'll bury him in a Christian place."

"Well, then, you hold on here," said he, "he'll not be struggling any more, I'm thinking, an' I'll get up the horses. We must get off at once, soon as the poor chap's right dead."

The young wife was left alone with the body of her husband. His eyes were closed; at intervals long laboured gasps for breath still stirred him, becoming fainter and more intermittent. She took his hand and called him by his name, but he had done with things of earth, and hearing had quite passed away. She held a cup against his lips, and tried to raise his head, to see if he could swallow anything, but there was no swallowing more for him, and feeling all the misery of her helplessness, she sat down sobbing on the bed beside him. And then her baby woke and cried, and she had to go into the next room to quiet it and make its food; and while the food was making she kept coming back to look and see if he was still the same. And then, when she had fed the child, she brought it in, hushing it mechanically in her arms, and found its father dead.

There was no mistaking now, she and the baby were left alone. And she stood beside the bed, too miserable and bewildered for more tears, rocking her body to and fro to keep her baby still. What she had lived through with this man, what she had had of joy and pain with him, passed through her mind; she thought of the time two years ago when he was courting her – this dead disfigured body – then a fine strong man, and how she had taken him to please her father, and how on the whole he had not been bad to her, though he was not the one she wanted; and then her father's death, now a year past, and the change in her lot which that had made, and the trouble she had known since then, when the love of drink had gained upon her husband, and brought him to this pass – dead, in his strong early manhood. And then she thought about her future with the farm, and all the work that she must now see to herself, and how she must keep things together for her boy; and it seemed to her that her pathway was very hard in life – and yet it looked so bright to her at one time.

But then the man came in, and she told him Jim was dead, and he said, when he had looked at him, "Missis, we most be starting off at onst, after we've put him straight."

So they took off the soiled clothes in which he lay, and dressed him clean and neat, and Sullivan fetched up the cart before the door, and put a mattress in it to lay him down upon.

He was a heavy man to carry, a six-footer, broad, and big, and bony; but between them (Sullivan at his head and the woman at his feet) they got him out and laid him in the cart. They sent a native to his father's place, to tell him Jim was dead, and they were going in with him to town, and he must meet them at Baylup, the half-way camping-place, by breakfast time next morning. And then the poor stunned girl collected the few things she wanted for her baby and herself, and locked up the house, and gave the key to an old native woman who would stop and mind the place – and so they started on their wretched journey through the night.

The road was rough and rutty, full of roots and crowns, and in the darkness Sullivan could not steer the cart so well, and Maria, sitting up in it alongside her dead husband, took his head upon her lap to ease the jolts; and so they journeyed on, over the ironstone hills, where the mahogany thickets and growth of saplings enveloped them in blackness; and through sandy plains, past swamps and water-flats, where the wind blew cold and damp, and the stars shone down upon them; and on and on in slow monotonous progress till sleep fast closed Maria's eyelids, and she forgot her trouble in her slumber, and did not wake before they reached the camping-place at early dawn.

His father and his mother were there before them; they had travelled faster in their little spring-cart than Maria had, and the distance of their place from Baylup was not so great as it was from hers. And as the cart came up, bearing the widow and the dead body of their son, they stood out in the roadway watching it – the father mute and stupid from the suddenness of the blow, from a sort of consciousness that some unusual demeanour was expected of him; and the mother, loud in her cries and lamentations over the untimely end of her firstborn. And Maria had to tell them the whole story, how Jim had been into town with a load of hay, and how he had brought out a gallon, and drank it on the road, as she supposed from seeing an empty case and broken bottles in the cart when he came home; and how when the horses brought the cart up to the yard last night Jim was lying dead drunk upon it, and seemed to have had a fall and hurt himself, for he had bruises on his chest, and arms, and loins; and then when they had got him in and laid him down upon the bed; how he took awful fits and struggled so Sullivan and she could scarcely hold him down, and how at last he had suddenly grown quiet and died.

And Sullivan had said that they must take him in, for the Government would want a cor'ner's inquest.

She said all this in a wearied stony way, and the mother got up into the cart beside her, and she turned down the rug to let the old woman see her boy. In strange contrast were the wife's stillness and the mother's lamentations as they sat close together, holding up between them his head and shoulders, looking at him who had been so near to both of them. To the wife there was little pleasure to look back upon, and much trouble, but still he was her husband – to the mother he had been her pride, her joy, though nearly her disgrace, when five-and-twenty years ago a timely marriage with old Pitman had saved her when she was with child of him. But what she had gone through on his account had made him dearer to her than the rest, born afterwards; and when he had grown up strong, and big, and hearty, she thought that none of the boys about were like her Jim, despite the radicalness of his ways – such a grand figure of a man, so brave and bonny. And she had chiefly brought about his marriage with Maria, who was an heiress in these parts, by reason of her father's farm and run, and the few head of stock, and she an only daughter.

Meanwhile Sullivan had told the old man more that was only suited to his ears of what he thought had happened before Jim got home, and then they boiled the tea, and called the women down to breakfast.

Chapter II

Three days after, they were all together again at Baylup, going home. Jim Pitman had been buried, and the young widow in her weeds was sitting on a log nursing her baby, her mother-in-law beside her.

Hitherto she had avoided all discussion about the future, and of what she was going to do about the place. It was all her own; Jim Pitman had nothing but himself to bring, and a few head of horses, when he married her. Her father had known old Pitman long, from being neighbours, and the boy Jim was quick and handy, and had been often useful to him, to help him with the cattle, and in other ways; and Maria had given up her own desires, and married him to please her father. But by her father's will everything he left was hers – the house, and farm, and run, and the cattle, and small flock of sheep. He had feared to leave his life's labour at the mercy of his son-in-law, in whom he had found himself much disappointed, and his prudence was now a cause of thankfulness to Maria, for even during the short time passed since her father's death she found her husband had run up a heavy bill in town, which she had made herself responsible to pay.

One thing she had made up her mind about – the Pitmans should not interfere with her; she was not going to be dictated to by them. They were talking, meddling people, and needy, too, and they would want her to themselves, she thought, to get all they could out of her, and this she was determined that they should not do. She would manage right through herself, with a man to help her; and she would ask Sullivan to stop, she thought that he would suit her. From a child she had grown up on this farm, and was at no loss to know what should be done. There was but a bit of hay to put in every year, and the potatoes and such things, and that the man could do, and she had an old native and his wife who had been with them many years to mind the sheep. The cattle were no trouble to her, she had handled them all by turns as calves; and with Sullivan to do the ploughing and rough work, and a little extra help at shearing time and harvesting, she felt she'd get along all right.

So she had managed until now to keep the Pitmans off the subject, and had refused on plea of her late trouble to talk with them about the farm and what she was to do.

But now the old woman said that she and Pitman had been talking, and that they would not leave her in the lurch. Tom, now the oldest left, should go up and live at Woodhill, they could box their sheep with hers, the runs being so close together, and Tom could see after both lots, and Maria could come down and live with them. Tom would then mind her place and live there by himself.

But Maria said, "No; thank you, mother, all the same; I'm going to mind the place myself. Sullivan will stop on, I daresay, and I'll be right enough. I'm not agoing to leave it."

And Mrs. Pitman answered, "A young female couldn't do the like of that, the menfolk were most good for ploughing, and minding sheep and cattle, and such like, and women's place was with the pots and pans and baby's messes; and she must just come down and make herself at home with them, and not be flabbergastering about the place like a mad heifer on the loose." And Maria, getting heated, said "she would not, that's flat, her father left the place to her, and she had done her share towards getting the bits of things together, and keeping of them straight, and what was her own she'd mind and stick to; and nobody should have a say in anything but she, or be poking in to mess about her place. And Tom could mind their own sheep, and make a job of that. And what she'd said, she'd said, and didn't want to speak about no more."

Mrs. Pitman – seeing her so resolute and so angry – felt that it would not do to ride the high horse over her; they did not want to quarrel with her, and lose her from the family. But it was not simply telling that would make her do their bidding, and that she saw right well; so she answered that Maria could please herself, of course; being grown now, and a responsible widow-woman, with a farm and baby of her own. But if so, she had enough on *her* hands, God in heaven knew, what with one thing and another; and she was not going to fash herself with stopping people's tongues when they wagged, as wag they would over a young female doing for herself, and keeping of a young serving man like Sullivan. That was not what *she'd* been taught to think respectable, but things was altered now, and Maria could just please herself, of course.

Maria sat still thinking, and gradually got very red, and said, Well, if mother could let her have one of the girls – Elizabeth Anne would do – to live with her – she thought that might be best; live on the place herself she must, and people would say less about Elizabeth Anne than they would say of Tom if he came stopping there; and with another woman to live with her, she need not fear their tongues. She was not scared, and never had much trouble to mind herself.

So Mrs. Pitman was obliged to content herself with this, and Elizabeth Anne, who had also been to town, was transferred to Maria's cart; and then they said goodbye, and went their roads, the Pitmans turning off at Baylup, and the Woodhill turn-off being further on.

Chapter III

Maria got out of bed at sunrise the next morning, and, opening the little square window of her room, put out her head, and leaned upon the sill to look at her domain – for the first time now sole mistress.

It seemed so long a time since four days back, when she went in with all her load of trouble, and the bright morning, and the sparkling dew, and the fresh air, and the piping of the birds, and the gambolling of the calves up in the stockyard, and all the merry life of early dawn, made her heart feel so glad – so glad, she thought it was quite wicked in her; so she shut down the window, and she sighed, and then she went before the little looking-glass to do her hair.

Maria's hair was red, deep red, and waved, and curled, and tangled so that it seemed quite a pity to touch it with the comb and bind it up, she thought; and she raised it up, back from her face, and, turning round looked at the masses of it thoughtfully. And then she took down the glass from the little nail on which it hung against the whitewash wall, and, going to the window, gazed intently at her face. Maria was not what one would call pretty; her forehead was rounded and projecting, and too large in proportion to her other features; her nose was of no type but still a pleasant nose, original and light: and her mouth – the women all said that it was large and ugly – but it had often made young fellows long to kiss her, and do it too. The lips were very full, and the teeth large; but the lips so red! so red! and the teeth so white! you thought it all the better that there was plenty of them. And when she laughed, her whole face lighted up, so bright and sunny, with such a soft, kind tenderness about her dark-grey eyes, that men all warmed to her at once, and thought not of defects, of freckles, and of tan that people said so spoiled her. And when she was not laughing, when she was grave, her lips were always pursed in such an odd, fantastic way, with so many shades of meaning as her thoughts came over her, that there was always something new to see when you looked into her face.

"Oh! dearie me!" she said, "I'm much changed since two year ago. I was a fuller figure then, and more white and red like it seems to me. The marrying, and the baby, and the work have taken it out of me to be sure." And then she sighed, and thought if only her face were as milky white and pure as the bare soft bosom and rounded shoulders she saw beneath them; and, putting down the glass, she washed herself, and splashed about, rubbing the water over face, and neck and arms, and shoulders; and coming back all glowing, sparkling and fresh, she smiled compla-cently at her reflection, and, dressing hastily, took up a bucket, and went out to the stockyard for the milking.

Sullivan was there before her; it was not part of the work that was regularly his; she generally did all there was to do about the cows and calves herself. But he said he thought that she might not be wanting to get up so early this first day, and so he had come up to milk. And Maria said it was good of him to think of that, and he could milk the cows that wanted bailing, while she did the rest. And while they were sitting at their work, with no sound save the munching of the cows at the green corn-stalks before them, and the regular squirt-squirting of the milk into the buckets, Maria thought that she would speak to Sullivan of what she meant to do, and see if he would stop with her; and before she spoke she turned her head round from its resting place against the warm cow's side to have a look at him.

He was a young man of some five-and-twenty years, about the middle height, strongly built, square, and stout, and sturdy, with thick, heavy limbs; a convict – sent out very young – but now he had his freedom, and on his otherwise comely face was that dull, sullen look so often seen in men of the same class. But he worked steadily, and got through a great deal more than most; and though he was at times ill-tempered and foul-mouthed, he generally kept quiet, and went about his work in silence, and so Maria thought that on the whole she might do worse than keep him.

But she scarcely knew what she should say to him about his stopping, for it would not do to let him think she could not do without him, and as she thought about how she should begin, he relieved her from embarrassment by speaking up himself.

"What are you going to do about the place, missis?" he said.

"I'm going to work it on myself, Sullivan," said she.

His milking now was done, and he came up and stood behind her, looking down upon her, with the bucket in his hand. He smiled, and his eyes glistened as he looked and heard. "I suppose you'll be keeping on a man?" he said.

"Oh, yes! I suppose I shall," Maria answered, carelessly.

"An' am I going to get the place?"

"If you want to have it, I don't see what's to hinder."

"Well, I don't know as I'm against stopping on, to help you out like, being now by yourself. I'm used to the ways of the place by now, and I daresay we'll suit."

"Oh, I daresay we'll suit right enough," she answered, annoyed at the manner of his speech, and rather uneasy at the tone he took.

"And for wages, you can give me ten shillings a month more than now; that won't ruin you, an' I'm worth it."

"No, I daresay it won't ruin me," she said, and went on milking without looking up, while he set down his bucket and folded his arms across his chest with an air of complacency.

She was angry at his way of talking, and she thought if he began like that he would be wanting to be master before long, and she wished to tell him that he need not think he was to get his own way in everything – she meant to see to things herself. But somehow she was bothered about the way to say it. So, Maria being nervous and hesitating, and Sullivan confident and strong, that was all they came to say about it.

Chapter IV

Maria had known much trouble since the time she married Jim to please her poor old father. Jim was a careless, lazy fellow, and fond of drink, and things would have gone badly with the farm had it not been for her. She had worked and slaved to keep all straight, and make up as far as a woman could for the man's shortcomings.

But now that Jim had died, and left her, although the shock at first was great, and the manner of his death had deeply wrought upon her, still she could but feel a sort of sorrowful relief; and – as when she looked out upon the bright early morning – a kind of exhilarating feeling would come her over now and then, the sense of freedom, and of trustfulness in her future and her own exertions.

She had her baby, that she dearly loved, to fill her heart, and – besides him – she had her hope.

Twelve years ago, when 'Ria, was a little girl of nine years old, she had a playmate in a little boy of twelve, George Ransome. In those days she used to mind her fathers flock of sheep – only a little lot – and in the fine long summer days she used to wander up with them along the river bank, over the steep grassy hills, spurs of the forest ridge above, and through the shady, moist, green bottoms, where little brooks purled gently on their way to the large river pools, and up to the "Long-point," the boundary of her father's run, and there would Geordie Ransome come to meet her, also with his flock of sheep. Geordie's father was an English gentleman, and man of good position in the district; but he was poor, and the boys did all the work of the home place, and Geordie was the shepherd, and brought his sheep down this way many a day from the homestead, four miles up the river.

Geordie had no sisters; if he had, he might not have been so fond of a girl-playmate. But 'Ria, as he called her, was a necessary part of his boy life. He was snubbed and bullied by his big brothers up at home, and had to play a very small and insignificant part in their republic, and it was delicious to him to find a human being in whose eyes he was a hero, to exchange the cuffs, and kicks, and sneers of what to him were towering, big-limbed, fearful monsters, before whom he trembled – and yet vaguely worshipped, as wonderfully clever evil beings – for the unfeigned admiration of a creature who saw in him the embodiment of greatness, strength, and wisdom. For Geordie was of vast importance in 'Ria's eyes – he had 500 sheep; she had but 200. He had shoes and socks; her little brown bare feet had to do their rough work unguarded by such luxuries. He had a fine big dog, that worked the sheep just like a man; she had but a miserable half-bred puppy, that showed no dispositions but for hunting rats. He had a gun; it's true it seldom would go off, but still it sometimes did, and then, if it contrived to kill a parrot or a cockatoo, her admiration knew no bounds, to think of the wonderful skill of Geordie! And she'd make a fire on the spot, and then and there they'd cook the dainty rarity, and religiously they'd eat up every bit. She had no gun, nor ever would, he said. And then he was a boy – almost a man, she thought – of twelve years old, and strong; she but a miserable little girl of nine.

And so their respective flocks of sheep suffered much driving. 'Ria's never would go fast enough, she thought, until they got to Long-point; and Geordie, once he was out of sight and sound of home, dogged his sheep down all the way. She was always there before him; she had only two miles to go, and he had four; and she would sit upon a stone, patiently waiting, looking up the river, while her flock was feeding in the hollow at the back. And then, when she heard his sheep-bells coming, her little heart beat fast, and she would jump up and run towards him; and when he saw her coming he would call out "Hullo, 'Ria! see me jump this log!" and would exhibit all his prowess in his feats of strength and skill, and his insatiable boy's vanity drank deep draughts of pleasure from her delighted admiration. And then they'd go down to the river, and fish for chelgies for the dinner; and Geordie sometimes would get in and have a swim, while 'Ria sat and cried upon the bank, afraid that he would drown. And they were always making fires, to cook the chelgies, and to roast the rats that 'Ria's Bobsy caught, or the rare birds that Geordie shot. And Geordie would give her orders and commands in a loud voice, like his brothers, and would call out, "Ha! spoony!" and "Go it, you little muff!" just like they did, when she was awkward in obeying his behests. And then sometimes she cried, and Geordie would look at her quite scared, and wonder what the matter was. But when he tried to comfort her she was soon better. And when, in the full swing of their delightful pleasures, they suddenly would think about the sheep, and looking up, would find them nearly boxed, 'Ria would run, crying aloud with fright, her little feet pit-patting on the stones and grass, to head back her flock; while Geordie swore at his, shouting out strange oaths he'd heard his brothers use, and calling to his dog, which made his sheep all rush together; and 'Ria thought, what a fine thing it was to be a man and frighten sheep so easily.

And then when the sun was high above them and glowed fiercely, and the sheep sought the shelter of the trees, and clustered closely round them, in sweltering, panting mobs, with opened mouths and heaving sides – and it was too hot to play – Geordie and 'Ria would seek some shady spot, down by the river, so that they could get a drink whenever they were thirsty, and then they'd sit and talk. Geordie would tell about the sheep, and all their tricks, and how he served them; and about the pony that was his, upon the run, and how he meant to catch it some day, and break it in; and how Charlie, his big brother, broke in a mare the other day, and shot her foal; and what his other brothers said when they heard the foal was shot; and what big, clever fellows those same brothers were, and how much they weighed, and how much they could lift, and how they licked him, and knocked him about anyhow, and all for nothing; and, under promise of great secrecy, he told her all the things he did to pay them out, because he could not hit them back, being so little. And 'Ria listened breathlessly, with opened eyes, to think of such great daring. That he should venture so fearlessly, and run such risk, to give them something back, she thought quite glorious. And she also told about her home affairs, of the garden, and the fruit, and of the cows and calves, and what her mother said, and what her father. And then, when it was very hot, they would lie down and have a sleep, while the sheep camped; but sometimes, when the flies were very bad, it was only Geordie got his rest, for he would order 'Ria to keep them off, and she would sit beside him, with a bunch of feather-grass, and fan him as he lay.

Sometimes they quarrelled, but not often. 'Ria would stand much from Geordie. One day, as they were sitting under some bushes by the water, eating their food, and waiting till the sheep drew off, Geordie suddenly burst out laughing, and then said – "I say, 'Ria, d'you know what Charlie calls you – 'carrots', 'cause your hair's so red. I say, ain't your hair just like a native's with his wilgee on!"

'Ria stopped eating, and put down her bread – which Bobsy seized at once – and her breath came quickly, and her little bosom heaved – as Geordie went on laughing at his joke – and the little lips began to quiver, and the tears to fall, which, when Geordie saw, he said, "Never mind, 'Ria, don't you be a fool, and cry; you can't help it if you're ugly."

When he said this she looked at him, and the great sobs heaved up, and then she walked away, and cried; holding her little ragged skirt up to her face, and drove her sheep down towards home, and would not hear when Geordie called her back, but went straight on, and when she was out of hearing of him, howled loud as if her heart would break, and for one week she did not go near Long-point.

Her little soul was sorely troubled by the dreadful thought that Geordie called her ugly. She did not care for ugly folks herself, and she felt clearly now that Geordie could not love her. She always thought that he was wondrously beautiful, just like the pictures of the angels in the book the parson brought her when he came on his rounds. She had not often seen herself; the looking-glass at home was high above her reach; but now she looked eagerly in the little pools, and when the moving surface distorted her reflection, she howled and cried again, and said that it was true what Geordie said, and thought that she was a poor wretched little child, whom nobody could care about.

And, oh! how miserable it was to be without her playmate, to wander about the bush, so lonely, and so sad, thinking of what he was doing, wondering if he missed her; but no, she felt he could not miss her, if he thought her ugly, and did not care for her. She did not understand that

Geordie, being a boy, wanted her with him, not because he liked her, but to amuse himself.

But as the long dreary days wore on, she wanted so to see him, and she drove her little flock towards Long-point, and camped a little way below, and hoped, and hoped that he would come.

And one day, as she was sitting mournfully beside the track, a black boy came in sight, riding down the river; and when he saw her he came grinning up, and said he had a paper-talk from Master George, and gave her a yellow, greasy bit of paper, and then rode away.

Poor 'Ria's little body could scarcely hold her heart, it bounded so. It was her first letter, and from Geordie; he had not forgotten her, he wanted her! Eagerly she ran into a little stinkwood thicket with her treasure, and sat down in this secret place, to try and read it. She slipped the paper out of the old bit of string that tied it, and inside she saw –

"Murier, – wy dont you cum bak. im tuired playing by myself, ef you dont cum il cum an lik you. Dont be a fule, Murier.

"G. RANSOM."

'Ria was no scholar; she had never had the chance of going to school, but her father had taught her a bit, of winter nights at home. Handwriting generally was quite beyond her, but Geordie's was large and sprawling, and she spelt out c-u-m two or three times upon the paper, and 'Ria knew that that spelt come – that Geordie wanted her.

How early the next morning she took out her flock, and how she yelled and danced about on her bare little toes as she hoorooshed on her lazy sheep in the well-known direction. But when she came near Long-point she pattered on ahead to look, and saw that Geordie had not come; and then she sat down in her old place to wait for him, longing with all her little soul for his appearance. But when she heard his bells, she hastily got up and ran back to her sheep and sat down behind a tree, and picked some grass to plait; she did not want that he should see her eagerness, and while her pulse was throbbing she assumed an air of perfect carelessness. Geordie came on and saw her sheep, and then he called out, "'Ria! 'Ria! Where are you hiding to? Come here at once !" but she sat quite still. At last a bark of Bobsy's betrayed her hiding-place, and he came tearing up.

"By George, Maria, I've a great mind to thrash you," he exclaimed. "How dare you keep me waiting when I called. Now, you just tell me what you've been about this jolly time that I've been waiting for you every day, and you didn't come."

"I didn't know you wanted me," poor 'Ria whimpered.

"You didn't know! What did you think I was going to play at, all alone? Now you dry up and come on here, and don't you let me catch you at these games again."

Crying made Geordie angry, and 'Ria hastily dried up her tears. She wanted so to kiss him, but then was afraid, and felt how very silly she must be, but as Geordie always said, it was because she was a girl; so she stifled her small sorrow; and in her joy to be again with Geordie, she soon forgot it, and was romping with him noisily. When they were tired they lay down to sleep, and Geordie let her sleep this time; but suddenly they were awakened from their slumber by a dreadful noise – the crack of a stock-whip above their heads. Over them was a great black horse's head, snorting hot vapour down upon them, and on the horse was Geordie's great big brother Charlie, in a towering rage. "Get up, you little cuss!" he yelled to Geordie, "and mind your sheep." And Geordie in great terror started up and ran away. And then he shouted out to 'Ria, "Now, you be off! and don't you show your red wig any more these parts!" And he flicked her little leg, and made it bleed, and poor 'Ria howled with pain, but she howled still louder when she heard young Geordie's yells as Charlie galloped after him to touch him up. And she went sorrowfully home.

And after that Geordie did not come down so often as be used, but when he did, 'Ria was there to meet him.

Chapter V

The years went by, and developed Geordie into a long, lanky boy, sixteen years old, while 'Ria was a fresh, bright, well-grown girl, three years his junior.

They did not meet so often now, though 'Ria still shepherded in summer time, for Geordie's flock was bigger than it used to be, and he now took a pride in it, and did it better justice, and so it was only every now and then that he could come to Long-point. But once or twice a week they met. They did not play so much as formerly, the shepherd life was making Geordie lazy; and after he had tramped about the hills, he thought his long legs wanted rest at camping time. And he would lie down at full length beside Maria, and talk to her about himself, about the life he led, and how he would not stand it, and what a shame it was to keep him grovelling after sheep this way, and doing nothing that could help him on in life; and how be meant to cut and run as soon as he could get a chance to sell his pony, and his dog, and gun, and scrape together a few pounds to make a start. And 'Ria pitied him, and was very angry with his father and his brothers, and comforted him, saying that he soon would be a big strong man, and then he could do what he liked. And Geordie one day said, "Now, look here, 'Ria, you and me have been good mates for long, since you were a tiny girl, and once I get away from here I'll be hanged if I don't marry you!" And this had been Maria's hope, from that day until now.

Truth compels to say that the relations between the boy and girl had a good deal changed their nature in the course of years, and that Geordie's dawning manhood had somewhat marred their innocence. 'Ria was too fond of him, and too ignorant to oppose his doing what he liked. She had had no careful bringing up, to make her what you call right-minded. But still she did not like the new state of things as she had the old, and she often cried about it, till Geordie laughed away her tears. And well it was for her that his father sent him off about this time to another station further up the country.

Four years passed away before they met again – as man and woman. Geordie's long limbs were well filled out; he had grown to his full six feet, and broadened, and a soft brown curly beard shaded his cheek. And he was very handsome – and knew it, too – as he came riding down to see Maria, dressed in his clean tight-fitting cords and blue serge coat, full of the sensation he was going to make upon the little 'Ria of his shepherding days. But when he saw her he forgot himself. She was a full-developed, handsome woman, her father's right hand now, her mother having died; and her face he thought so pleasant, and so fair, and so merry, and so kind; and when he swung off from his horse and kissed her, she blushed so rosily – that blush gave Geordie quite a new sensation. And then she gently freed herself and led him in, and made him tea, and gave him cake, fresh butter, and good things – she knew just what he liked – and then, when he had eaten, they began to talk, and told all that had happened to them since they last had met.

Geordie told how he and his brother Ted were starting on their own hook now, to take a farm up in the lake country, thirty miles away. They had some cattle, and Geordie would look after them while Teddie worked the farm. He did not know how it would pay, but it would be a jollier kind of life than the knocking about for other people's profit he had had till now. And the home-place would be kept up right and comfortable, for Ted was going to marry; "but by Jove, Maria, if he'd seen you before he got his girl I bet she'd have stood but a poor chance," said Geordie, laughing. But that laugh and speech startled poor 'Ria with a sudden pain. Was it not he who was to marry her – he who had promised that he would, only four years ago, when they were last together? And now he laughed about the attraction she would have for Ted, as if he did not mind at all, and had forgotten all about what she had always treasured in her heart as a great good from God to her to come.

And then he asked her, what about her sweethearts? And she burst into tears; she could not help it, and, sobbing, said, "Geordie, you know I never had a sweetheart in the world but you!"

"Oh, oh! ’Ria – and Jim Pitman; don’t you be cramming yarns, you little witch; I’ve heard all about Jim and you."

"If you’ve heard anything about him and me, you’ve heard what isn’t true," said ’Ria passionately, lifting her tear-stained face; "he’s been about the place, of course, and father wanted me to have him, but you know why I couldn’t, Geordie."

"I know, why should I? He’s a jolly fellow, Jim; if I were you I’d take him, ’Ria."

Maria’s tears stopped flowing, and her face grew white. She answered not a word. What could she say? This was her playmate of days gone by – her boy lover, and her promised husband, the idol of her heart, and soul, and body, counselling her with careless laugh and jest to give herself to a Jim Pitman!

She remind him of his promise? – Never! If he could forget, if four years had wrought this change, that she was now to him as any other woman – let it be so. Her joy in life was gone. Had not the thought of him, and of the time when they should be again together, made the earth bright, and all things pleasant? And now – the sun might shine, the earth bring forth fair fruits, all nature smile – what did she care! It was all blackness, void, and misery, now Geordie did not want her.

But Geordie did – only he did not want to marry her. Not care for her! By George! he’d never cared so much for her before. Was he not twenty-one? Was not this splendid woman something more in his man’s eyes than the girl-playmate had been in the boy’s? But ’Ria had forgotten the difference in their stations. His father was a gentleman, and by virtue of that fact he was received in circles where she could not follow. If he married her, he could not raise her; it was but his father's name that kept him up, and she would pull him down.

And then he was so young; he wanted so to have his fling, and take his fill of pleasure. All this wide world of plain and forest, range and creek, and stock and farm, was such a thing of joy to him; he never saw the loneliness or the monotony of the life; existence in itself was to him ecstasy, and pleasure madness. All day long he galloped, and he whistled, and he sang, and laughed at everything; trouble drew from him but a passing curse; he did not understand it yet, and from flower and weed alike he drew some honey.

But underneath this boisterous exuberance of his young manhood there lay the groundline of his character, which the realities of life would soon bring out – strong selfishness. His youth might burn for 'Ria, but his selfishness bade him loudly have a care. "Don't you be the fool to marry her," it said. "Look at your brother Charlie, with four squalling children on his hands, and he not twenty-six; and his hair beginning to turn grey, and so glum, and stupid, you'd think the fellow was a patriarch! When you marry, your life's ease is of the past, my lad!"

And so unreasonable it was of 'Ria to remember the absurdities of a spoony boy; he thought she would have had more sense. Of course he recollected all about it; he knew the meaning of her tears, and said what he had done on purpose. That time four years ago, what he had said, what he had done, sometimes stirred him somewhat uneasily; and he thought, in saying what he did, Maria would have sense enough to take the cue. But when he saw her evident real pain, and her distress, and had to face the chilling silence of her wounded pride, the lad, who was withal good-natured, felt vexed and sorry, and he tried to talk cheerfully of other things, and so bring back her smiles; but it would not do, she could not speak about indifferent things, she could but feel her misery.

The sun had set, and night was coming on, so he said that he must go, and got up, and stood looking at her. Why did she spoil his pleasure with her woe? He did not wonder that she loved him, he thought it was but natural that the poor girl should, and it was pleasing to his vanity to know he was so loved; put he thought she should not worry him, and annoy him in this way, causing him to feel uncomfortable about his doings. But then, again, thoughts of old times with her came to him and of how good, and patient, and loving she had always been; and he felt sorry for her, that he could not keep that boy promise he had made. But love, if she would have it without that, he was ready enough to give. And he went up to her, and whispered caressingly, "'Ria, come down with me as far the garden gate, I want, to speak to you." And they walked down in the twilight there together.

Under the banksia tree beside the pool they stood, and Geordie took both hands of hers in his, and gazed down in her face, with his black eyes all aflame. She looked up at him wistfully, with a little patient smile parting her trembling lips – the first kind word from him had driven out her pride, and only left her sorrow – and when he drew her closer to him, and clasped her in his arms, and did not withstand him, or hinder his caresses, but closed her eyes as he kissed her face and hair, and felt that this was her goodbye to him.

But presently she freed herself, and sprang aside, and with face all crimsoned she told him he had better go, and would not let him touch her, or take hold of her again, but with her hand upon his arm, gently, but firmly, she held him back. "Geordie," she said, "don't make it worse; it's bad enough for me now as it is."

"Oh, well," he answered, baffled and irritated, "I thought you cared for me a little bit, if only for old times' sake, 'Ria; but now I see you don't, so I'll be off." And he unhitched his horse and mounted, but, turning, he saw her seated on the ground where he had left her, and her face was covered with her hands, and she was sobbing quietly. And then Geordie's heart smote him, and he rode up to her, and leaning down, said, "'Ria, what you want can't be, you should not be so foolish as to think of what I said when I was but a silly boy – it's no use crying, it will all come right."

"Oh yes, I daresay it will all come right," she answered drearily.

"Now, don't send a fellow off in the blue dumps like this; get up and kiss me, 'Ria, and say goodbye." She rose and held her face up to him, and let him kiss her, and said goodbye quite quietly as he rode away.

And that night, when her father again spoke to her of Jim, she told him it was all the same to her, and if he wished it, she would have him.

Chapter VI

The arrangements for 'Ria's marriage were soon made. Jim was all eagerness to enter upon the enjoyment of the good things it would bring him, to exchange the scrambling hard life of his over-crowded home for the plenty, and the comfort, and the pleasures which were hers to give.

Her father, also, growing old and feeble, was impatient for the time when he could pass the labour and the toil of looking after farm and stock on to the younger shoulders of his son-in-law.

And to 'Ria – sooner or later, it was all the same.

And so the wedding day was fixed, just one month from that night when she had said goodbye to Geordie under the banksias, by the river pool.

The house was filled with neighbours and with friends; the parson from the township had blessed their union; the eating and the drinking had begun; the old homestead rang with mirth and laughter, with shout, and song, and jest; all hearts were merry, and all eyes were bright – save only 'Ria's.

She was in the kitchen, busy with the pots and pans; she said that they must just sit up without her – she could not leave the things to cook themselves. And so she kept apart, during that riotous afternoon, with an old neighbour woman to help her do the work; and often, as she laboured, providing for the appetites of the noisy band that was gorging and drinking in her honour, the tears fell down her heated face, and she thought what this day might have been had things otherwise turned out. But now she had taken Jim, she would be a good wife to him and do her duty, and by and by perhaps she would feel less about that other love that she must now root out – her only love – for Jim was but – her husband; and when she thought of that she shuddered and grew pale.

While the rioting was at its height Jim came in to her with staggering gait and bloodshot eyes, and took her by the arm to drag her in and make her share their mirth; and she resisted him, and begged that he would let her go. But, with a drunken laugh, he clasped her round the waist, and tried to force her out. 'Ria was nervous and excited, and could not keep from crying, and when he saw her tears he left her with a curse, and went away. And when she had sat down again to calm herself and wipe her eyes the old woman who was with her handed her a packet which had fallen on the floor out of Jim's pocket. Her name was on the cover; she opened it, and this was what she read:

"Dear 'Ria, – You need not have been in such a hurry. You must have known I was in joke when I told you you'd better take Jim Pitman. I've thought about it since, and if you'll have me, say the word. Throw old Jim over, that's not difficult, and write back by the bearer to say when I may come. – Yours affectionately, G. RANSOME."

The hand that held the letter trembled so that she could scarcely see the words – she let it drop upon her lap – her head fell down against the dresser at her side, and she sighed forth a long, low moan of anguish, and was still.

"Oh dearie me! what is the matter?" cried the old woman, hastening up, and throwing water in her face. "She should have gone into the parlour, and not 'ave stopped in this hot place, and so I telled her; and now it's took her sudden, but I'll get a drop of brandy, and she'll soon be right."

Wearily 'Ria opened her eyes again, she heeded not the woman, she only felt that she should like to die; this added misery was too great.

But her father called out for more beer; she must help on the mocking gaieties of her wedding day, and without flinching do her part. So she got up, and with a sad and wearied gesture passed her hand across her eyes; and there in the doorway she saw the native who had brought the letter and given it Jim, waiting to go back with his answer. She went to a little cupboard, and took out a rusty pen and an old ink bottle, and on a bit of paper traced the words – "Too late; I'm married. – 'Ria."

She folded up the paper, and gave it to the black, put Geordie's letter in the bosom of her frock, and went back to her work without a word.

Night was come, and the wedding guests had all gone home. And 'Ria had put things straight about the place, and settled her old father, who was shaky from the drink and the excitement; and then she tremblingly went into the front room, where Jim was lying on the sofa.

She went up softly and stood beside him, leaning against the table at her back, and looking down upon him. He was fast asleep – dead drunk. His handsome, rough, brown face was flushed and moist; his head thrown back, supported by one brawny arm; while the great carcase of him stretched across the sofa, and his legs dangled to the ground, and deep, strong breathing swelled his chest.

This was her husband – and her wedding night.

But 'Ria felt a great thankfulness that Jim was drunk, and thought that Heaven had been merciful in this. Then she took out the little note that was hidden in her bosom, and looked at it again, and smoothed it tenderly upon her knee, and looked down drearily, thinking of what she had lost. No tears came to her; her face was calm, and white, and stony, though a sad smile came over it now and then, when she thought about old times, and the joys and sorrows of her childhood, when she was a bare-footed little shepherd lass, and Geordie's slave and playmate, and knew not of the troubles that her womanhood would bring.

But Jim stirred in his sleep, and groaned; and 'Ria started, and woke again to the realities of her life. Henceforth she must blot out her love and live for duty. And her duty she would do; she felt that that might be her comfort in her trouble.

So she tore up Geordie's letter, bit by bit, and threw it in the fire, and calmly watched it burn, till the last cinder of it had blackened and collapsed. And then she went back to her husband, took off his boots, and put his feet upon the couch, fetched out a pillow for his head, and covered him with a blanket, and settled him down straight and comfortable for the night.

When she had done all that she could for him she went into her room, and locked the door.

Another door in 'Ria's bedroom opened outside into the little thatched verandah, and through this she went to breathe the cool fresh air, sweet with the smell of wallflowers and verbenas she had planted in her little garden. She let down her long thick hair, and held it out, for the night wind to cool her throbbing, heated head; and looked up at the little stars, and thought how strong-hearted they must be to shine so brightly upon joy and woe alike, and wished she could be with them, up in the pure sky, and as untroubled as they seemed to be. And so she sighed, and went inside again to rest.

'Ria had taken off her wedding-dress, and her shoes and stockings, and was standing all in white before the glass, with arms and shoulders bare, thoughtfully brushing out her long red hair, when a low knock sounded at the verandah door, and turning hastily round, she saw before her – Geordie!

With a faint cry she sank down on the bed, trembling and white, her staring eyes fixed on his face in terror. He stood still in the doorway, his hand upon the hasp, frowning down at her silently.

"So this is the way you serve me, 'Ria!" he said at last; "playing me false as soon as my back is turned. Did not you get my letter?"

She had but strength to answer tremblingly, "I did not get it till today."

"And if you did not, you might have had the decency to wait a little longer before you threw yourself into another fellow's arms straight out of mine!"

When 'Ria heard these words she rose up from the bed, her white bosom heaving, and her eyes flashing scorn at him. "Geordie, how dare you say those words to me!" she cried. "Have you so soon forgotten? When we were children both together, I was fond of you with my whole heart; when we were girl and boy, you know best if I didn't love you; when you were away those long, long years, I thought of nobody but you, and what you'd promised me, and counted up the days till you came back. When you came back, you laughed at me, you tore my heart, you told me to marry the man father was pressing on me; you told me I must not think about your promise – and you went away. And now I've done it, as if it was not hard enough, you come back on my wedding day, and say those words to me! Oh, man! when you threw me off, when I found that all my love from childhood up was spurned, and that you and me were to be nothing to each other – what did I care for more! They could do with me as they liked; and I just did what father wanted – what you told me to."

She faltered as she finished, and sank down upon the bed again, pressing her poor worn face against the pillows to still her sobs.

When Geordie heard those words – heard the confession of her love for him, and saw her thus before him, beautiful in the abandonment of her distress – he forgot his anger, and felt but the fierce power of his passion, and a wild regret for what his selfishness had lost.

But lost she should not be to him! She was his 'Ria, always had been his! What cared he for the mocking rites that gave her to another! She should not be another's!

And eagerly he threw himself beside her, and tried to raise her up, and showered kisses on her round white arm and her shoulder; and, drawing back the long thick hair that hung disordered round her, poured passionate entreaties, and prayers for flight, and words of love into her ear, pressing her closely to him.

But she rose and freed herself, and told him as calmly as she could that he must go, and never try to see her any more. "Have mercy on me, Geordie, and do this for my sake," she cried.

She might as well have asked for mercy from madman. The fury of passion and desire was upon him. He seized her again, and drew her to his panting, throbbing breast. He heard not what she said; his ears were deafened, his eyes were blinded by the wild, surging of his tempestuous, boiling blood. And 'Ria sank down, kneeling at his feet, with a wail of fear and helplessness, and dragged herself towards the bed, and clutched hold tightly, kneeling there beside it, begging him to leave her, and struggling to hold on, while he madly tried to raise her up again. And she, with straining muscles, held tight on, and prayed of him, with despairing sobs and cries, to leave her and be gone. And at last, enraged and baffled, he dashed out again into the night, cursing her and himself, and all things, in his wrath.

And Jim, awaking with the noise, called out, and the poor fainting girl unlocked the door, and he stumbled into bed.

Chapter VII

I t was in this wise Geordie's midnight visit came about.

Some time after he got home to the place where he and Ted were living – after that night on which he said good-bye to 'Ria, and freed himself, he thought so well, from his entanglement – he heard that she was to be married to Jim Pitman. Their old man told him so, 'Old Joe', who had been with them since they both were boys. "It's been a long time making, has that match," said he, "and Jim, they say, he blames it on to you. Ah, Master George, but you're the lucky man."

"How's that, Old Joe?"

"Oh! you're the boy the females is a runnin' after. I hear that they should say you had but to stretch out yer hand and you'd have had her, sheep, an' run, an' all. Well, well, yo' was but a babby yesterday, an' now it seems yo' might be having babbies of yer own. Well, well, how time goes, to be sure!"

As soon as they were left alone Teddie said to him, "You are not going to tell me, Geordie, that you've been such a fool as to let that girl slip through your hands, if what Old Joe says is true?"

"If you mean to say I might have had her, if I wanted to, it's true enough."

"And why didn't you want to, then? Do you think you're going to get a farm, and run, and flock of sheep, and cattle, all for the asking, any time you want."

"But they are not hers."

"They will be right enough."

"I've sweethearted with the girl for years, but I never thought of marrying her," said Geordie in an offhand, airy way.

"And who do you think of marrying, pray? What princess d'you suppose is going to throw herself at the head of a fellow such as you. Now look here, Geordie! Don't you be a fool, if you can have the girl, you take her. You might be working all your life, and yet not get together what she can bring you for a start. By Jove!" Teddie went on, "I'll be hanged if I know what the girl can want you for – she never would me! I suppose it's the height and breadth of you that's done it." And Teddie critically looked, and measured Geordie up and down.

"Perhaps," said Geordie loftily, "others may set a different valuation upon me to what you do, Ted."

"Well, I can't say, old man, I set a very high one on you, apart from looks," Ted answered laughing.

"I dare say you do not. A man's no prophet in his own country," said Geordie with great dignity, while Teddie roared; "but that others have a different opinion, you'll soon see for yourself – for, Jim or no Jim, if I find that girl worth having, you'll see I'll have her." And with that he went away.

This conversation made a great impression upon Geordie. Strange to say, the heiress side of 'Ria had never struck him. In their former shepherding days, she had a brother and a sister, but they both had died since he had left the river; and 'Ria in the character of an heiress was to him a new idea. It's true her heritage was not great, but still a most desirable one for a penniless man like Geordie. The pill of her lowly birth would be a much easier one to swallow with this coating. It was not breeding or refinement he missed, for them he did not care. If he gave up his freedom, what he sought was his advantage as a compensation. And he began to see that his advantage clearly lay in marrying 'Ria – which, when he had looked upon her merely as a rustic bush girl of lowly station, and had not taken into account the property that would be hers – was not so apparent to him.

And now Geordie became as anxious to be on again with 'Ria as he had before been to be free. And the more desirable he came to think would be the acquisition of her, the more uneasy he became as to whether he was in time to get her.

And so he sent a black boy down to Woodhill, with the letter 'Ria got upon her wedding day. The black boy was a long time on the way, and in his eagerness he followed up himself. And, finding that he was too late, and, angered by his disappointment, he began to think his haste had been unwarrantable, and indecent, and a personal injury to himself, and working up his wrath, he waited round the place until he obtained that midnight interview.

During the two years of 'Ria's wedded life that followed, Geordie did not trouble her. His violence at that last meeting had not cured 'Ria of her love for him, but that, together with his former conduct, when he gave her up, had, to some extent, taught her to form a juster estimate of his worth and character, and to know the measure of his selfishness. And the further experience of the ways of men that marriage had brought to her, had not the effect, now she was free, of making her over anxious to be wed again. She was now a developed woman, of strong common sense, somewhat hardened by the trouble which she had known, and which she had learnt to bear as something which must come, and must be suffered without fuss; and somewhat sceptical of others, with very few hallucinations left; but withal a womanly woman. And the good, healthy spirits of her girlhood were but subdued, a very little made her glad, and her heart light and merry as in the old days when she and Geordie used to play at Long-point. And now – she often thought of him, but not as in old days when he was all in all to her; she had learnt prudence now, and meant to use it.

Chapter VIII

Midsummer had come on. The river pools were drying up and brackish; the grass along the banks and in the open flats was dry and stubbly; the cattle sought the shady creeks back in the range and the lagoons, where beds of tender rushes grew on last year's burnt ground;

curtains of yellow smoke hung in the hot sky from distant fires; and all around nature lay hushed in sweltering lassitude.

It was washing day, and 'Ria and Elizabeth Anne were busy at the pool. On four forked sticks stuck in the ground they had raised a leafy arbour to shade them from the sun. Beside them a trypot full of clothes was boiling, and with skirts and sleeves tucked up, with faces flushed and moist, they bent over their foaming wash-tubs, hard at work.

Elizabeth Anne belaboured an obstinate pair of Sullivan's moleskins. "'Ria," she said, "them breeches won't come clean. What with the cooking of their grub, and the washing of their clothes, and the minding of them when they're drunk, the men's more trouble than they're worth. They get their legs into a pair of breeches, and there they stick, until the thing's that black you can't do nothing with it." And she scornfully held aloft the offending garment.

"They're bad enough, the men; but with the women-folk to mind them, they're of some use in the world," said 'Ria, "when they keep their place."

"The fellah to them breeches ain't a keeping of his place," said Elizabeth-Anne, emphatically.

"Here! give them me," said 'Ria, flushing: "and you do out the child's."

Both women were somewhat out of temper, and kept silence for a while.

The owner of the breeches was doing his work upon the place with steady zeal; from early dawn till night he toiled and strove, and the missis had no trouble. A hint from her, and what she wished was done. Hard work was child's play to his strong arms and shoulders. He often growled and cursed – that was the nature of him. He had a bulldog's temper. But while he swore at what he did not like, he worked the harder, and no disinclination made him flinch from doing well the part that had been given him.

But Elizabeth Anne, with her quick female eyes, thought that she saw a motive for this ardour, and she had said with purpose what had made 'Ria flush.

'Ria knew it well; she had gained more experience in such matters than had Elizabeth Anne. She knew that he was working for love of her and her's, and it pleased her to see what power she had over him.

Elizabeth Anne could not be silent long, or she would burst; "'Ria," she went on, "what's it like to be in love? Is it a good thing to be?"

"Why? What are you talking, you great silly."

"'Cause there's a young chap as wants to try it on with me, I think," said Elizabeth Anne with dignity, "and so I want to know."

"It's most times trouble to the woman," 'Ria answered, sighing; "the men want so much and give so little. You mind yourself, Elizabeth Anne, and don't be doing foolish."

"Oh! I'm all right, he'll not be getting over me – I'm not in love – I'm not that far gone as yet."

"Who is the man?" said 'Ria.

Elizabeth Anne made no reply except to giggle, and 'Ria, looking up to ask again, suddenly left off washing, and screamed out "My God! what's that?" and rushing up the bank towards the house, where the ground was open, stared in terror down the river.

Elizabeth Anne flew after her, and when she had looked, she said, "How far away?"

"Close up; it's at the Half-way Creek," 'Ria answered; "Elizabeth Anne, you run and tell the men; say I've gone on, and stop and make some tea, a lot, and bring it with you in a jug. The child is safe up here with Dinah."

'Ria then saddled up a horse that was standing tied up in the yard, and galloped down across the paddock, and soon was lost to sight in a thick cloud of smoke that was sweeping up the river. Steadily and silently the yellow cinder-laden fog came on, enveloping all things, darkening the sun. And every now and then, out at the back of it, with a loud roar, a swelling mass of blackness shot up into the sky, surging up, flame-laden, with fierce swiftness as it left the earth; then billowing out, wider and slower as it rose, until it hung a flat black cloud, high overhead.

A terrible bushfire had broken out upon them.

Elizabeth Ann ran off up to the barn, which lay some distance from the house across the small corn paddock. Sullivan and another man were there at work threshing the barley. Breathless with running, she called out to them that she wanted to speak to them.

They stopped their work, and asked her what it was.

"The missis says will you go down at wonst – the fire's broke out on us – down to the Half-way Creek; an' she's gone on ahead, an' you're to go, an' I'm to make the tea an' follow after."

The men threw down their flails, put on their flannels, and rushed out; and Sullivan, after he had looked, flung down his hat upon the ground, and stamped, and yelled out, "Blast the fire!" He knew the work that was before them, and the trouble they would have – two hands – to put out such a mighty conflagration.

Meanwhile, 'Ria galloped down through the gathering smoke towards the Half-way Creek.

The afternoon breeze was getting up, and lazily began its work, gently driving the smoke-clouds up the river, and every now and then, rousing to energy, it rolled up a black, suffocating mass towards her, which choked both horse and woman. Then, again, it lulled, exhausted, and the smoke cleared suddenly off and rose straight up through the quivering trees, showing a long, flickering, crimson line upon the ground, steadily creeping on with fiendish dance and cackle in its devouring course; roaring out an exultant mass of whirling, dazzling flame as it caught some larger leafy prey; leaping madly up the dry and flaky bark of the mahogany stems, to fall again in glowing showers to the ground.

'Ria tied up her horse beside the track, where he was safe, and breaking off a leafy bough rushed down to begin her work of beating out the flames.

The fire had run across the river, and was coming up in a straight line, square to its course; and she thought if they could stop it at the Half-way Creek, on the house side, it would be best. There was less grass there, and the track would help them. So she set the feed alight along the track and creek, and let it burn to meet the larger fire. But before long the wind got up again, and the red flames bent forwards under it, and licked along in maddened haste, in fierce derision leapt track and creek, and raced and tore its way over the long grasses of the river flat.

How desperately 'Ria began to beat, and tried to stem the rushing flames, and cooeed for the men to help her. The fire scorched her face and singed her hair, and the choking smoke enveloped her, mocking her impotent endeavours. But she was fighting for her home and for her boy, her all; and madly she swung her bough about, wildly she beat and swept, the flaming grass, to save her homestead from destruction. And now the men came up, and set to with a will, and the wind lulling, the fire no longer ran so fast; and above the roar was heard the regular plash-plashing of the boughs upon the ground, as they followed one another up, sweeping back the flames into the blackness they had left behind.

Eagerly they worked, with panting haste, the fire seeming at one time to be almost conquered, then again breaking out savagely; in front of them, behind them, roaring and swirling on with every puff of wind – to stay again its haste and give the weary workers time to get it under, as they thought, only to break out afresh with fiendish glee, as if it felt its power, and was playing with the toiling men and woman making their frantic efforts.

But at last, Sullivan, and his mate, and 'Ria had worked round to the river, and on that side the fire was safe. They flung themselves exhausted to the ground, the perspiration running in streams from off their steaming bodies, their faces blackened and begrimed with smoke and ash, throats parched, and eyelids red and sore. And then Elizabeth Anne came up with the welcome jug of tea, and laughed at the scorched, grimy figures of the men, and screamed out to her goodness when she saw 'Ria's disordered, burnt, and tattered clothing: and gave them round the jug, and they drank long draughts of the warm, weak, sweety compound, and lay back with a sigh of pleasure as they wiped their mouths.

But their work was not yet done. Beside them was the deep river pool that ran up to the house. The fire raging on the other side could not cross that as the wind then blew; and 'Ria had no fear – now the house side was all put out the other side could go; she thought it would be just as well, for the scrub over there was old and dry, and stood in need of burning; so they lay still and rested.

But by and by, shrill yodels from black Dinah, at the house, warned them of something wrong, and starting up, they saw masses of black smoke rising swiftly from the river bed above the pool and billowing down towards the house. The wind had shifted, and the flames had swept across the river bed up there, and were feeding gloriously on the tangled masses of rush and ti-tree bush, and dry dead stinkwood sapling, that lined the banks, and lighting up the grasses, were bearing down upon the paddock, doubling back upon their former upward course.

The men rushed off towards the house, and Elizabeth Anne, bearing the jug, ran shrieking after them, while 'Ria followed with the horse.

It was but a passing blast that bore the fire down, and the burning patch on the house side was soon put out. But while they worked, making all safe, throwing the burning logs and sticks within the black, charred stretches over which the flames had passed, and sweeping in the smoking cinders, 'Ria was startled by the sudden crash of a tree falling close behind her, and a wild yell from Sullivan. She fled before the showers of dead sticks and cinders that fell around her, and when the noise had ceased, and she looked round, she saw Sullivan lying still upon the ground, half covered by the splintered ruins of the tree. She rushed up to him screaming out for help, and dragged him from out of the smoking heap. And his mate hurried up, and then Elizabeth Anne; and they knelt down on the black ground beside him, frightened to touch him for fear of what they might discover.

But Elizabeth Anne yelled out that there was blood upon his head, and they found an ugly cut across it, from which the blood was slowly dripping. His eyes were shut, and he breathed heavily, and the healthy red-brown of his face was gone, and the skin shone greeny-white through the wet, black grime upon it. His mate ventured to feel his limbs and body; apparently, no bones were broken, but there was another nasty cut upon his thigh.

And now they had to get him home, and with some trouble the women helped the man to take him on his back, and he carried down his heavy senseless burden across the paddock to the house. Then they laid him on the couch in the front room – the same couch, on which 'Ria had sat when Geordie told her she ought to marry Jim – the same couch on which poor Jim had lain when he was drunk upon his wedding night

"We must be taking off his duds and seeing if anything else be wrong," said the man to 'Ria; and Elizabeth Anne loudly expressed her sorrow, and her sympathy, and her willingness to help. But 'Ria shoved her out, and locked the door; and then they cut away the short, thick stubbly hair from around the wound upon his head, and took off his blackened clothes, and found some few hurts of not much amount; but upon the swelling outer muscle of the thigh was a bad cut and bruise. They washed him clean, and dressed his wounds, and put a shirt upon him, and before they had quite done their work the man came to, and after he had drunk a drop of grog they left him, sleeping quietly.

Chapter IX

It was now night, and their supper over, the women and the man went down towards the Halfway Creek to see that all was safe, to throw in burning logs, and make sure that the flames would not spring up again upon them in the night.

The sky was thickly charged with smoke, and browny-black; but down below the Half-way Creek, and across the river, all along the wide track of the morning's fire was a grand, rich, red illumination.

The burnt, ashy ground was streaked with splashes of vivid crimson from glowing logs, and against the glare stood out in bold, stark blackness the trunks of the charred forest trees, while up them now and then ran sportive tongues of flame, crackling and flashing up in the loose hanging bark of their dead limbs, spluttering showers of fire-sparks around, while through the broken funnel of many an old tree trunk the flames were wildly rushing, breaking out high aloft in a great flaring blaze, impatient to finish off their work and to bring down the towering mass in crashing ruins to the ground.

Crash! crash! they came, to right, to left – trees that had stood upright against the winter wind for many years – a storm of fire, ash, and smoke dashing up from them as they fell. And the vivid flashes, and the shifting lights, and showers of red sparks, and shooting flames, filled the old forest with what seemed a wild, grotesque, satanic, life, while through the thick brown gloom spread overhead the moon looked down like a dusky blood-red ball hung over it.

The weary workers thought not of the strangeness or the beauty of the scene; mechanically they moved their tired limbs, and finished off their tasks and went up home. And 'Ria, when she saw that Sullivan was getting on all right, and her boy sleeping peacefully, sat down outside in the cool air, to rest and think upon the troubles of the day.

Old Mother Pitman had spoken right that time at Baylup, when she said it was not for young women to be minding of a place; the men-folk were some use to see to things. It was all very well, she thought, having a good serving-man like Sullivan to do the work, but the bothering when fires came, and such like, and the worry of the thinking and the ordering of what was to be done, was more than she could stand with the baby on her hands, and the cooking and the keeping of the house. And 'Ria felt very miserable this night, and wished that poor old Jim with all his faults were alive again, and with her. But Jim was dead and gone, and then she thought of Geordie.

She often thought of Geordie now; she had tried to banish him from her heart while Jim was living, but now she wondered if he would come back to her; she thought that it was cruel of him to leave her thus alone with all her cares. He had never come to see her, never let her hear a word of him, and he was living only four miles off, for his father had gone to live in town, and he had taken the old place up the river.

She was free now, why did not he come to her? Two years ago, when she last saw him, he had been mad to have her; had her possession by another so cooled his ardour? 'Ria did not think so, she had more to bring him now than she had then, and she smiled sadly as she thought that that would bring him back. She knew Geordie well by now.

But she felt sure that, if he took her, he would work for her, and do well with the place for his own sake. And he would be her husband! And 'Ria trembled and cried with pleasure when she thought of that, her one ambition since she was a little girl. She forgave him all his selfishness, his violence at their last meeting; she felt herself the little 'Ria of old days, and he, her lord and leader, her only love through all these years. She was so weak and tired tonight, so weary of her loneliness.

When she had first been widowed, she had thought she would be prudent, would not blindly risk her fate with him, but then she had felt sure that he would come at once and seek her. But now he kept away, and left her to herself, and showed no sign; she longed for him, and thought if he would only come, and say a word of love to her, she would risk all and take him.

And while she sat, and cried, and thought, Sullivan on the couch inside was groaning out in pain and heaviness. And 'Ria listened and was sorry for him. She knew he thought that he would get her, and the place – for that it was that he was working like a slave, for that he was now lying wounded in her room; and she pitied him, and sighed and smiled as she thought about the ways of men.

But Sullivan, with all his pain, was happy; he thought that this would conquer her, that he had nearly met with his death in working for her service.

When he first came to Woodhill, while Jim was living, he stopped on for the missis' sake; she always gave him a kind word, and looked well to his comfort and his victuals. Bred up in vice, and crime, and ignorance, with the good side of him lying dormant, used to evil thoughts and evil ways, he thought bad things more readily than good; he thought all men were bad, and women, too, only that some were lucky, and had not the ill fortune of poor devils such as he. And so, when 'Ria was good to him, and kind, it never struck him that it was simply because she was good-hearted, and would be kind to any poor dog that might cross her path – he thought she had a fancy for him, and he would stop, and reap the crop that it might bring; and when Jim died, he schemed how he might take his place.

But the missis was more wary than he had supposed – it was not cheap that she was to be had – she would not see it, when he tried to make advances; and, afraid to lose the precious prize, the poor fellow worked, and slaved, and laboured anxiously to do her pleasure.

It was a prize worth working for to him! He had never but a pound or two to jingle in his trousers pockets, and it had been hard work when he got that, and the bit of money was no use to him, except to have "a drunk." What was the use of a poor man like him trying to get on and save? He might save the few pounds wages he could screw together, after he'd filled his pipe and clothed his back, for many a year, and be no better off to speak of. But here was a wondrous chance of a big fortune, ready made to hand, that he might pick up if he only willed and set about it right. And a fine woman with it, too, and he'd show her it were best to have him. He set about to do it, and anxiously he brooded, and he thought, at night after his day's work was done, over the progress he had made, and how to make the best of the next day. And when the task seemed hard and slow, and the end no nearer, a creeping heat would sometimes run along his back and neck, and break out on his brow in a cold sweat of fear and indignation, when he thought his work might be in vain, and he might not get the widow after all. And then he swore and cursed her for a deluding jade.

But as the time wore on he began to think much less about the place, and more about the woman.

Hitherto a woman, any woman, had been to Sullivan – but a woman; if young and fresh, so much the better, but one and all about the same, and held at a cheap rate.

But he began to think the missis was different from the rest. In the first place, she was hard to get, and the getting of her involved the possession of so much more, that her personality acquired fresh importance in his eyes. He began to see what she was like; to feel pleasure as he listened to her voice, and looked at her; his untutored eye wandered down the graceful outlines of her form, and was satisfied and pleased; his dull imagination began to work, and lifted her in his mind out of the herd of common women, into something that he did not understand, but longed for – something graceful, good, above him. And this new feeling even subdued the passionate desire that he now began to feel for her possession, and made him timid. Sullivan was in love!

He combed and greased his stubbly hair; he washed his face until it shone again; he even washed his body, kept his clothes clean, and made himself as pleasant looking as he could; but still he had a dissatisfied, vague feeling that he was not up to much beside her. But then he worked like a slave, and vowed again that he would have her. She could not get a man to do for her better than he could do, and but for his misfortune he was as good as any, and better, too, than many he knew, who had kept out of trouble. And now that he was lying sick, and sore, and wounded for her sake, she must hear him, she must pity him, and yield. And when the missis came inside, and he feigned to be asleep, and when she laid her small, cool hand compassionately on his head, to see whether the fever was abating, and settled the bandage comfortably, poor Sullivan's heart and body thrilled with a strong yearning. He would have caught her, had he dared, and drawn her down to him, and then and there have told her that she must be his missis, and have kept her imprisoned in his arms until she said she would; and then he felt what a proud man he would be, and how he'd snap his fingers at the world and its ill-usage. But instead of that he lay quite still, and shivered as her hand rested on his head, and lightly touched his hair, as she smoothed the bandage. And when she went away the salt tears started from his eyes when he thought of the miserable poor devil that he was; and being weak, and ill, and faint from loss of blood and fever, he doubted that she would ever care for him, or have him; and his dull life would go on as it had before.

So he lay back through the night watches, nursing his misery and self-pity.

Chapter X

One day Elizabeth Anne was riding up the river, driving the cows. The water in the pool at home was brackish, and the cattle would not drink it, and up at Long-point was the big pool out of which, in former days, Geordie and 'Ria used to haul the chelgies, that was fresh and good. And up to the Long-point pool Elizabeth Anne was bound to drive the cattle every day.

This work was a great satisfaction to Elizabeth Anne. When mid-afternoon came on she threw poor Jim's old saddle on the mare, and mounted straddle-legged, rounded the cattle up down in the paddock, and took them off.

Once started, they did not need much driving, and Elizabeth Anne could take her pleasure. She galloped after kangaroos and rats; she yelled and sang; she performed wild evolutions in the saddle; best of all, she liked to lie down at full length, her head over the old mare's tail and legs upon her neck, and then she cautiously would raise her feet, till the flat soles of them faced the blue sunny sky, and with them so she'd clap her heels together gleefully, and with a bound resume her straddle-legged position. This she called circus-riding; Sullivan had told her that they did like that. She tried to stand upon the saddle, but could not quite succeed, she always tumbled off; but she knelt upon it beautifully, and that was not far from the right thing. And often, when she was tired with her exertions at these clever tricks, she would tie up the mare and have a sleep, and, waking up near sundown, would gallop up to Long-point and fetch back the patient cows. And then, when she got home, she had wonderful, things to tell — of how they had split on her, and some gone up the creek; and how it took her all her time to fetch them back; and how the calves were all that wild, there was no doing nothing with them, and she was nigh a breaking of her back, and the mare's heart, a keeping of them all together, and a getting of them up and down before the night – and such-like fictions.

But on this day that she was going up it had been very hot, and Elizabeth Anne felt heated and uncomfortable, and thought that she would have a bath and cool herself up in the Long-point pool. So she drove the cattle steadily, when she got close up she galloped on, and tied the mare up to a tree.

The pool was deep, and off the reed-grown, sandy banks the bather stepped into 10ft. of water; only at the upper end, where the pool narrowed, it was shallower, with rock and gravel bottom, and, here the trees arched overhead, the banksias and the flooded gums, and gave cool shade.

Elizabeth Anne, when she came up, thought that before she had her bath she would step in and just see what the water felt like. So she took off her hat and bared her feet, and taking up her petticoats, stepped gingerly upon the rocks. The water was so pleasant that she raised her petticoats higher, and waded till her knees were under water, and then turned round and shouted at the cows and calves that had come down to drink.

The poor dull creatures were standing off, and vaguely gazing at the strange figure of their driver disturbing their quiet watering place. But, by and by, a strawberry cow with more spirit than the rest shook up her horns and snorted, and stepped down nearer to the water's edge. And then Elizabeth Anne yelled out, and brandished up her feet, and splashed the water, and the strawberry cow moved back, and shook her horns again. And then a little runty calf walked solemnly from the bank, and put its moist white muzzle down to drink. But Elizabeth Anne scooped up the water with her hand, and threw it in its face, and shouted, and the runty calf ran bellowing to its mother. And so she laughed and teased them, and kept them all at bay.

And now she found a clear flat stone where the water came to midway up her calves, and standing on this stone she danced a furious jig, such as she'd seen the men dance at the shearing time at home when they were drunk. Her garments she held tight about her waist, and throwing out her shapely limbs kicked up her toes in mockery at the frightened cows, and leapt and stepped it merrily, churning up the quiet water into frothy whiteness. Her curly hair hung down, her cheeks were reddened with a glow of pleasure, her merry mouth laughing with impish frolic, one white arm curved above her head – just like the men did – and all around her and overhead she splashed the water, and the spray flew up sparkling like diamonds in the tiny flecks of sunlight that danced about, and shone through the breeze-stirred leaf-masses overhead.

But all at once a man's laugh rang out merrily from the bank, and Elizabeth Anne in startled terror lost her footing, and plashed down sitting on the stone, breast high in the water.

The tumble hurt Elizabeth Anne, and made her yell, and the water she displaced and agitated in her fall splashed into her eyes and mouth, and made her gape, and gasp, and shake her head, while she threw her arms out wildly to keep her balance, for her feet were off the ground, and beating on the surface of the water. But when she was righted, and had wiped her eyes, she looked up to the bank and saw young Geordie Ransome – the cause of her discomfiture – sitting on the leaning trunk of an old paper-bark, making the woods ring with his boisterous laughter.

Elizabeth Anne now raised herself, and thought to run away, but her dripping garments clung treacherously to her lithe form. So she was ashamed and sat her down again with burning cheeks, while Geordie laughed still louder.

And now the cows and calves walked steadily down to drink, their mistress having ceased her troubling of the waters. And Elizabeth Anne put her brown fists into her eyes and cried.

"Good evening, miss," said Geordie, "I hope I see you well. Chosen a nice dry place to rest in, haven't you?"

"Get out, you beast!" said she.

"It's you that should get out, miss – I'm not in. But I'll get in if you like," said he.

Now she howled loudly, and splashed the water at him, and screeched and cried, and called him all the bad names she could think of. But Geordie quietly took off his boots and socks, and began tucking up his breeches. Elizabeth Anne, when she saw this grew desperate, and, bounding up, rushed out upon bank, the water streaming from her skirts on to her bare legs and feet, and the frightened cattle stampeding every way.

Geordie ran after her, and caught her just as she neared the mare.

"Now, missy, don't be frightened, and don't bite," he said; "I only want to be your sweetheart."

Now Elizabeth Anne had never had a sweetheart – what she told 'Ria was a pure invention, just for the sake of talking, and she suddenly bethought her that this was a new and most desirable experience she might make. So she stood still at once, and looked up at him, and thought him a most proper sweetheart for a girl to have. And then he asked her who she was, and she said she thought every one knew that – she was Elizabeth Anne Pitman, sister of Maria Pitman's husband, from Woodhill.

When Geordie heard that she had come from 'Ria, his face grew grave, and he let go her arm, and asked how 'Ria did.

"Oh! she's nicely, thank you," said Elizabeth Anne.

"And how does she get on about the place now that poor Jim is dead?"

"Oh! her and me, we gets on pretty well! We has our troubles – the cattle's very wild, and is always a-splitting about the country on us. And then the sheep is that contrary, they're a-losing theirselves on us every day, but we mostly gets them back. The paddock bothers us, but Maria's young man does the work."

"Who's her young man?" growled Geordie.

"Oh! that's a young chap called Sullivan, he's a fine feller, and me and 'Ria likes him well enough, and now he's lying with a broken head and leg, a-groaning terrible, an' she's a-nursing of him. But I know something, only you must not tell," and then she came up closer to him, pursing her mouth, and looking very cunning. "He wants to be her sweetheart, and when I tell her of it, she won't let on. Your widows is that close!"

As she said this, young Geordie gripped her arm, and frowned down fiercely on her, with clenched teeth.

"Owch!" screamed Elizabeth Anne, "what's that you're doing?"

But he never heard her; he dashed headlong up the bank, sprang on his horse, and galloped down the river.

"Well, if that's what you call sweethearting! – well, I never!" Elizabeth Anne exclaimed. "It's more like the contrary thing."

And then she wrung out her skirts, got on the mare, and gathered up the cattle, and made them run as fast as the poor tottering things could go, sparred by a gnawing curiosity to follow Geordie with all possible haste, and find out what was up.

Chapter XI

Geordie was on his way to 'Ria when he stumbled on Elizabeth Anne. He was going with some diffidence. When he cooled down after that last scene on her wedding-night, and thought of all that he had done and said, he felt ashamed; he felt that he had been a brute, to make her trouble worse – a trouble he could but own he had brought on – by his violence and his unjust reproaches. But though he knew it was unjust, he still felt angry with her, angry because he had lost the game; angry and mortified because she had repulsed his passion; angry because he knew that she had cause for strong complaint against himself. And so he brooded on his fancied wrongs through those two years.

But when Jim died and she was was free, he determined that his rightful possession should come back to him again. He had seen no women he liked so well as 'Ria, so suited to him – knowing him so well – so unselfish and so unexacting, giving all, and content to take so little from her lover – at least he knew that so she had always been with him, since they were boy and girl together.

And then he saw no chance to get a wife whose hand would bring him better things than hers, so he felt generously-minded to forgive his wrongs, wipe out the past two years, and make it up with her.

Still he had sufficient pride about him not to be too hasty, or show too great an eagerness, and besides he was not sure how she would look upon him after what had passed. But, on the whole, when he thought of what she had been to him during those long early years, he felt some confidence that she must have forgiven him ere now.

But when on his way down he stumbled on Elizabeth Anne, and the fun that he had meant to have with her was stopped by finding that she was 'Ria's kinswoman, he thought he would find out from her how 'Ria was disposed.

But when she told him, early in their talk, her yarn about the man, Geordie was suddenly filled with rage and indignation, and alarm, and forgetting all his pride and caution – with a wild determination to have it out and settle matters then and there; and so he broke away to speed to her, in strong excitement.

Elizabeth Anne, with her poor cows and calves, was down at home in half an hour after Geordie left her, and rushing in the front room, found only Sullivan lying on the sofa, pale and sulky.

"Where is he gone?" she cried.

"Where's who gone?" he grunted.

"That young chap in the boots and breeches, on a black horse."

"I haven't seen no horse, but young Ransome – Geordie they call him – was here just now a-wanting of the missis, an' a-cursing up an' down the place; an' he's off up the Washpool Creek to look for her."

"Oh lor! Oh lor!" exclaimed Elizabeth Anne; "if that was not 'Ria's sweetheart afore she married Jim. Oh, I say, Sullivan, what a lark!" and Elizabeth Anne ran out and danced and shrieked with glee, to think of the delightful mischief she had done.

Sullivan sat up, and glanced after her, as she went away. His pale face worked with rage and anguish, the sweat stood on his brow, and his breath came short and heavy in his strong excitement.

Was this intruder come to spoil his game, to rob him of his prize, to cheat him of the woman he was living, suffering for – to obtain with a hand's turn what he was toiling to get – to treat him like dirt beneath his feet? And with an intensity of rage he felt that a poor devil such as he had but a poor chance beside a swell like that?

But 'Ria must have seen his aim, and he swore that he would be no laughing-stock for her, and for her jackanapes. Him she should have, or no one else, so help him all the powers; he swore it with a fearful oath, and lay back panting on the couch.

That afternoon the native women had come in to say that they had lost some lambs. Sullivan was sick, and Elizabeth Anne away, up with the cows; so 'Ria said that she would go and find them, up in the Washpool Creek, where they were lambed, and for which they mostly made when they were lost. And Sullivan had told Geordie that she had gone up there, and to the Washpool Creek he followed her. He went down by the river pool, and across the black charred ground, the track of the late fire, and over a low, rough hammock, powdered with white quartz gravel, and so down into the long grass of the Washpool Valley. The spreading thick leaf-masses of the redgums shut out the sinking sunlight, and had preserved the grasses fresher than on the wider river flats. The soft rounded slopes were painted in pale greens and browny greys, with splashes of warmer yellow where the silver grass had found a lodging, while close in along the creek, beside the running water, were borders of deeper, brighter hues, a groundwork of rich green grass, and a mass of tangled loveliness above, clusters of golden wattle-bloom, thick patches of ground runner of a vivid blue, showers of crimson creeper flowers, and giant fern fronds shading every little sparkling pool.

Geordie cantered fuming up the bank until he came to a long sloping grassy ridge, round which the brooklet wound. The ridge face nearest him lay in deep shadow, but the rays of the sinking sun just touched the crest with a streak of golden colour, and beyond was the hazy grey-blue of the distant hills at the creek's head.

Out on the ridge-crest, in the mellow sunlight, Geordie now saw the small, grey, curly bodies of five little lambs, followed by the darker, bony outline of a mother ewe, and rising up behind them, from the other side, first the white sunshade, then the black folds of 'Ria's dress, and the bright blue of the toddling child's figure at her side, standing out against the glowing orange of the western sky.

Geordie, now that he saw 'Ria coming, peaceful and quiet, driving the sheep before her, felt his blustering mood grow fainter. What was he to reproach her with? What was he to say, now his angry haste had brought him face to face with her? How was he to use the yarn that impish girl had told him in accusation? And if it was not true, how would he look? And if it was, what right had he to interfere, except that in his own intention she was his; but what had that to do with her? 'Ria was free to do whatever she might please, without his sanction. And so he felt abashed, and angry with himself, and her, and everything; and he got off his horse, and stood aside, waiting and watching as she came.

The little group of woman, child, and sheep had left the sunlit space above and entered the deep gloom of the ridge side. 'Ria had taken up her boy, lest he should fall on the steep slope, and with him in her arms was manoeuvring behind the stupid, wilful lambs, to get them back on to the cattle path that ran along the creek, which she thought they would then follow up, and she would have less trouble. At last she got them on to it, and they set off bleating towards the house, the miserable old ewe in front, with the anxious lambs in tail.

And now she gathered up her skirts, and settled the child more comfortably on her arm, to follow after them. But suddenly she stopped, and gave a little startled scream, for there, in front of her, stood her old lover, Geordie Ransome!

Geordie looked at her, all his wrath gone, in an anxious, deprecating kind of way, as he nervously held out his hand, and said, "Well, 'Ria!"

'Ria was still more nervous than himself; she hastily set down the child, and gave her trembling hand to his with a little quivering smile. And so they stood, face to face once more, for the first time since that stormy night two years and more ago.

They spoke not, but they looked at one another. Geordie, seeing how pale and thin she was, felt sorry for her, when he thought of all the trouble she must have known to alter her so much in a short time. And he, she thought that he was handsomer than ever; only there was a more restless and less joyous look about his eyes, and work had somewhat roughened him.

They looked at one another with a sort of shy and troubled smile upon their faces, their hands still lightly clasped. 'Ria was wondering if her time of joy had really come; and Geordie, softened by the sight of the pale face of his old love, was wishing that he knew what she thought of him now, and whether she would have him if he asked. 'Ria was the first to speak, and overcome her trouble; she told him about her worry with the sheep, and how there were fifty lost from out of the flock, and how she had as yet got back but these miserable six; the man was sick, and she had nobody to look for them.

Geordie listened to her, and did not speak, as she went on talking nervously and fast; but all at once he drew her to him with a sudden grasp, and held her tightly, looking down at her with a flushed, quivering face, and said in a rapid eager way, "'Ria! I'll find your sheep! I'll find your sheep for ever, if you'll let me; you know well what I mean! Now, will you, 'Ria? Come, tell me."

There was something of the old masterful manner of his boyhood in the last words, and he grasped her arm so tight he almost hurt her. But she could not speak, the tears were coming fast; and he thought that she was angry, and let her go, and she sat down beside him on a log, and cried and cried most heartily, with a hard-earned enjoyment. "Oh, Geordie!" she sobbed out at last, "I am so glad. I thought that you were never coming to me."

So she was waiting for him! She loved him still! She had forgotten all his wrongs! And Geordie for one short minute thought he was a brute, and was not worthy of her. But his great satisfaction with his good luck, and his gratified man's vanity, overpowered every other feeling; and being now perfectly good-humoured and self-satisfied, he lifted 'Ria up and kissed her, and swung her laughing on his saddle, and gave her up the boy, and asked if she had forgotten all about the lambs, that had gone on ahead. And she said, as she wiped up her tears, "Oh! bother take the lambs," she did not care; they'd find them somewhere on the road.

So he walked along beside her down the creek, with his long arm round her, saying he was frightened she would fall off the man's saddle travelling this rough path, for the mare stumbled in the darkening twilight. And now it was Geordie's turn to talk, and he laughed and chatted gaily as they went; and when they came to the white quartz ridge, above the river valley, they found the ewe and lambs on an old camp beside the track. And Geordie said he'd fetch them home, if 'Ria would go on and get the supper ready. So he set to work to do the job, cursing and swearing at their contrary ways and horrible pigheadedness, until they came in sound of their mothers bleating, up at home, and so made straight their paths.

When Geordie reached Woodhill, it was almost night. Elizabeth Anne was setting out the table, and when he came inside she stopped and stared at him, and laughed. She had already teased and questioned 'Ria, and found out pretty near the truth, and then she mischievously had told the tale to Sullivan. And now she said, "Well! you're a pretty sweetheart! When are you coming sweethearting along with me again?" Geordie reddened, and laughed, and Sullivan, with a groan of pain and rage, rose up, and crept out, down along the yard, and into the low lean-to place beside the shed, where he had slept before his hurt, and laid him down upon his wretched bunk. And there he tossed about in suffering and anger, muttering hoarsely to himself, and in low growling tones, telling his troubles and wrongs to the inanimate sticks and slabs around him.

They did not think of Sullivan inside, they had forgotten all about him, they did not even notice he had gone. Geordie was in boisterous spirits, rattling away to 'Ria and joking with Elizabeth Anne, and 'Ria was sitting at the table, subdued and quiet, but happier than she had been for years. She felt no trouble, no misgivings about what was to come. She cast aside her reasoning prudence – she knew his faults, his selfishness – she knew that she would have to be his slave, and sacrifice herself in everything to him; but such sacrifice would be no hardship to her. She loved him – not only as a woman does her lover, but as a mother does her son – the more for all the suffering he had given her, the more for all that she had done and would have to do for him.

Elizabeth Anne was somewhat disappointed with their ways. She was a young thing was Elizabeth Anne, and had not much experience. She had thought she would have found out in her own person what the men did in their spooning, when Geordie had caught her up at Long-point; but that satisfaction, to her regret, had been denied her, and now she thought she would at any rate learn something as a looker-on. But Geordie and 'Ria did not spoon at all, and talked but of indifferent things, and Elizabeth Anne kept wondering when they would begin; and every now and then she would get up and run away and leave them to themselves, and then come back on tip-toe behind the door, and take a look in through the crack, but to no purpose, and then she felt indignant and much aggrieved. But later on she had some consolation, when Geordie went away, and 'Ria and he had said their goodbye, alone together as they thought, beneath the banksia trees beside the river, where they had said goodbye before; for Elizabeth Anne, unseen in the deep shadow of the garden fence, watched all that passed, and was more satisfied.

Chapter XII

All was still about the house, on which the noon shone down, and 'Ria was sitting in deep thought alone, in the front room. Her hands were folded upon her lap, and her eyes cast down. A smile would break out now and again upon her face, and linger there, while her soft grey eyes grew moist and bright, and then the smile would softly die away again, and she would sigh and sink once more into grave pensiveness. Her sweet face flushed and paled as the thoughts came over her, and those full red lips of hers, now parted, and now firmly pressed, and now again trembling and twitching nervously, took on such manifold meaning, you could see her woman's heart was working passionately – love, hope, joy, sorrow, fear, were struggling in her breast; but love kept up the mastery!

The little lamp upon the cupboard burned low and dim, and through the opened door the pale light of the moon shone in, and blended with its softened yellow haze; and gentle breathings of the cool night air swept softly through the heated room, while the tick-tick of the wooden clock upon the mantel shelf struck sharp and clear on the oppressive silence. No other sound was heard save the gentle breathing of the boy, asleep in his little cot beside his mother, as she sat and thought and dreamed of her past and future life.

But suddenly she started up; she heard a sound of shuffling feet outside the door. Who could it be at this late hour of the night? A shadow filled the doorway, and a man came fumbling in.

"Sullivan!" said 'Ria somewhat anxiously. "I thought you were asleep in your own place tonight. Do you want anything?"

Sullivan came slowly up and stood before her, leaning upon the table at her side. Sullivan – his disordered hair bound round with a white cloth, his eyes bloodshot and wild, face pale and damp, and all the comeliness gone from it, working with passion and excitement. He glanced at her awhile, and then he said, with grating, trembling voice, "Missis! what is this you're doing?" She answered not, she was too frightened, but sat quite still.

"What is this, I say, you're up to with that man – that Geordie Ransome?" he said again in louder tones.

"Nothing," she answered tremblingly. "What have you got to do with it, Sullivan?"

"Nothing! You lie!" he shouted. "You mean to marry him! But, by God in heaven above, you sha'n't!"

He paused, and for a moment nothing could be heard but the quick excited breathing of the man and woman, staring at one another with fixed eyes.

Then he began again more quietly, but working up ere long into a howl of passion – "You know I've not been serving you as most men would. You've known well what I meant while I've been slaving for you all this time. You've smiled at me, and you've talked fair. You've been a-kidding of me on, you black-hearted, fair-faced, false-tongued woman, you! And now you think to cheat me, to throw me over, do you? By God, I'll let you know that I'll not stand humbug from the likes of you! Do you think I've worked for nothing at it, day and night, to please you? Do you think this goes for nothing, missis?" he shouted, plucking the bandage from his head, and dashing it upon the ground before her. "This blood-let that I got a-bothering after you, a-slaving for your favours, which you led me on to hope. Now, look you here," he yelled, shaking his clenched fist in her face, and quivering with rage, "you just throw up your game, and if you play me false I'll work hot mischief upon the place, I warn you!"

His shouts woke up the boy, and he began to cry, and this gave 'Ria courage. She snatched him up, and, clasping him close to her, standing up bravely before her maddened would-be lover, she pointed to the door, and told him to be off, and not to let her see his face upon the place again. After such words to her it was no place for him to stop, where she was mistress. She scorned his lies, and he might go and tell them somewhere else.

Sullivan laughed, a harsh and grating laugh, and seized her firmly by the wrist, and with his other hand pulled up his trousers, and showed the bandaged wound upon his leg. "Have you forgotten this," he sneered, "you tender-hearted woman? For whom did I get well-nigh killed, and who has been a-nursing of me while it suited her, and a-pretending she was sorry, and were kind, and now's a-going to kick me out like a mangy dog, 'cause she don't want me any more an' has got another mongrel cur she wants to pet. She didn't think the dog could bite – she didn't, eh?" he went on viciously, and shaking her, while 'Ria struggled, terrified, to free her arm; but he held her with an iron grip, and his face flushed crimson, and he shouted with hoarse vehemence, "Put down the boy!"

Poor 'Ria screamed aloud in agonising dread, and a shrill yell of wild defiance answered her from out the bedroom doorway, where stood Elizabeth Anne in her white night-dress. She seized an iron bucket full of water that was standing in the room, and, rushing up, she hurled it at the man with all her strength, and felled him to the ground, deluged and stunned. Then she and 'Ria hastily sought refuge within the bedroom, and locked the door.

Maria sat down shaking on the bed, while Elizabeth Anne applied her ear to the keyhole and listened. She heard low groans and muttered curses, and before long Sullivan got up and crawled away.

"You've brought this on yourself, Maria," said Elizabeth Anne. "When you saw what the beast was up to, you should have sacked him. Long ago I told you."

'Ria said nothing, but she sat up all that night, too frightened and excited to find sleep until the daylight dawned, when she sank back exhausted on the bed, just as Elizabeth Anne got up.

The girl peered cautiously about, but saw no sign of Sullivan. She ventured then to take a look through the slab-work of the shed into the lean-to where he slept. His bunk was empty; and so, waxing bold, she went right in, and found his things were gone – his rug and clothes and all his traps – and he was nowhere to be found. The man had left the place.

When 'Ria woke again and heard that he was gone she felt a great relief, but later in the day they found that Sullivan had left his swag with the natives at the tittle-house, and had said that he would fetch it by and by. So then they thought he must be skulking somewhere round about, and 'Ria said she would not stop another night upon the place alone – she would send up for Geordie.

So they sent a native up the river to ask him to come down.

Soon after dark he came, and they told him how Sullivan had given 'Ria cheek and been abusive, and how she had given him the sack, and

how they thought that he was hidden somewhere about the place, and
had got frightened and sent for him, because they didn't feel safe at
night.

Geordie, not knowing what they knew, laughed at their fears, but
he was glad enough to stay with them, and offered to come down there
every night until the time when he should come for good and all, and
he counselled 'Ria to make it short and spare his horseflesh. But 'Ria
could not take things merrily. Sullivan's threats and the terror she had
suffered had weakened her and made her wretched. She wondered if
he really meant what he had said; she feared he did, and she endured a
misery of apprehension. And when Geordie asked her later in the evening to come outside with him, and have a chat alone in the cool night
air, she hesitated, and would not have gone but that she feared Geordie
might be vexed, and she felt she could not tell him all and make him
understand.

They went outside together and sauntered down towards the garden;
and Geordie said he wanted to talk to her about their marriage, so they
stopped beside the garden fence, and 'Ria sat down on the bank, while
Geordie leaned upon the rails beside her.

The night was cool and calm. Behind the distant misty hills, up the
wide river valley, the lemon-coloured moon was rising, and all around her
a soft bright haze of tender yellow-green shone forth, paling on the outer
ring, till it melted in the dark grey-blue of the sky. The upper valley lay
bathed in shining light, and the bold serrated outlines of the nearer hills
stood out in black relief against the misty brightness, while long shadows
from the trees beyond the paddock stretched their distorted shapes across
the clearing, and for the moment cast deep gloom upon the garden and
the house.

'Ria sat listening to Geordie while he told her all about his plans, and
asked her to decide about their wedding. And then she told him what she

felt about her boy, and how she must do her duty to him, and that she thought before they married it would be well to see the lawyers, and get some papers made out about the place, so that in case she died he might have his share secured. She had been thinking of it, and she felt that this she ought to do.

But Geordie said this was all nonsense; did she think she could not trust him to see the boy got all his rights? If she got messing with the lawyers, she'd see the place would be so fixed up, that neither the boy nor anybody else would profit by it; that was all humbug about settlements, and she'd better give it up.

But 'Ria was quite firm. She felt that this was her duty to her boy and her dead husband. But her heart feared to anger Geordie; she could not bear now, so near her goal, to vex him, and she got up and came close to him, and put her hand upon his shoulder, looking up at him lovingly, and pleading with him to see things as she did. And the moon rose up above the trees, and shone upon her bright pure face, and lighted up her tender glistening eyes, and glorified her with its radiance. Geordie was startled and softened by the beauty of her that the moon brought forth, and he yielded to his better nature and his love, and told her she should have her way. And then he took her in his arms, and pressed her to him. But as she turned her smiling face aside, and laid her head upon his breast, she saw, in the deep shadow of the house, a blacker object close against the wall, and in front of it a long bright glittering line.

With a wild cry she threw both arms round Geordie's neck and clasped him tight, while a loud report broke suddenly the stillness of the night, and its echoes rolled and thundered up the valley, breaking afresh in all the gorges and ravines, and travelling on till the distant, soft, faint wave sounds were lost in the far-off hazy hills.

When the last lingering murmur had passed away, 'Ria lay dead in Geordie's arms.

Chapter XIII

Elizabeth Anne rushed out, and came down to the garden in answer to his calls, and set up a wild yell of grief and rage when she had seen, which was taken up and echoed shrilly by the frightened blacks up at the tittle houses, while they brandished high their flaming sticks round the red glow of the fires.

They brought her in and laid her down, and when they found that life had gone, Geordie upstarted with a furious oath, calling down vengeance on this doer of this fearful crime.

He started back in horror when he saw the man before him – Sullivan – standing in the dim light, at the bottom of the couch, gazing intently at his victim, leaning on the muzzle of the gun.

His pale face, beneath the soiled white bandage, looked ghastly and horrible in its expression of frenzied mute despair. He was still as death; his protruded eyes were fixed on 'Ria's face; his lips were parted and drawn from the set teeth, through which his long-drawn breath came hissing.

Geordie now bounded forward to seize the murderer, but the man looked up, and instantly the shining barrel was pointed at his rival's breast.

"That shot was meant for you," he said, in hoarse excited tones, "and not for her! Stand back! There's another shot left yet for you – or me!"

Seeing himself helpless in the madman's power, Geordie stood still, while Elizabeth Anne clung to him, in terror lest a second tragedy should happen.

Sullivan turned again, and gave one last long look at the dead woman lying there before him; and then, without a word, he passed outside into the bright calm moonlight, and, opening the garden gate, followed the little path that led down to the pool.

Geordie, with trembling hands and wild white face, took down Jim's gun and loaded it, and roughly tried to free himself from Elizabeth Anne's despairing clasp, when suddenly another loud report rolled up the river valley and died away.

***

They buried her in the garden beneath the banksia tree, at rest from all her trouble – her love, her hope, her joy, her sorrow at an end; and bitter tears of grief fell from her lover's eyes as he stood at the well-known spot beside the grave of the woman who from childhood up had loved him so – who had suffered, lived, and died for him.

Where the track runs steeply up the scrubby range above the river, and a bare sandy patch lies at the foot of the smooth granite rocks, they buried Sullivan.

Through Fire and Water

"Wilga"

"An honest tale speeds best, being plainly told."
– Shakespeare

Chapter I: Through the Fire

"Yes," he said, "they look out of place there, don't they? A lifebuoy and a set of horse's hoofs silver mounted are not only about the last combination you would think it likely to find hanging in a hall, but seem stranger still among old suits of armour and swords, and spears and antique guns. Yet I would sooner part with the whole collection of curiosities than with the lifebuoy and the horse's hoofs."

They certainly did look out of place. The time was Christmas Eve, the place a large square hall in an old English mansion. It had a great fireplace in it, with a chimney like a cavern; and doors opened in its oak panelling in every direction but the one expected. It was hung around, as has been said, with old weapons and suits of armour and other relics of the days when war and battle were the greatest and most glorious things on earth. But over the fireplace were four horse's hoofs set in silver; and these were so arranged as to form a kind of centre-piece inside the ring formed by a lifebuoy.

The host and owner of the place had just shaken hands with me at the door, and was welcoming his son's college chum in the hall, which was well lighted up, and had a great fire of Christmas logs roaring up its wide chimney. I had come to spend Christmas with Tom Cotswold's people, and there was his father – a fine, stalwart, active, man, who did not look his fifty-five years of age.

And later on that evening Mr. Cotswold, without much entreaty from his son and daughter, and with a fond look first at his handsome wife, who seemed ridiculously young for Tom's mother, told us (his half-dozen visitors) the story why a lifebuoy and a set of horse's hoofs occupied the place of honour amid helmets which had been dented by sore battle strokes of old, and swords and spears which had made widows and orphans in many a fight. He said –

"Those horse's hoofs came from Australia. Thirty years ago, though her goldfields had made her name known throughout the world, and though people of all kinds and degrees crowded there in search of fortune, Britain was not as intimate with her nor she with Britain as they are today, when the passage to and fro is but a pleasure trip, and the Association Cricket Ground at Sydney is as well known to our crack cricketers as Lord's or the Oval is to those of Australia, and when it only wants an Australian horse to come over and show them his heels in the Derby for Australia to be first in the field in all that Britain has claimed for herself before. First on the cricket ground, first on the sculling course, and first on the green turf. Ah, well, I suppose you young fellows are laughing at me for 'blowing'; but, remember, I am an Australian born and bred; and so is Mrs. Cotswold; and we're proud of it, and of those four Australian hoofs on which stood the stoutest, truest horse whichever looked through a bridle, and brought me and my young wife (she was my sweetheart then) through the hot flames of a fierce bushfire, which, as the Bible says, 'has compassed us about on every side.'

"It was Christmas time, as it is now; and she and I and half a dozen more lads and lasses were riding to a Christmas party which some friends were giving. Those were the days when the old families of Australia (they call it New South Wales now) lived on their land in houses, which nowadays are called old-fashioned, but are modern compared with that whose roof shelters us tonight; and in those days hospitality at a homestead meant something. The garden was loaded with fruit; the cellar was full of good wine.

"Well, well, if I moralise like this I'll never tell my story. Your mother, Tom, and I were the only couple in the party who were not heartwhole; and so we lingered behind the rest; letting our horses walk until the others were far ahead of us. We had to cross a deep gorge, on the sides of which the scrub grew thickly. The narrow road wound down one side, and, after crossing a clear stream, wound up the other. There was open country above on either side. The air was hot with the smoke of bushfires; and away down the gorge one was burning. But, as our horses went at a foot pace down the road, I was telling your mother the old, old story which Adam told to Eve, and which Tom and you young fellows will sometimes be telling, if, indeed, a few of you have not told it already. When we came to the stream, and let our horses bend down their curving necks to drink, my lass had promised to be mine for weal and woe; and it was only then we noticed that the bushfire had crept up the side of the gorge we had passed, and had crossed the top of the road we had come down by, wrapping it in flame and smoke. And there, on the other side, up which wound the road we had to climb, the fire was coming swiftly up on the summit like a fringe against the sky. It was foolish of us, who should have known better, to have let ourselves get caught in such a trap. A glance round as we descended, the smallest thought, a little quicker pace with our horses, and we should have been all right. But, as Adam said to Eve, 'With thee conversing I forget all time.'

"And sure I am I thought of neither time nor place, nor sky above, nor earth beneath, nor anything around me that day, when I was telling my love to my love."

I declare that while Mr. Cotswold was speaking like this his face lit up with a radiance which made us all forgot how unfashionable it is nowadays to be anything but prosaic; and not even I, though a most irreverent youngster on occasions, could feel anything but the deepest sympathy with him as he told his story. As for Mrs. Cotswold, she only said —

"You cannot wonder that I was forgetful to all around me as was your father. Hear how well he talks now; and judge how well he talked then, and made me think of nothing but him."

The story-teller went on: "I believe it is not considered good form in these modern times to make love in sweet poetic fashion; and certainly it would in one sense have been better for us thirty years ago if we had been more matter of fact. I do not know, though; for then most likely my wife and I should never have gone together through a danger which knit our hearts together for ever after.

"There was no time to be lost. We dashed through the river, and up the road as hard as our horses could travel so steep a way. We could hear the fire crashing and crackling through the scrub, and roaring as it twisted up the tree trunks, and caught the branches above. But as yet the road was open; and, though smoke was filling it like a fog, it gave safe passage. But just as we got within a hundred yards or so of the top when we should be clear of the scrub, and where the short grass on the open land would let us pass through the fire in safety, my darling's horse stumbled and fell. She herself dropped clear and unhurt, and did not faint, as I believe it is customary to do in these cases. Her horse gave a stretch of his head, or rather a queer shiver of it, and was dead. His neck was broken. And there beyond me was the fire coming to cross the road, lick up the scrub on the other side with its hot mouth, and make the road itself a furnace. You see, there was no way out of it for us but along the road. The dense scrub and undergrowth prevented escape by any but one way. I took off my coat, wrapped it around my darling's head and shoulders, took her in front of me on the saddle, and started Starbeam, my good horse, up the sloping road which led to death or safety. He carried us through unharmed, though the last fifty yards felt like a furnace for heat;

and the smoke nearly suffocated me. But it could not have been long after we were out of the scrub and in the open where the fire was not to be feared, that the road we had come was a sheet of flame.

"Now, you can guess why Starbeam never wanted the kindest care I and my wife could give him while he lived, why when I had to take to an English home and an English life with my wife, Starbeam was brought to England too, and why when he died from sheer old age 'in clover' the four hoofs which had borne us so well from death were mounted, and placed where you see them."

Just here Mr. Cotswold looked at me, and went on – "But why with a lifebuoy around them? I can see you say by your looks. Ah, that explains why Starbeam and I had to leave Australia and come to England; and of course my story would not be finished without that."

Chapter II: Through the Water

"After your mother and I had settled between ourselves that Christmas time that we would each marry none but the other, the course of true love, as the saying has it, ran particularly smoothly for a time. In fact, as one of her girl friends thought, there was not half romance enough about it. Our parents, instead of being obdurate and quarrelling about our engagement and forbidding us ever to look upon one another again, not only consented readily, but absolutely told us that they had seen what was coming for some time, and approved of it altogether, but did not wish to let us see their approbation lest, on the principle that stolen fruit is always the sweetest, we might not have cared for that which was offered to us so freely. It was settled that we were to be married in a couple of years, when a run in the north, which I had just taken up for my father, would be well stocked, and provide a home fit for us to live in; but in less than six months after that day on which we plighted our troth we were in the midst of romance sufficient to make half a dozen three-volume novels.

"Mrs. Cotswold's father got a letter one day from England, which told him strange things. Like many a man who had made his home on Australian acres fifty years ago, he was a cadet of an old and rich country family in England. He was the younger son of a younger son, and was an encumbrance when he sailed for Australia, and rid himself of the trouble being regarded as an encumbrance. He was of an independent spirit, and had since carved out his own somewhat modest fortune, exchanging few letters with the old country during his earlier years in Australia, and none at all of late. Therefore, during the silence he did not know of the strange things which had happened. His race had become almost extinct. Some died in peace and honour, but childless. Others had died in shame and disgrace, but childless. Young men and women had gone down before the grim reaper, death. Husbands and wives, old bachelors and old maids, had done the same; and now, of all the Cotswolds, there were left but a soured and disappointed man of sixty years (to whom the possession of the family estates had come too late to bring even content), and my future wife and her father. It had so happened that to this old gentleman, when he was a grown up poor relation – and Mrs. Cotswold's father was a boy poor relation – the latter had shown attention and kindness at more than one family gathering which they had attended. And the old gentleman had evidently remembered this, for he had set his lawyers to make inquiries quietly of a firm of Sydney lawyers, and had thus ascertained exactly how his relation was situated. That was simply stated. My father-in-law was comfortably, was, indeed, well off in Australia, but not too well off to let pride stand between him and his daughter, and an old English estate worth £5000 year. And the letter from his relative's lawyer, put plainly before him a position which left it to himself to decide whether by staying in Australia with his daughter, he would risk losing the £5000 a year.

"The old gentleman made the following offer: 'If his relative in Australia and his daughter would come and live with him in England, and be to him as a son and a granddaughter, then he would do nothing to prevent the family property from coming their way at his death. But, if they declined to do this, then he vowed he should marry, even if he had to ask his gatekeeper's daughter to have him; and it would not be his fault if a young heir did not step in between the Australian branch of the family and the property.'

"Now, these, did not seem very hard conditions but for the unfortunate fact that I had to be counted in as a difficulty. What would the old gentleman think about his young relation's intended husband? In such an important matter as her marriage he would surely like to have a word! There was a family consultation over this matter; and finally it was settled that my intended father-in-law and his daughter should take the offer made to them, let the place in Australia, go to England, and if they found their new parent reasonable even in the matter of my marriage, stay with him; but if he demanded too much compliance with his wishes, and those wishes were tyrannical, then they would leave him, and come back to Australia and to me. Here, you see, were doubt and romance, and all the elements which some people think go to sweeten love furnished gratuitously for us. And though these elements, as you shall presently see, soon disappeared, yet I have to undergo another great danger and come out from the clutch of death at another Christmastide before the fruition of my love was given to me. This last part of our story I can tell you by reading a letter and a newspaper paragraph which I always keep in my pocket-book at Christmas Eve. Hearken to the letter:

"'The Priory. Downshire.

"'Dearest Tom, – I am so glad to be able to write and tell you the very best of news within a bare month after our arrival here. I got your first letter yesterday. Of course, you did not wait to hear from me before writing, but sent your letter by the mail following our leaving. I read it over again for the twentieth time just before starting to write to you; and, as I am in the library here, I just had a look at the Globe and a peep at the place on the opposite side of the world where I came from so lately, and where you are now. Well, everything is all right, Tom. That may not be elegant English, but it is the truth. Uncle (the old gentleman insists on father and myself calling him 'uncle') is a dear. He took to us and we to him at once; and last night, after getting your letter, I told him everything about you and me. And what do you think he said? Well, this–

"'I was waiting to hear this from you, Mary; for I heard it all from your father two days after he arrived here; and I have made up my mind.'

"This rather frightened me, Tom. Do you remember your Aunt Jane, who, whenever she said 'I have made up my mind,' made you feel as you were used to say, as if a 'Southerly buster' was coming. But I need not have been frightened. Uncle went on –

"'You can marry your young man.' Uncle has picked up some rather common ways of saying things while he was a very poor relative. 'You can marry your young man with my full consent, and my promise that your father shall have this property after me on two conditions. Those are that he comes to England to live with you in this house, so that I may see your children's faces, and hear their voices round me when I die, and that he changes his name to Cotswold, yours and my name.'

"I'll not read any more of the letter," said Mr. Cotswold. "You have got the facts. The rest only contains expressions to which all you young fellows will get quite accustomed when you are in love, and send and receive love letters. The next thing is the newspaper paragraph. It is from the Downshire Gazette of nearly twenty years ago. It reads –

"'A WONDERFUL ESCAPE.

"'In connection with the marriage which has been arranged between Miss Agnes Cotswold, of the Priory, and a young Australian gentleman named Thomas Deepdene, who is, however, to change his name to Cotswold, a most wonderful escape from a fearful death amid the briny horror of the deep'" – "I don't like the newspaper fellow's English half as much as father's," whispered young Tom Cotswold to me – "'has to be recorded. Mr. Deepdene was a passenger in an Australian vessel which arrived a few days ago, and when the pilot was being put on board at the mouth of the Channel, while watching the process (a dangerous one, as a very heavy sea was running), fell overboard just as the pilot was being 'whipped' on board. Lifebuoys were thrown to him from the vessel, but missed; and, strong swimmer though he was, he must have gone down had not the wind and sea carried him rapidly past the pilot schooner lying near the vessel, waiting for her boat to come on board. This lifebuoy he reached; and he was picked up by the pilot schooner's boat, put on board the schooner, and subsequently safely landed at Plymouth. The crew of the schooner were handsomely rewarded by Mr. Deepdene, who, however, insisted on keeping the lifebuoy as a memento of his escape.'

"That's all," said Mr. Cotswold. "But I think you'll own that few ordinary people have had to go through more danger in order to be married than have Mrs. Cotswold and myself; and I think you'll also own that we are right in keeping as treasures of this house, old Starbeam's hoofs and the lifebuoy which saved me."

Christmas Sketch
The False And The True

J.M. Barr

Chapter I. The Prospectors' Camp

Tom lay sick almost unto death with that terrible malady, colonial fever, which seemed to have burned up the strength and vitality which was such a prominent part of his youthful countenance. Now, the long limbs lay inert and powerless, and the once massive frame was painfully emaciated, and the strengthless fingers, like birds' claws, moved restlessly upon the thin blanket, his only covering. The beads of clammy perspiration stood upon his brow and the former light brown curls lay damp and limp, unkempt and uncared for. His mate Ralph entered the tent bearing a pannican with some kangaroo soup, and roused him from a dreamy doze.

"Wake up, old fellow, and take this. It will strengthen you before I leave. I want to ride down to the township and get some medicine for you, as well as a few stores, for we are nearly out and as you are not able to be moved just yet we must get some tucker for Christmas. Cheer up Tom! It will be evening before I can be back, but Rover will keep you company." The sick man tried to raise himself, and a faint look of animation gleamed in his tired eyes.

The sick man tried to raise himself, and a faint look of animation gleamed in his sombre eyes.

"Oh Ralph! Do call and see if there are any letters for me, I sent my poor old mother my last address and asked her to write. It may be she has done so. Don't fail now, matey, for I am awfully anxious and it may be the last I shall ever read from her. I want you to go, although it will be something dreadful to lie here in this little tent all day with the fierce heat and closeness of the weather. There is thunder about I am sure." After a pause he added, faintly, "I am an awful trouble to you, and if I have not seemed to hit it with you just as I would have liked, pray forgive me now before you leave."

The other hastily rose to take the hand wearily held out to him, but a deep growl came from under the stretcher, warning him to keep his distance.

"You hear that? Neither Rover or yourself have had that confidence in me which there ought to be between mates of six months' standing, but never mind old fellow, I forgive you. Dare say you can't help it. Well ta ta, I am off. Twenty miles ride on a hot day like this is no joke. I'll see about the letters, and there's a billy of water handy for you to reach." So, mounting his horse he rode away, muttering to himself; "Yes, if you knew me as well as I know you, you'd have less confidence than ever. However, you're not likely to last much longer, and I have your pocket-book and papers. Pah! You'll never need them, and they will be of great service to me."

Meanwhile, poor Tom's hand hung down, and the faithful collie dog Rover crawled out and licked the wasted fingers. In a few minutes the invalid fell into one of those fevered dreams in which the past is brought vividly before the brain, and memory awakens the visions of long ago. He saw himself once more the only son of his honoured parents – the heir of his rather proud, but just father, and the idol of his tender mother, the athletic leader of the sports at the public school, the joyful feast on his coming of age, the sweet love of the brightest and best girl of the county, and their affections agreed upon by the parents on both sides. Oh, what happiness to recall those blissful scenes, and as he slept, the thin wasted lips wreathed into smiles of pure joy and rapture. Then the cloud, dark and threatening, fell in blackness over the scene: that fearful and dishonouring charge against him – his utter ignorance of it and inability to prove his innocence – his father's wrathful refusal to permit investigation – in vain his mother's pleadings – his spirit roused and his indignant denial doubted, and the harsh words and bitter rejoinders – until he was cast out as unworthy to be called the son of an honourable family. Mad in righteous anger, he had turned his back on his home, with the father's words ringing in his ears – "No son of mine. Go dishonored, go." The parting with his mother – "I believe in your truth, Tom. Wait, God will prove the right." The farewell of his sweetheart – "God bless you Tom, I will never doubt you. They will not allow me to marry you now, but I will never marry any other while I live. You will be cleared yet." Then passed like a vision as in a moment the five years at the Australian diggings, the search and gain of gold – the new mate – the prospecting tour, and then he awoke to murmur piteously, "And this is the end of it, dying far from friends and home, dying alone, deserted by all, save my poor faithful dog." Then he thought how, his heart yearning for his mother and lover, he had enclosed letters to each under cover to the family lawyer, and had learned from him that it was his father's intention to leave the estate to an Irish nephew of his that Tom had never met, but who appeared on the scene immediately after he had fled to Australia. How he had received one such sweet reply from each of the dear ones reiterating their love, and confidence, and then came a long lapse of two years, with not a word from home or friends. Can it be wondered that the once strong man wept as he prayed for blessings upon those dear heads he might never see again.

Chapter II. The Desertion

The day was close and sultry; the sun hung like a huge ball of red-hot copper in the lurid sky; the mountains loomed vast and indistinct through the haze-like, thin, blue smoke which hung over the face of the land; not a leaf quivered on the trees, not a bird twittered in the bushes; all that seemed alive were the quick-glancing lizards, or the gliding snake, as it swept its folds across the dust. But Ralph, as he urged on his horse, had no eye to see, or ear to listen; he was brooding, thinking over a great scheme, a cruel monstrous injustice, which grew stronger and more fully developed as he rode along. That thought had sprung up in his mind a year ago, and had become an abiding presence with him ever since – the thought of Cain, the murderer. He had brooded over it until it had mastered him in its might, and a thousand opportunities had been given in that close companionship of six months to have turned the thought into the deed. Yet he had hesitated, and now he congratulated himself that the illness of his mate would save him from all need for crime. He had only to wait and let him die – it was better so. What had he to fear from the disinherited outcast, save that the father's pride would give way at last, and the mother's unfailing love conquer in the end. And, therefore, it was a stroke of diplomacy on his part when he volunteered to his aunt to secretly go out to Australia and find out how the cast-off son did fare, while he was supposed to be travelling on the Continent. When he had found this cousin, who knew him not, he had wormed out his secrets, and now was going for his letters, which should decide the future course. As he rode, the gloom grew more oppressive, but he knew it not.

When he arrived at the rural township store and post-office combined, a packet was handed to him, with the address, Thomas Wentworth Warren, Esq., and bearing the Melbourne post-mark. He hastened to the quietest corner of the hotel bar, and while his horse was being attended to, opened the packet and read. It was from the firm of Ward and Safe, solicitors, and requested their respected client to come down to their office at once, as they were instructed by their London agents to inform him that matters of importance to his personal interest and advantage required immediate attention. They also enclosed a bank draft and a letter from England, which he also read, and gnashed his teeth as he did so. It was from Tom's mother, full of the outpourings of maternal love, but to the reader the most important words were these – "Do not delay; come at once; your father is failing, and thinks (though as yet he will not say so) that he was too harsh with you. Besides he has heard something – I know not what as yet – which causes him to have doubts about your cousin Robert. Have you not met him yet? He promised to search for you and bring you back with him as a brother would do. His last letter said he was still searching for you. I enclose a photo of him, so that you may know him should you meet."

As he read, a look of black ferocity settled on his otherwise handsome face, as he muttered, "So you doubt me; he never will now." Then he read again: "Since I last wrote, your poor girl has lost both her parents at a stroke, and has gone out with her uncle, Major Campbell to Victoria, the name of the place I cannot tell, but the solicitors in Melbourne can easily tell you where they are to be found. Go to them at once, as soon as you receive this letter."

"So," he said, with a deep, black frown on his forehead, and his eyes contracted with hate, "this hurries matters. If he had received this letter, it would have been all up with me, exposed and disgraced. Fortune is with me, however. I will not return for a day or two, but will ride to Beechworth and cash the order, money is always handy. But to make matters sure, I must have proof of his death to satisfy the lawyers and my kind uncle and aunt. Well, I can leave word with the shepherd or stockman about the poor fellow dying in his tent alone while I ride off for a doctor to Beechworth. Of course we will be all too late. I can then go to town at once and hey! for home, money and beauty. I will soon find out his lady-love and it will go hard if I cannot persuade her and her uncle too, to let her return to England with me."

Accosting the landlord in an open, eager manner he asked: "Is there any medical man about here?"

"None nearer than Beechworth. Anyone ill?"

"Yes! I have a friend sick in the bush and must get a doctor. How far to Beechworth?"

"Sixteen miles, and a bad road too. You will scarce go there tonight. I'm sure the bush is on fire between here and there. But if you will go, there is a track to the left, about six miles on, that takes you to a shepherd's hut on the creek. You'd better make for there, and he will show you the way. The station is about two miles further."

The horse was brought out and he dashed away into the deepening gloom, and the smoke that hung like a pall.

Chapter III. The Station

In a wide and deep verandah which encircled a large and roomy house, there sat a group of ladies overlooking a nice garden well stocked with fruit trees and flowers. Although the latter were drooping in the dull heat, the cherries gleamed like coral on the branches, the currants shone white and black in clusters, and the scent of strawberries mingled with the perfume of honeysuckle and roses.

"I do not know, aunt, how you can stand such a climate as this. I am completely melting," said the youngest and most beautiful of the three. "I am sure if I had known of such weather I would have hesitated before leaving England with uncle. And by-the-bye, where is he on such a day as this?"

The elder lady replied to the last question first: "The major has ridden out to visit the shepherds. He said this morning we were likely to have bushfires about, and Sam has gone with him to carry fresh provisions to the outstations. The waggon will not come back empty for the major generally shoots a kangaroo or something to bring home. But we do not have such weather all the time, even in the midst of summer, Daisy, so you must not be too hard upon our climate after the dismal rain and cold we experienced when at home. But see, the heat has not been great enough to prevent Dr Parker from riding over from Beechworth. Doubtless he will spend the Christmas with us, and the attraction is plain; Miss Daisy, you have made the doctor the captive of your spear and bow," laughed the lady.

But Daisy replied with a pained expression on her face:

"I hope you are mistaken, aunt, for I respect Dr Parker, and would be very sorry that he should waste his affection where it cannot be returned. I cannot speak to him on the subject, but you know that I am pledged to Tom Warren, for good or ill, so long as we both shall live, and if you think there is any occasion, I wish you would let the doctor know in your own quiet way. I am now free to act as my own mistress, and the principal cause of my coming to Victoria was to try to find poor Tom, to let him know that the stigma is cleared from his name, as well as to escape from the importunities of that evil cousin of his, who, like Jacob, tried to rob him of his birthright."

In a short time the guest had arrived, and received a hearty welcome, although he appeared rather disappointed at the tinge of reserve which mingled with the greeting of Daisy. After some refreshment the conversation turned upon the weather, and the doctor informed the ladies that from the heights he had crossed he had seen the gleam and smoke of a large bushfire in the Black Range, in which direction the major and his man had gone, but as he was a good bushman and well mounted no anxiety was felt.

Chapter IV. The Bushfire

Alone in the small tent, the heat was awful to the poor fever-stricken man. As the afternoon came on he had exhausted the supply of water, and the dog suffered with him, panting with its tongue out, as it lay or sat looking at its master. The water-hole was not a mile off, but the dog remained by its master's side; there was no desertion in its faithful heart. On the hills behind the tent the ominous dark clouds hung deeper and denser, and a hollow, sullen sound, like the distant breakers, could be heard. It came nearer, and now loud reports, like infantry firing, mingled with the roar and heavy crashes as the big limbs fell down. A rush of wild animals went past at full speed, as the denizens of the forest fled before the destroyer – for the bush was on fire. Flocks of parrots and cockatoos passed screaming overhead, the wallabies and kangaroo rats leaped away, and the dingo slouched behind them. Yet Rover remained by his master while the fiery death drew nearer and yet nearer still. There was no wind as yet to fan the flames, to send them springing forward fast as a horse could gallop, but it was coming. The heavens were black, and at intervals, flashes of lightning rent the veil, but no thunder was heard. The heat became beyond endurance, and the sick man raised his hands towards heaven and cried, "Merciful God, it is hard to die thus. Let me be resigned to Thy will. Bless Daisy – mother – father," and then nature could bear no more, he sank back unconscious, while Rover lifted up his voice in melancholy howls, as if his heart would break in its agony. Who will say that the despairing cry of the man, or the inarticulate prayer of the dog, were unheard or unanswered?

* * *

Hurriedly driving the waggon laden with the spoils of the chase, Sam was hastening homeward, when the major riding beside him cried suddenly, "Stop! There's a dog howling. Something's wrong! Turn to the right and follow me."

Dashing through the smoke drift, meeting the shower of sparks, right almost to the face of the flames, rushed the gallant major. Tearing into the tent, now ignited on the top, he caught the senseless form in his strong arms. "Hold the horses! Make room for the man. Cover him with the rug, and now drive for your life to the water-hole. Good dog!" he cried, as Rover with one bound leaped into the waggon and lay down by his master's side. The spirit flask was put into requisition, and a slight fluttering of the pulse followed. "Thank God he is not dead yet. Pour some of the water over his head and drive, for life or death hangs on your speed."

* * *

In just the contrary direction from the station, a man is goading his overdone horse along as if pursued by the furies. The heat and passion combined appears to have maddened him. He bursts into hoarse laughter at times, and drinks from the flask he carries. The shepherd's hut is reached, and the wondering man points the way to Beechworth, but pleads with the rider to stop. "The storm will be on you in a few minutes. Your horse cannot carry you far, it already trembles beneath you. You had better bide a wee till the storm is over."

"Curse the horse and you too. I'll make him carry me. I must go on —" and he dashed forward.

"Take care of that branch!" shouted the shepherd. "My God! He is down." The animal, goaded by the spur, had galloped beneath an overhanging limb, and Ralph, struck on the forehead, fell to the earth. Justice had overtaken him at last, The False Mate.

Chapter V. Retribution and Reward

There are two patients at Campbell's station on that Christmas morning, when the storm of the night had passed, and the earth, fresh from its bath, sent up a grateful steam. The fires had been quenched by the thunder rain, and the flowers looked up and smiled at the clear blue sky. The windows were open in the cool chamber, where the breakfast was laid, but none were there to partake. In the verandah the major paced restlessly, until the doctor appeared:

"Come, Major! You are a justice, and I wish you to witness a dying man's deposition. He cannot live for an hour, his consciousness has only returned for a little while, but cannot last. He is terribly smashed. I opened his pocket book, and found letters and papers addressed to Thomas Wentworth Warren. I think that must be his name."

"That cannot be," said the major; "Tom Warren is the man I brought home last evening. He was recognised at once by Daisy, who is with him now."

Draw the veil over the death chamber, where Robert Warren, the false mate Ralph, gasps out his confession of the wrongs he had done to his cousin, both at home, by the lying accusation made by his tool and slave, a poor fallen girl, and in Victoria, by his retention of letters and final desertion of him who was thought to be past recovery. The confession is full and complete before the pale Angel of Death seals up his lips for ever. In another chamber, surrounded by all the comforts that wealth and affection can give, lies Tom Warren, with the hand of Daisy clasped in his. All is explained, the dark shadow removed from his life, his father's letter asking for his forgiveness and return has been read to him, and the love pledges renewed between him and his recovered darling.

Joy seldom kills. His countenance is happy and peaceful, the great weight has been lifted from his heart, and his position now is like Paradise when compared with the Inferno from which he has been snatched. The doctor comes in, and is amazed at the change for the better in this patient. Of the other he simply says, "He is gone, and it is better so." A silence falls upon the group; Daisy's hand is still clasped in that of Tom, and seeing the doctor's look of astonishment, she simply introduces him: "This is Tom Warren, my affianced husband five years ago. We took each other for good or ill when all seemed against us, and I thank God that I am permitted to try to make up to him for the sorrow and suffering he has had from his false mate."

And Tom said, faintly, "I will forgive him all; I have now my father's blessing, my mother's love, and you – true and faithful mate once more."

The sweet calm of the holy Christmas morning falls like balm upon their hearts, and the only sound is the tattoo of joy which Rover's tail beats upon the floor. He is happy too.

One Night at Gorringe

A.M.

Charlie Mackenzie came walking up from the woolshed to the house, one warm morning in last November. He bore about him an air of great importance, and frequently referring to an open pocket-book in his hand, alternately made notes therein and talked in a voluble and dictatorial manner to big Dugald Cameron, the overseer, who was with him.

Charlie's sister observed them from the open doorway, and gave a little laugh as she noted the droll sidelong look with which Dugald listened to Charlie's conversation, and she said half aloud, "Well! isn't that boy putting on airs!"

'The boy' came in presently, and dropped into his chair at the breakfast table.

"Oh, by the way, Bessie," he said, "you'll have to go to town without me. Dugald expects some trouble with those union fellows, and says I'll have to stop here."

"Then I shan't go," she declared.

"Oh, yes, you will, old girl," said Charlie, much flattered at being so sought after on both sides. "Stay at the Trigs'; you know they are for ever asking you, and I'll give you a sov. to lay on Ensign. Wonder what will win the Cup, though? It's hard luck for me, for I've wanted awfully to see it run."

"Oh, Charlie, what is the use of listening to Dugald, as if he cared whether you stayed or not? You ought to be ashamed of yourself, Dugald, when you know quite well that I won't go to town without him."

Dugald had taken no part in the conversation. "Well," said he, "it's my humble opinion that I might pull through without Master Charlie, but as he suggested himself it would be better to have 'the boss' on the spot, as the men might take advantage of me, I just agreed to what he said." And then Dugald winked at Charlie's sister, with an air of appreciation at his own joke.

"Oh, Dugald's too soft with the men," said Charlie, who had not seen the wink, and felt indulgently towards his ally; "but for all that I've learnt a wrinkle or two from the same old boy."

"To go or not to go," that was the question she set herself to think. She had really wanted Charlie to go for his own sake, and, of course, she depended upon him to take her everywhere. They had arranged to stay at Menzies' and have a splendid time, and now the idea of staying with those slow-going Trigs! But, on the other hand, there was her Cup dress, fresh from the hands of Madame, and which she was dying to wear. And, as a kind of secondary consideration, there was Jack Armstrong. Some few months before her betrothed, one Doctor Armstrong, had given her the diamond ring she wore, and somehow this latest thought of hers seemed to decide the matter.

When "Cup week" falls at shearing-time there is a struggle in the squatter's mind as to which comes foremost, and, as a rule, he managed to snatch a day or two for the great event of the year.

Old Mackenzie had bought this Victorian station for his son simply because he did not know what else to do with that good-natured but not over-wise youth. Leaving him under the charge of his old overseer, who managed Charlie cannily, he spent most of his time on his New South Wales stations, occasionally pouncing down upon them at Gorringe at the most unexpected times, just to see how they were getting on.

So, when Dugald explained that Mr. Mackenzie might make one of these invasions and not be over-pleased to find Charlie away from his post, Bessie, being a sensible girl, agreed with him. He had already placed the suggestion before Charlie in a more diplomatic light.

"Remember, Mrs. Betts," said Bessie, on the eve of her departure, "you will attend to your master's meals while I am absent; and you are not to put him off with cold meat, or anything that may save you trouble."

Mrs. Betts was really the best of a long list of domestic failures, and had some culinary ability, though she was not dependable.

It was gay in Melbourne last November, and the Trigs proving more sociable than Bessie had anticipated, she had not at all a bad time. Charlie was not forgotten. He duly received a society paper containing a paragraph marked with ink describing "pretty Miss Mackenzie's charming gown worn on Cup Day."

Dr. Armstrong's profession did not allow him so much as he would have wished of his sweetheart's company. But one night he took her to 'The Mikado,' at 'the Princess.' It happened that she had seen it before, though neither he nor Mrs. Trig had, and while they were both taking a lively interest in the stage, she sat and reflected, and her thoughts carried her far away to Gorringe.

"What is the matter?" Jack asked, noticing with surprise the sad look upon his beloved's face.

"I'm thinking of Charlie," said she, dejectedly. "Poor boy; I wonder what he's having for supper tonight? I've quite made up my mind, Jack, to go home tomorrow."

"Now, may you be forgiven," said Jack. "Did I take you here to think of such an incongruous subject as Charlie's victuals?"

Next morning Bessie left Spencer Street by the early train, and somewhere about 4 p.m. arrived at the wayside station. "No one to meet me," she repeated, in dismay, after the stationmaster. "Is it possible that Charlie has not received my telegram?"

"They have not sent for their mail for these two days," said Mr. Brown. "On account of the bushfires the men have all been kept busy." And going into the little office, he reappeared with a large pile of letters and papers and Bessie's telegram to Charlie, which Jack had sent for her that morning.

"I'll tell you what," said the stationmaster sympathetically, "there's Tom, from Macpherson's, come with the cart for those floor-bags, and he could leave a message at Gorringe as he passes."

"Oh, couldn't I go in the cart?" asked Bessie, imploringly; and when 'Tom from Macpherson's' permission had been solicited he replied surlily enough, "Kin if yer likes." Bessie, nothing daunted, clambered up and seated herself on the ends of the flour-bags.

Eight miles to Gorringe. What a drive it was! They jolted off straight in the face of the angry sun. Blackened stretches of country lay on each side of their road, and all that was left of the boundary fence between Gorringe and Woodlands were a few blackened posts, with the wire helplessly dangling or lying flat. A thick smoke shrouded everything within a hundred yards.

At last they arrived at the home paddock gate, and Bessie intimated to Tom that she would walk the quarter of a mile up to the house. She came in so quietly that no one noticed her, not even the dogs, and she was so thoroughly exhausted after her drive and walk in the scorching heat that she threw herself down on the sittingroom sofa, and lay there resting for ten minutes or so.

"What a surprise she would give Mrs. Betts if she came in just now, and Charlie and Dugald when they came home in the evening." Bessie was fond of giving surprises.

After drinking a glass of not very cold water from the sideboard she peeped cautiously into Charlie's room, which opened off the sittingroom, as though expecting to find him there; but the room was empty and in a most disordered state, actually! And her wrath rose. The bed had not been made. "I must go and see Mrs. Betts," she said, and on her way out to the kitchen the thought struck her that the place seemed wonderfully silent and deserted; but it was natural to feel it so coming that morning from the noise and bustle of the big city.

The kitchen, an old wooden structure, detached from the house, was without an occupant. The door of the servants' room was wide open, but here again was emptiness.

"Mrs. Betts! Mrs. Betts!" the girl called impatiently, and then, receiving no answer, she ran inside and opened every door in the house, and not in one room did she find a living object. "Good Heavens!" she said, in a frightened voice, and flew over the garden, down to the swamp at the foot, up to the poultry-yard – only some hungry-looking hens there – down to the haystack and stables – not a horse.

"Where can they be?" she thought in bewilderment, and then came back and made another fruitless search over the house, ending in the kitchen. Here she saw what had escaped her notice before, that on the table was a heap of unwashed dishes, apparently from breakfast. There was a long form lying on the floor, feet uppermost. The fire was dead out and on the whitewashed hearth – her eye fell on it now – was a pool of blood.

"Oh God!" she said, and her heart stood still.

"Those union shearers! Had Charlie in his boyish presumption been too bold with them?" She pressed her hands hard against her head. If she let her imagination run riot she would go mad.

The garden at Gorringe slopes down to a neat rush-grown swamp haunted by waterfowl, which every night send forth weird cries from their green beds. Here Bessie came to try and think in a dazed kind of way. "The silence of that great swamp!" Not the smallest wind came to stir the dull waters or move the drooping leaves.

An aged terrier, half-blind and totally deaf, had crawled after her, and lay at her feet. All was intensely calm, noiseless, and solitary. The atmosphere was heavy and hot. Almost she seemed to be in another world.

Anyone who has tried it can testify that it is a more than a solemn thing to be alone in the Australian bush; but here, the deserted house that should have been filled with life, and the terrible uncertainty, the bloodstains on the hearth – all this was enough to tax the heart and brain of any one, let alone a helpless, inexperienced girl.

The night was closing in, and through the darkness and smoke came two men with swags upon their backs. She heard their footsteps as they stumbled round the kitchen, and knew instinctively that they were strangers.

Then some unseen agency seemed to move her to a line of action. She roused the dog and made him follow her, and came to where the men were – not pleasant-looking men. To neither could she tell her distress, therefore. She must take pains to keep them in ignorance of it.

"Was the boss at home?" one asked – a bold, disagreeable-looking man.

"Not yet, but she expected him shortly; in the meantime they might stay in the hut."

"Thank ye, miss," said the same man, civilly; "but my mate and I'd be glad of a bit of tucker. We've come a long tramp today."

The mate, a red-bearded slouching man, chewed a bit of tobacco and said nothing. "I will ask the cook," Bessie said, so strung up by this time that she was ready for anything, even entering that awful kitchen again. She knew where the matches were kept, and lighted a candle, then got some bread, tea, and sugar, and took some time looking for meat, but could not find any. When she turned around the man was looking curiously in.

"I suppose your cook will let me boil my billy here," said the man, looking suspiciously into the empty fire-place.

"No," she answered, boldly, "you can light a fire in the hut."

He mattered something about "having no matches," and she gave him a box.

When they had gone her courage fled, and too weak to stand, she sank upon the floor, almost fainting. Sad tears rained down her white face, and presently she commenced to weep passionately. Her overchanged heart seemed calmer after this outburst. Once more she must put on the strain, and try to live through this awful night.

She took the candle and went inside. The faint light could not penetrate the gloom of the long dark room, and she cast furtive glances into the shadowed corners. Her workbasket she noticed was in its accustomed place, and taking from it a bundle of Charlie's socks, which had been placed there for mending, she sat down by the table, and took a long, long time threading her needle.

Had anyone looked through the window? The blinds were down: they would have seen a girl calmly engaged in darning, and because the light was feeble they would not notice how white was her face, or how peculiarly rigid her movements, as she laboriously drew her needle in and out, or how cautiously she would lay the scissors on the table, as though she dared not break the silence. The silence was so profound that the ticking of the clock sounded like the stroke of a heavy hammer. That sudden cracking noise which is only noticed in the stillness of night time would set her heart beating and nerves tingling.

Loudly the clock struck ten. Almost simultaneously there was a step in the verandah. Her heart gave a great jump, could it be Charlie? Then a knock at the door dispelled the hope, leaving her sick with disappointment and fear. For some seconds terror chained her to her seat, and it seemed impossible that she could ever find courage to open the door.

She rose slowly and painfully; like one fettered with heavy chains she walked. Standing at the door was the same man who had spoken to her before.

"My mate's taken bad with cramps, miss; and if you'll be so good as to give me a drop of brandy, I'd be obliged."

The man's tone was civil, but he looked cunningly at her.

"I will see if there is any," she answered, in a voice that to her ears sounded miles away. In the cupboard she found half a bottle of brandy, and poured some into a glass.

"I might as well take the lot," said the man, coming boldly into the room. "You see, the chap's so damned bad, he'll want to use it outside as well as in."

She answered not a word, but let him take the bottle – a fatal mistake, she knew.

"Thank you, miss; much obliged," with a sneer. His hawk-like eyes fell upon her diamond ring. "The place seems uncommonly quiet. No men about. The boss not home yet. I suppose?"

It was her last chance.

"I hear them coming now," she asserted, with great presence of mind.

He started, and looked doubtfully at her. A strong wind had risen, and a rumbling noise was heard which might be the tramp of horses' feet and wheels. Then, with an oath, he seized the bottle and walked off.

If she had any hope, it left her then. And if she had at any time thought of trying to hide or make her escape, that was impossible now, for her limbs seemed dead – she could not move to save her life. In all this old wooden house there was not one lock on door or window.

So she sat on, never quite losing consciousness, yet never wholly conscious. She saw that the candle was slowly burning down; there was only an inch left now. And the table was doing such mad things; it would rise slowly up right under her eyes, and sink down again.

By this time they would have discovered that the sound was not of horses' hoofs, only the distant thunder, which was coming nearer now. Above the moaning of the wind there came the sound of men's voices raised loud and fierce in angry quarrelling. They must be having an angry dispute, for the hut was some distance off, and she could hear them distinctly, and their voices were coming nearer. Then there was a silence.

Someone was walking stealthily in the verandah, cautiously the door handle was turned, and it opened creakingly.

Bessie still sat looking at the table.

"My God! Bessie, what is this?"

Slowly she lifted her stiff eyelids, and as Charlie sprang forward, stood up with an awful shriek of pent-up agony.

"Lord save as! What is it? Oh! my goodness, oh! What's to be done wi' ye," gasped Dugald, stumbling about in an agitated and singularly helpless way.

One shriek followed the other, till Charlie caught his sister by the shoulders and shook her violently.

"Stop that!" he roared. "Stop it at once!"

She stopped, looked wildly at Charlie, and burst into tears. Thereupon he followed up his treatment by throwing a jug of water over her, after which he made her drink some brandy and water which Dugald had procured. Then, thinking a little kindness might be beneficial, he kissed her affectionately and carried her to the sofa, where she lay for some minutes, unable to speak.

Under judicious treatment Bessie slowly revived, and was able to tell her story. Charlie became very excited over it, and interrupted continually with fragments of "his adventures."

Briefly told, his explanation was this. He had been out all night working at the fires, and about five in the morning got home, feeling dead beat. He had a nip, turned in, and slept till eleven o'clock, when little Billy the rouseabout burst into his room to say Mrs. Betts was dead. So he was up and out, and found Mrs. Betts with her head on the stove, and her feet near a bucket, which induced Billy to think she had kicked it. They found her insensible, with a wound on her head. She evidently had a fit, and struck her bead when she fell. The only thing to be done was to drive her to the township, 27 miles off, and leave her at the hospital. It was necessary to take Billy to open the gates, as the woman was still unconscious, and that was how the house came to be deserted. Of course he had to stay and rest his horses for an hour or two, which kept him late. "But I never imagined," said Charlie, "that Dugald would not be home before me, and was astonished when I met him with the two men about three miles from here."

Then Dugald explained how the fire had gone on to MacPherson's, and it had taken all their labour to beat it down.

"Why I came so cautiously up the verandah was because I wanted to find out who had a light in here, when I knew there ought to be no one in the house," Charlie told Bessie.

Dugald had made some tea for Bessie, which she drank gratefully, and also provided a queer kind of supper.

"Those brutes!" said Charlie presently; "we must go down, Dugald, and kick them out of the place."

"You leave them to me," said Dugald sternly, "and I'll make them remember this night's work." But when they went down to the hut, there was no sign of Bessie's friend, only the red-bearded man sat smoking by the fire.

"I'm darned if I'm going to be treated like this," said the man, wrenching himself out of Cameron's grasp. "If you want to collar anyone, you can go after that other chap as took to his heels when he heard you coming. You know me, Mr. Cameron?" It turned out that this man had been woolscouring at Gorringe last year, and though noted for his surliness, bore a good character. Taylor had fallen in with the other man on his way to the station. And the latter soon found out that there was no one at the place save Miss Mackenzie, and wanted Taylor to join him in a general pillage, which he had refused to do, and they had come to high words over it, when the arrival of the five men had caused him to decamp. And although the police were ordered to keep a look out for him, he was not seen in that district again.

Bessie's nerves were so unstrung by her night's vigil that Charlie took her back to Melbourne immediately. A great doctor prescribed medicine, and a trip to Tasmania. This doctor bestowed on Mr. Charles Mackenzie a word of praise for the prompt measures which had rescued his sister from hysteria or something worse, "though it left her with a very bad cold," and the young man carried his head very high for some days, I assure you.

Bessie recovered her health, and last week I noticed her wedding announcement in a society paper.

Kitty Dunolly, My Schoolmate: A Victorian Sketch

G.E.C.

Chapter I

"Corrie!"

"Well?"

"They think me the veriest wretch that ever wore shoe-leather, don't they?"

"Whom do you mean, Kitty?" I ask gently.

"The people here, of course," answers my companion, impatiently. "I don't care. I'm not good for much, I know, but still, they might give one a chance!"

I looked up gently from my sewing as I answered: "they mean well towards you, dear Kitty."

"They don't!" persisted Kitty, obstinately. "They hate the very sight of me. I wish I were dead!"

"Hush! dear." I had risen and put my arm around her shoulders, as she dropped her head on the table with a stifled sob.

"I have nothing to live for; I am only a burden to myself and everybody else!"

"I love you, Kitty!"

"Thanks! If it wasn't for you, I'd have made a hole in the Yarra long ago!"

"Oh, my dear, do not talk so!" I cried, with sudden pain, for I, who have been so tenderly cared for, so perfectly loved as an only daughter, felt chilled at the utter despair and desolation in my school-fellow's voice. It was seldom wild Kitty got so low-spirited as this. As is very often natural to people of highly excitable temperaments, Kitty generally had a bout of "ennui" and inertness, after any unusual excitement or "grand lark;" but seldom had she despaired like this. Although our schoolmistress and governess did not exactly consider her, as she so forcibly expressed it, "the veriest wretch that wore shoe-leather," they did, however, condemn her as wild and intractable, and by no means an acquisition to Runnymede, as our school was called. But they had not discovered the soft, sweet womanly part of Kitty's character. I had. Surely there is never a nature so bad as not to have one redeeming point, at least! But unfortunately, people, as a general rule, are always more ready to seek out the faults and failures of their fellow creatures, than their virtues. So it had been with Kitty. For six years the poor girl had been thrown from one home to another; misunderstood and neglected on every side, with no kind guiding hand to show her right from wrong, no fond heart to feel truly grieved if she came to any harm. "Wild, thoughtless, no one can do anything with her," her aunt had said, when she handed her over to the tender mercies of Mrs. Graves, just a year ago; and whether the words were true or not, no one had seemed inclined to find out.

The way I discovered that Kitty Dunolly, my schoolmate, was not utterly lost and irreclaimable, was this – but first let me enlighten my readers as to "the people here." They consisted of Mrs. Graves, head teacher, three governesses, two visiting masters, and twenty-six boarders. Mrs. Graves could not have been better named. She was tall and thin, with short, crisp, grey curls, each side of flat, shiny ears; pale, green, fishy eyes, utterly devoid of lashes, and, moreover, enclosed in hot, red lids, drawn in Chinaman fashion at the corners. Her hands were long, pale, and thin, with hard, sharp nails, kept always scrupulously clean, but seldom paired. She had a thin, sour face, and she was religious – coldly, sternly religious – a bigotted Calvanist, and a hard-hearted woman. But she did not mean to be so, not at all! She thought that she was doing all that was most virtuous and proper in forbidding laughter or merriment in her school. "Better to be in the house of mourning than in the house of mirth," she used to tell us. So the girls wore long faces and spoke in low tones when in her company; but once out of her sight and hearing, they (to use a horsy but expressive phrase) "kicked up" and "larked." For who doesn't know that the harder you press down a jack-in-a-box, the sooner will he leap to freedom again when you take the pressure off? But I am only speaking of a few; for the girls were mostly so crushed in spirit by the everlasting weight of drilling, psalm-singing, and penances, that they sullenly succumbed to the chilling influences that surrounded them, and seemed, indeed, as if they could "never smile again."

But Mrs. Graves' "bête noir," was – rings. Immediately a ring was seen by her on the hand of one of her girls, she tore it off, and strung it on to a bit of cord, kept for the purpose. Some of the girls were daring enough to try and see how long they could wear one without her noticing it – hence the increasing number of rings. But one day, and never shall I forget that day as long as I live, Kitty Dunolly entered her class with a thin black ring upon her left hand. She was in my class, the first which Mrs. Graves taught today. I looked up in startled surprise as I saw it, for Kitty had never shown a taste for such ornaments, not even with which to annoy Mrs. Graves. I could not say anything to her as she sat a good distance from me; nor could I catch her eye which was bent, with unusual thoughtfulness, on the floor.

"Miss Dunolly," called Mrs. Graves, and Kitty stood up. She repeated her task with perfect steadiness and correctness; and, was about to resume her seat, when Mrs. Graves cried sharply:

"Let me see your left hand please, Miss Dunolly?"

Kitty left her desk and went to the governess.

"Ah! A ring," she began adding, peremptorily. "Give it to me please, Miss Dunolly!"

"But, Mrs. Graves!" pleaded Kitty.

"Silence, Miss!" cried the governess, snatching the pretty, slim hand in her lean cadaverous one.

"But Mrs. Graves! Let me explain!"" cried Kitty, wrenching her hand away, white with anger and distress.

"Hold your tongue, Miss! How dare you dictate to me? You know that rings are my greatest aversion. Now! not a word," as Kitty again attempted to speak. "I allow no girl to speak back to me!"

As she spoke she again attempted to get her hand, but Kitty said firmly, and with a face white and fixed as marble:

"I will not give you the ring, Mrs. Graves."

"You will not?" almost screamed Mrs. Graves, her eyes dilating with anger. "You will not! You won't!"

"No. I certainly will not," returned Kitty, with blanching lips. "You will not let me explain, nor would I now do so if you desired it."

I never saw anyone in such a fury as Mrs. Graves was then. For an instant her calm and icy nature seem convulsed with passion; her lank fingers twisted viciously; her face seemed quite contorted. But she soon mastered herself, and, in a sharp, cutting voice, said between her teeth:

"To your room, Miss!" And Kitty obeyed.

Chapter II

The girls exchanged glances of mingled surprise and apprehension; while I felt my heart laden, and my eyes fill. But Mrs. Graves continued the studies quite composedly, her fit of rage, however, leaving her more pale-green and drawn than ever. How the long hours dragged that morning! How my head and heart ached! We had no recess, as the heat of the day was too intense, but worked on wearily at our arithmetic, till at last – O! be joyful – the hands of the clock reached to top, and twelve strokes quivered through the room.

After having given the signal to disperse, Mrs. Graves retired; and, leaving my books and belongings to their fate, I hurried up to our room, just in time to meet Mrs. Graves at the door. I turned to retreat, precipitately, but her frosty voice bade me stay, and, trembling and anxious, I followed her into the room.

Kitty was standing by the window, her hands clasped loosely before her; and on the white finger, the ring still shone. She turned her head slowly and proudly as we approached her, and her rich, red lip curled scornfully as Mrs. Graves began:

"Miss Dunolly, I trust that you have had time to repent your violence; if not, I shall find it my painful duty to make you do so. Give me that ring on your finger."

She did not look as if she thought it would be a painful duty, for a bitter dislike shone in her pale eyes, and her long-nailed fingers were pressed, viciously, into the palms of her hands.

Kitty made no answer. I saw her bend her head forward and swallow something very hard, and her loosely-clasped hands tighten, swiftly; but, otherwise, her face and manner did not alter.

"Will you give me that ring, Kitty Dunolly?"

"No, Mrs. Graves."

How strange and far-away poor Kitty's voice sounded. It had lost all its sweetness, and was harsh and cutting. There was no bravado or bouncing in her manner; no wild rebellion or despair; but a steady firm determination, that shone through her steadfast eyes, and marbled her face till it quite terrified me. I pressed the palms of my hands together, and looked at Kitty in an agony of dread and supplication.

"Oh! Kitty, give it up!" I cried, involuntarily.

Mrs. Graves waved her hand imperiously towards me and turned once more to Kitty. I saw her temper was rising again, and I dropped my face in my hands with a low cry, as she demanded, this time with livid face and clenched teeth:

"Kitty Dunolly, give me that ring, or I shall take it from you."

"Mrs. Graves I cannot, and shall not give it to you!" was the firm, answer.

"Then! –"

She did not stay to finish her sentence but seized Kitty's hand, and with the other was about to pull the ring from her hand, when Kitty, her whole bearing altered, threw her off, wrenched the slender circlet from her finger with such force as to raze the skin in places; and, with a mingled cry of triumph and despair, flung it on the floor, crushing it to atoms with her heel.

I fled from the room in terror, and crouched in the corner of the hall till Mrs. Graves came out. Her face was ashy-white, and she said to me sharply as she passed:

"You will not enter Kitty Dunolly's room until I give you leave," and then she swept away.

"Not enter Kitty Dunolly's room until I give you leave!" Hopelessly the words rang in my ears as I sat sobbing in another room with aching head and dull heavy heart, trying to realise it all. What could be the matter with Kitty? Why should she so determinedly refuse to give up the ring? It was not obstinacy; for that was not one of Kitty Dunolly's faults. So I sat sobbing and anxious till the bell boomed for dinner, and I was obliged to go down.

I could not eat a morsel; the food stuck in my throat, and I kept my head bowed through the meal. Mrs. Graves had outwardly quite regained her equanimity, but I noticed that she sent her dinner away untouched, and looked at me furtively now and again. As we rose from the table she stayed us with her imperious hand and began coldly and distinctly:

"Young ladies, I forbid any of you to enter Miss Dunolly's room or hold an intercourse with her till I give you permission. You may go."

I dragged myself wearily out into the courtyard, and sank upon one of the seats, while my companions drew together in lots conversing: some eagerly, some apprehensively, about the unusual disturbance, and now and again plying me with questions that I was too weary and miserable to answer.

It was worse in the afternoon; a hot, withering north wind sprang up, dulling all our faculties, and making the atmosphere almost insupportable. It did not improve Mrs. Graves' temper either. The governesses were tired and cross, and, altogether, we had a hard time of it. One poor girl fainted, and, at last, half an hour before the usual time, Mrs. Graves said we might go, as it was so hot. My first impulse was to run upstairs to our wing, but remembering her orders, I went softly down the hall, but how could I pass Kitty without speaking to her? I stopped at the door.

"Kitty! Kitty!" I softly called. There was no answer.

"Kitty ! Kitty dear!" still no answer.

"Answer me Kitty! It is I – Corrie!" and risking detection, I turned the handle of the door and entered.

She was kneeling by the bedside, her face raised towards the picture of her mother that hung before her; her hands clasped above her head; and the intense pallor of her face contrasting strangely with the deep darkness of her eyes. In a moment I was on my knees by her side, with my arm round her shoulder, forgetting everything but that Kitty, my darling favourite, was in distress, and I must help her.

"Kitty, dear."

She rose heavily from her knees and put her hand upon my head, saying softly:

"Corrie, dear; you should not have come here, you will get into trouble."

"I don't care!" I cried wildly, in a passion of love and sorrow as I pressed her cold hand to my hot cheek. "Kitty! Kitty! tell me what is the matter! Why do you wear the ring?"

"Hush! Corrie. Sister dear. My mother – my darling lost mother, gave it to me on her death bed, today six years ago. 'Wear it, Kitty darling, she said to me as she took it from her finger and placed it on mine, 'Wear it my child on every anniversary of this day. It will help to remind you of the mother that loved you well.' As if I wanted that or anything to remind me of her! O! Mamma, mamma! Can you see and love me now? Your poor desolate child!"

She flung herself on her knees again in an agony of tears and sobs, her slight frame shaking like a leaf in the wind.

Suddenly she rose and put me from her with a quick gesture. "Go away, Corrie dear, before she comes," she began, stroking my hair, caressingly. "Oh! my dear, my dear. You are the only one that loves and understands me. Mind," she added, as she gently pushed me out of the room, "that you don't tell her what I told you. Goodbye! Don't let anyone see you." Then she closed the door.

Chapter III

I went slowly and sadly down the hall, when Mrs. Graves met me at the end of it. She looked at me, suspiciously, and, in her acrid voice, inquired:

"Have you been to Kitty Dunolly's room?"

My head dropped, and I answered, feebly, "Yes."

"You have disobeyed me, then, Miss Grey?"

More feebly I replied, "Yes."

"Follow me, Miss."

I obeyed. She went quickly down the hall, and turned into our room.

Kitty was sitting on the bed, reading. She raised her head haughtily, and closed her book. Mrs. Graves began:

"Miss Dunolly, have you made up your mind to do as I desire?"

"No, Mrs. Graves."

"You will not apologise to me?"

"Certainly not."

There was a deep silence for a moment; the governess biting her lips, nervously.

"Now mark, Kitty Dunolly," she began, at last, bending her green eyes full on her face. "Unless you do as I wish, I shall –"

"Mrs. Graves," I interrupted, too eager to feel timid, "had you not better let Kitty explain?"

"You hold your tongue!" was all I got, however.

"I was about to say," continued Mrs. Graves, "that unless you do just as I desire, I – shall – expel you; and," she added, as she saw no change on the marble-white face, "not only that, I shall inflict a severe punishment on – on others." She glanced at me as she spoke, and I saw Kitty's face change like magic; she laid her hand heavily on the dressing-table, while the tears welled into her eyes.

"That ring was given to me by my dead mother, this day six years ago – the day of her death. She charged me to wear it on every anniversary of that day. Is it any wonder I wished to keep my ring?"

Her voice was perfectly clear and distinct, and she kept her eyes fixed upon Mrs. Graves' face the whole time. The lady, to say the least, looked exceedingly foolish; she mumbled, something about being "very sorry," and that Kitty should have "told her before," and left the room.

A few minutes after, she sent one of the under-governesses up to say that Kitty might go, and, never after did she mention the subject again.

"I would never have told her," Kitty said to me that night, "if she had not hinted at punishing you Connie, I couldn't stand that love!"

That was how I discovered that Kitty was not wholly void of natural affection, not utterly lost in her wild recklessness. From that day we were faster friends than ever.

Kitty and I were quite unlike each other. She wild, merry and ingenious, I – quiet, sober and reserved; Kitty dark, tall, black-eyed, and rosy-cheeked. I – pale and slight, with quiet blue eyes, and sleek yellow hair, that never ruffled like Kitty's raven locks, which blew all over her head into short silky curls, confined by neither comb nor band.

Christmas was drawing near. We were now deep in the examinations, and everything was upside down. I did not feel nervous but I was anxious, for I was not quick and clever like Kitty, but rather slow and dull. But I came in third, and Kitty was first. How rejoiced! Kitty after all had beaten her class and no one could rob her of her victory, for there it was in black and white.

After a great deal of persuasion Kitty prevailed upon her guardian to allow her to spend her holidays with me, at my home – Tildersley Station, up in the ranges.

On the twenty-first of December we started from Melbourne and after three days travelling, reached the township of L, now only twenty miles or so from home. We stopped at the inn and very glad was I to see the good old lady's familiar round form coming down the well-lit passage, with open arms and a face shining with smiles to welcome us.

She hurried us inside with hospitable haste, divesting us in a trice of hats, cloaks, and gloves and bustling about in her motherly way, at last leading us down in triumph to the supper-table, which had been stocked more plentifully then ever for our especial benefit. Next day we were up almost at dawn, and wended our way through the broad, green paddocks, brushing the early dew from the grass, and drinking in with keen delight, the balmy freshness of the morning.

Along the grey road we saw a horseman galloping towards us. I needed no voice to tell me who it was, and in another moment I was in my brother's arms.

"My darling girl! Coming home again!" he cried, heartily, as he pressed his cheek to mine.

"Jack," I began, turning from his embrace, and laying my hand on Kitty's arm, "this is Miss Dunolly, my schoolmate."

Jack bowed, and, after the usual remarks, turned again to me.

"I have brought Laurie and Sportsman down, for I presume Miss Dunolly can ride," he added, interrogatively. Kitty bowed, gravely. "One of the stock-boys is following with them. If you are ready, Constance, it would be better for us to start almost immediately. Miss Dunolly has a good, stiff twenty miles between her and home."

Jack hurried on in front to order a speedy breakfast, while Kitty and I followed more slowly.

Mrs. Brown, the good landlady, bustled about to some purpose that morning, for in less than half an hour she had a good, steaming-hot breakfast on the table, and everything ready for starting. The ride was a beautiful, though rather risky one – up-hill and down the whole way with very often fearful abysses yawning beneath us, or frowning mountain-peaks towering overhead. But we enjoyed it immensely, all the more, perhaps for having been cooped up in a town for so many months.

At last, about 12 o'clock, we reached the plain on which Tildersley stands. Through the glossy, ever-green trees we saw the gleam of white roofs, and above them the pale wreaths of smoke, curling up from the chimneys to the bright sky. Oh! home! home! Truly "there's no place like home!" My heart yearned towards it. Every blade of grass, every flower that bloomed there, was dearer to me than worlds!

I saw Kitty's fine, dark eyes sparkle with pleasure, the ripe lips parted into a sweet and tender smile.

"This is home!" she said softly, as her eyes wandered from the blue-veiled hills in the distance, to the dimpling lake that lay bathed in dusky, ever-shifting shadows beneath the grove at our side – "Truly this is home!"

Chapter IV

We had been home just three weeks, when one evening, soon after tea, Jack entered my little parlour with an anxious cloud on his brow.

"Constance," he began, earnestly laying his hand on my shoulder. "One of the stockmen has come home from Deadman's Creek. He says there's a terrific fire up there, and it is rapidly coming down on us. You are not afraid to stay here with the women and old Cob, for father and I must go off post haste?"

He looked at Kitty as he spoke, and she said eagerly:

"No! O, no! We are not afraid," while I added more tremulously, "No, Jack, go dear."

He bent down and kissed my forehead as if to reassure me, and then, waving his hand gaily to Kitty, hurriedly left the room.

As soon as he had gone, Kitty and I went to the verandah to try and see some signs of the enemy. But there was no change in the fair, pale, evening sky; the dark belt of wood that encircled the flat before us was even more void of smoke than usual, for in these parts, during the summer, there is nearly always smoke lurking somewhere in the woods. The golden stars began to pierce through the Heavens as we watched; the curlew whirled past us with his plaintive night-cry, and the solemn stillness of the evening fell on us like a spell.

"Look! Connie," suddenly cried Kitty, pointing excitedly towards the western horizon. "Do you see that blush-like red upon the sky yonder?"

I eagerly followed her eye, and sure enough there was a faint pale-red reflection, very slight, very distant, but still a reflection. And as we gazed, with a chill, indescribable kind of nervousness creeping over us, the flush broadened and deepened, stretching along the sky with appalling quickness, till at last, from behind the front range there rushed up a dense, black cloud of smoke, followed, in a moment, by one long pale finger of fire. Kitty and I clung closer together, while we heard the excitable shouts of the servants who were assembled near us on one of the lawns, and saw one of the selectors dash past us on horseback, crossing the flat in the direction of the fire.

That one quivering flame was followed swiftly by others, and the fire, gaining in strength and quickness every moment, soon had the sloping, thickly-wooded range one living mass of flames. Oh! dreadful and appalling sight, a bush-fire, and yet, how grand! The red-hot trees with the fiery flames licking their blackened trunks. The intense and awful darkness of the forest which they have not yet reached; while, standing out, in marked and startling distinctness, was every object over which their lurid shadow had been thrown!

"The Flat! The Flat!" shrieked old Cob, the gardener, wringing his hands that had withered in my father's service. "They must stop it in the Flat, or we're done! If it gets a hold among them dry rushes, it'll make a clean sweep of everything!"

It was evident the men had seen that, for presently, on the edge of the Flat, a jet of flame shot up, running well round it, and effectually stopping the track of the destroyer.

Old Cob clapped his hands in delight. "We're all right! We're all right! Fire kills fire! God be praised for't."

And so it did; the fire, baffled, receded quickly, while its opponent burnt slowly across the Flat, two or three men beating it out when it had spread far enough. There was no immediate danger now; the fire spread farther back into the forest, and the wind, providentially changing, moved it altogether from our direction. How thankful were we to see father and Jack safely back again! Begrimed with smoke; burnt on hands and face; spent with fatigue – they were, pretty objects!

"It was a near toucher," Jack said. "If the wind had not changed, the whole station would have gone, for, though the Flat was safe enough, it would have had us at the back, to which it had been rapidly working."

"Connie," began Kitty, that evening, as we stood by our window, watching the dark mountain that, but a couple of hours before was raging in flames, and which now was darker than ever, although a lingering curl of flame and an occasional burst of smoke, told us that the foe was still to be feared. "Connie, dear, I have a feeling that something is going to happen to me. I cannot explain, dear girl, but I feel it, Constance! I feel it!"

I gazed at her earnestly, as she passed her arm round my shoulders, and drew me to her.

"You are nervous and excited, dear Kitty," I answered reassuringly, "and no wonder!"

"No, my dear, I am neither nervous nor excited, my heart is quite steady, Connie."

There was an ineffable and tender loveliness in her eyes as they met mine – a strange, fond yearning in her smile, as she turned her face to me – pallid in the moonlight.

"Kitty? Dear Kitty!" I softly whispered.

"Connie! Dearest Connie!" she answered, kissing my forehead.

Chapter V

The fire was as bad as ever! Not at the homestead, but on the North run, fifteen miles from us. Father and Jack, poor fellows, had to start off again; and we were left as before. There was no help for it; all the station-hands were wanted, though father left behind one of the stock-boys with old Cob. This was the next afternoon. We were not frightened for ourselves, for there was no possibility of the fire reaching us again, but I was terribly anxious about my dear ones, and so, indeed, was Kitty.

"You needn't feel anxious, Miss Constance," said Mrs. Thorn, the old housekeeper, joining us in the garden. "Mr. Grey and Jack can take care of themselves – don't you young ladies worry."

"Yes, Miss," added Cob, leaning on his spade, as he joined in the conversation with all the self-assurance of a privileged domestic, "Don't be a-feared, Miss Constance; they'll be back in no time."

"I'm sure, I hope so," I answered faintly, watching with sinking heart, the red-gold disk of the sun falling behind the range. Somehow he seemed like a friend, and my eyes wandered, wistfully over the quiet landscape warmly touched with his departing rays.

"You are not having a very enjoyable time, I fear, dear Kitty," said I, as we passed into the house together.

"Connie," she answered, stopping under the flaming chandelier in the hall, and placing her fair, slim hands on my shoulders. "My dearest friend, nay, my sister, Connie – if you will have me –" (I laid my cheek, caressingly, on one of her hands.) "Dear sister, my happiest hours have been spent here. This is the first rest that I have felt since my mother's death, I should like to stay here all my life, Connie: I should like to die here!"

Oh! Kitty. Oh! my sister, yes, as dear and dearer to me than if we had, indeed, been born so! Sitting in my desolate room I remember your words now – words, that despite the lapse of many years, are as fresh in my memory as yesterday. Last night it had been more mad, wild excitement than anxiousness; but tonight it was slow, torturing anxiety, with nothing but our own thoughts to entertain us, everything outside being very quiet. Now and again there came the shriek of a passing black swan;

or from the forest, the wild, trilling of a night-bird, and the howl of the dingo; but that was all.

I went to the piano, struck a chord, but it echoed so through the quiet room, that I felt almost startled, and quietly crept back to Kitty's side.

"Perhaps you would like me to sit with you, young ladies?" asked Mrs. Thorn, gently insinuating her long form through the half-open door.

"Certainly," answered Kitty, cheerfully, seeing that the old lady was feeling lonely, and was speaking one for us and two for herself. "Certainly," I echoed, dreamily. So Mrs. Thorn with a brightened smile, sat down before the fire-screen, and complacently took out her tatting, every now and again glancing kindly at us girls as we reclined together on the sofa. Somehow I felt nervous and unhappy, and longed most intensely for father's return. Kitty, too, seemed restless, for she rose and paced the room with hurried steps, now and again stopping at the window to gaze keenly out into the night, or lay her hand, in a soft, caressing way she had, upon my head. Suddenly she stopped short by the window, and raised her right hand in a listening attitude.

"Don't you hear voices, Connie? And you, Mrs. Thorn?"

We went to the window and listened eagerly, but before I could speak the door leading into the hall flew open and Martha and Jane, two of the servants, rushed wildly into the room, crying, in terror-stricken voices:

"O, Miss Connie! The bushrangers! The bushrangers, Miss Dunolly!"

"What do you mean Martha?" asked Kitty in her calm, collected voice, passing her arm with an unconscious action around my shoulders.

"Johnnie, the stock-boy heard them talking, in the yards, Miss Dunolly," explained Jane the younger and less terrified one. "They said it would be a good chance to stick up the station as all the men were away. Johnnie heard 'em say so, and he run home as quick as he could, and told us."

"Where is he now," asked Mrs. Thorn.

"He ran off into the bush. O, what shall we do? What shall we do?" wailed the first one, wringing her hands.

"Where is Cob?" asked Kitty, quickly.

"He's down in his hut, Miss Dunolly."

Kitty paled, but, as she was about to speak again, the door re-opened and Cob appeared. He had a revolver in his hand.

"O! Cob is that you?" cried Kitty eagerly. "Come in! Come in!"

"What are we to do?" he asked quietly.

"Defend ourselves till Mr. Grey and the others return. It cannot be for long," answered Kitty promptly, and with her face pale but fearless. "We have no time to fly; besides that would be cowardly. There are some fire-arms I suppose?"

"Yes," answered Mrs. Thorn, producing a brace of pistols and a revolver from a press seldom used, in the next room.

"How many bushrangers are there Cob?" I asked faintly.

"Only two I think, Miss Connie, but there may be more near at hand, Johnnie only saw two in the stock-yard."

"Give me the revolver," said Kitty, taking it from Mrs. Thorn, "I cannot use a pistol. Is it loaded?"

"They are all loaded, Miss Dunolly."

Kitty and Cob, after scouring all the back doors, stationed, themselves at the two front windows, poor old Mrs. Thorn standing at the side one with her pistol, for neither of the servants nor I could use fire-arms.

"Hark!" cried Mrs. Thorn, "I hear voices!" and Kitty without a word, though with hands that trembled a little, bravely threw up her window.

"Who goes there?" Her clear sweet voice rang through the air.

I shuddered all over.

"Who goes there?"

"I – Rollicking Jim! Jest open them doors my pretty miss, and let me an' my mate in," came from without.

I was not frightened now; but intensely, terribly, excited. I saw the same feeling in the faces of my companions.

Kitty answered, promptly, "I shall not let you in."

"O! come now," answered the man evidently greatly tickled at the last – "That's too good! that is, jest open that ere door a leetle bit, my pretty miss!"

And now we saw his face, a wild, shaggy, wicked-looking face; leering and repulsive.

"I will not let you in," repeated Kitty, her lips whitening.

"Here, none of this!" said another man, pushing himself forward. "You open that door you wench, or I'll make you!" and his revolver gleamed in the reflection of the lamp, as he pulled it from his breast.

"You wouldn't like a pill of what this holds, I suppose?" he asked, glaring at the white, determined, young, face. "But open that door or I'll give you one."

"What do you want?" asked old Cob, thinking it time to show himself.

"We want money and food, and don't object to a pretty girl or two, either," answered the man Rollicking Jim. Then the other one clambered up on to the window-sill and glared ferociously in on us all. The men evidently did not know we had fire-arms, but now Kitty showed hers.

"If you come an inch further I shall fire!" she cried, wildly. The man with an oath, sprang to the floor, nimbly followed by his mate. I saw Kitty's face set; there comes a "click click!" and a groan, followed by a long, piercing cry – and all is dark!

When I returned to consciousness I found myself in bed, with the sun shining brightly in upon me. I looked round bewilderedly, and at the foot of the bed saw Mrs. Thorn.

"Where is Kitty? What has happened?" I cried, sitting weakly up and putting back the hair from my eyes.

"Lie quiet, Miss Constance, I will tell you bye and bye."

"Have I been ill?"

"A little dear. You fainted the night before last. Don't you remember?"

I shook my head,

"Where is Kitty?!"

"I will tell you bye and bye."

Presently Mrs. Thorn left the room, and Jane came up and took her place. Her eyes were red and swollen, and her face very pale.

"O, my dear, dear Miss Connie!" she sobbed, falling on her knees by my bed-side. "I'm so glad you're better."

"Thank you, Jane. But where is Miss Dunolly?"

"O! Miss Connie, you mustn't talk, the doctor says!" answered Jane, hurriedly and anxiously.

"Doctor!" I echoed.

"Yes, Miss Connie. Mr. Jack went for him yesterday."

Just then Mrs. Thorn returned and gave me wine and white jelly.

Martha slipped from the room in a minute or two, and the good housekeeper established herself in her former place.

Another night came and past, and still she sat there, never scorning to go away – always there!

In the morning father and Jack came in to see me. Both their faces were worn and haggard. They kissed me tenderly, and soon went away. But I cried for Kitty! What had they done with my Kitty, my sister?

"Mrs. Thorn," I implored, "tell me about Kitty! Where is she? Why doesn't she come to me? Tell me!"

"My poor child, you had better know the truth!" And kneeling by the bed she gathered my hot and trembling hands in hers. "My poor Connie, I have sad news for you. Listen, my dear, patiently."

What was this cold breath creeping over my heart? I pressed my hands over it to still its beating.

"Kitty – dear noble girl! shot the man, Tim, dead on the spot. The other one fired at her and – and wounded her. Just then your father and Jack returned, but the wretch escaped through the window. O! My poor dear Miss Connie! Kitty died the next morning!"

***

It is by her grave I am standing now – Kitty's grave. A quiet mound that lies alone by the side of the lake. No need of epitaph or monument for thee, dear Kitty! No need. The soft lapping of the water with the wailing wind is thy requiem, and for those who care to be reminded of it, the solitary grave tells its own story.

Rover. A South Australian Story

Sylvia[1]

Chapter I. Destroyed By Fire

"Fire! Fire!" shouted a horseman as he rode rapidly past a lonely cottage in the densely timbered district a few miles south of Willunga at a placed termed the Square Waterhole.

Upon hearing the shout and clatter of the horse's feet a man only partially dressed, for it was yet early morning, appeared at the door of the cottage and saw a mighty volume of smoke rushing towards him from the northeast, while a raging hot wind fanned the flames that belched forth like furnace blasts. The horseman rode rapidly onward, and the lonely resident saw that he would have to fight for his life with the demon of destruction that was approaching his home. He turned indoors and said to his wife, "quick Jane, there's a terrible fire coming; we must see if we can save the horse and cart."

"Oh, Fred, how can I leave baby?"

"He will be right enough. The fire won't cross the road; but be quick lass, it's coming on at a great rate."

The horse and cart referred to were in an enclosure about 200 yards on the opposite side of the road, where sheds had been erected and a few acres had been cultivated. The land was now covered with cockspurs and rank dry grass.

In the spring-cart were the few personal possessions of Fred Williams and his wife. For two years Williams had struggled to make a living in this wilderness, but becoming tired of the hard life and loneliness he had resolved to try his fortune on the Victorian goldfields. He intended leav-

---

[1] Charles R. Hodge

ing on the following morning for Adelaide, and spending Christmas with some friends in Melbourne before going to the diggings. The vessel in which the passages were taken was to leave Port Adelaide two days later. If now the fire proved the master Williams would at once be penniless and homeless, for after the expenses of the voyage had been defrayed he would have very little left, and if his horse was lost it meant that he could not reach Adelaide in time for the boat, and would therefore lose the money paid for the passages to Melbourne.

"Come, wife, come," he exclaimed; "leave Georgie on the floor; Rover will mind him." Mrs. Williams put the cooing crowing little cherub on the floor, and calling Rover, the dog, she patted him on the head and said, "good dog; mind Georgie."

The old dog licked her hand, and wagging his tail as if in assent lay down between the child and the door.

Together husband and wife went forth to save their little all. The fire had come on with great rapidity, and was roaring and crackling in demoniacal fury. The whole country was parched with the intense heat that had prevailed during the previous week, and the flames now leaped from tree to tree and swept through the thick undergrowth with alarming speed. Sometimes a gust of wind would send the glowing embers a hundred yards, and almost before they fell the undergrowth was ablaze.

Williams and his wife made all speed to the sheds, but before they could get the harness on the horse an arm of fire shot swiftly through the dry grass between the shed and the road. Williams knew then that in a few moments they would be surrounded.

He rushed out, tore down a green bough from a tree, and shouted to his wife to fire the grass close around the shed, so that fire might meet fire, and he hoped by thus burning immediately around him that they might be saved. Jane Williams sprang forward a few yards and set the grass on fire, while her husband beat it back from the shed so that it should burn outwards.

Williams worked like a horse, while the sweat rolled in streams from him. The fire roared and hissed, the smoke was blinding, and the heat almost unbearable.

On three sides of him he saw a gradually widening space, but just as he thought all was safe a gust of wind carried a shower of sparks on to the thatched roof of the shed, and in a moment that was in flames.

Williams seized the shafts of the cart, while his wife ran the horse out, and they succeeded in getting on to the burnt and blackened foreground without hurt, but panting with exhaustion and thirst.

When they felt themselves safe they sat down on the cart and looked around them. To the north, north-east, and south nothing could be seen but blackened earth and smouldering trees, while to the south-west the fire went roaring on in a mighty wall.

Williams and his wife were both so dazed and exhausted that for a few minutes they could hardly realise where they were.

Suddenly Mrs. Williams exclaimed, "Oh, Fred, my baby, my baby."

Williams ran forward towards the road by the house, but he could distinguish no road, nor could the house be seen. All around was blackness and destruction.

Husband and wife were nearly frantic with grief and horror, and ran hither and thither until they were almost distracted.

At last Williams tripped and nearly fell into a well. He knew then that he was in the vicinity of the spot where his house had stood. To his left there was a smouldering heap. He ran forward and kicked through the heap until he found a pile of stones. This then was all that remained of his home. The house had been built of wattles and plastered with clay (known in the country as wattle-and-daub) with a chimney of stone.

When he realised the truth, and thought of his dear little son, he threw himself down on the blackened earth, and his muscular frame shook with convulsive sobs, while his poor wife moaned and cried for her darling boy. "Oh, my baby, my baby," she wailed. "Oh, God have pity on me. Oh, that my darling should have perished like that. Oh, Georgie, my boy, my boy."

Words are, however, unable to depict the heart-rending sorrow of this stricken couple.

When they realised that nothing could be done for their darling they determined to put the horse in the cart and start at once on their journey to Adelaide. They did so, and arrived in Willunga in the afternoon, where they told their pitiful story, and received the sympathies of the few people in the township. Some suggested going back in the morning and looking for the child, but the poor mother could not bear the thought of their finding the charred remains of her beautiful boy. "Don't let them Fred," she pleaded.

"Let me remember my darling as I last saw him, bright and rosy after his sleep, with a smile on his baby lip. Oh, my poor, poor baby, my darling, my darling."

Ah! many a mother in Willunga wept that night over the terrible fate of poor Jane William's winsome little baby boy.

Early the next morning Fred Williams and his wife left for Adelaide, but their hearts were heavy, and the events of yesterday seemed like a horrible dream.

Chapter II. Rover's Sagacity

Within a mile of the Square Waterhole, to the eastward, lived a farmer named Jones. His house was in a sheltered gully, and was fortunately beyond the radius of the bushfire that destroyed poor Williams's home. During the day Jones anxiously watched, for if the wind changed, as it sometimes suddenly did, to south-west, then it would bring the fire down upon him in a very short time.

Jones and his wife stood at the door watching, when Mrs. Jones said, "Henry, I'm afraid that fire will be bad for Fred Williams, it's burning in a direct line for his place."

"Oh, but he'll be gone by how, Maria."

"No, he's not going till tomorrow. Poor chap, then I'm afraid he'll be burnt out. I would go and see if I could help, but I'm afraid I couldn't get there, the fire's all around, and if the wind was to change the fire would soon pay us a visit."

However, about 4 o'clock Mrs. Jones said, "I'm awfully anxious about Jane Williams. Henry, couldn't you ride over and see if they want help. There's no fear of the fire here now and it must have passed Williams's long ago."

"Yes, Maria, I'll jump on Nugget and go over;" and in a few minutes Jones was on his way to look for his neighbour. He struck a beeline for the Square Waterhole. There were no fences to stop him, for beyond the limits of his land everything except the big green gumtrees and smouldering logs had been swept away.

Yet he had great difficulty in locating the spot where Williams's house had stood, and when at last he found it the poor fellow stood aghast. As far as he could see they had all perished. However, after a careful search he found the tracks of the horse and cart over the burnt ground, and came to the conclusion that although the fire had gone over the place Williams and his family had got away safely.

Mrs. Jones was much upset at the news, and wondered why the Williamses hadn't come to them. "Well, Maria," said her husband, "Fred couldn't very well drive over that country, and I expect after the house went they just drove over to Willunga."

This explanation seemed satisfactory, and was mutually accepted by Jones and his wife.

During the night they were aroused by the barking of the dogs, and listening they thought they heard something scratching at the door.

Jones jumped up, and going to the door, he asked "Who's there?"

There was no reply but a terrific row amongst the dogs, followed by a yelp and a scampering in the direction of the creek.

Jones then opened the door, but could not see anything, although he could still hear the dogs in the distance. He called them, and in a few minutes the two cattle-dogs came panting up to him. He ordered them to lie down, and then returned to bed.

"What was it, Henry?"

"Oh, a wild dog prowling about, I think, but Growler and Lass have sooled him off."

Nothing more disturbed them during the night, but when Jones came out in the morning he saw a strange dog a little distance from the house. He called it, but the animal would not come any nearer. Mrs. Jones came out, and at once said, "Why, Henry, that's Fred Williams's dog, but he's afraid of Growler and Lass. Chain 'em up, and perhaps he'll come to us." Jones chained up his dogs, and then called "Rover! Rover!" The dog came up and suffered himself to be patted, but when they tried to coax him indoors he trotted away a few yards and then stood and wagged his tail.

Jones went up to him, and then the dog ran on, and again stopped. "Look here, Henry," said Mrs. Jones, "that dog wants something; you best follow him."

"Well, I believe he does, wife," and, so saying, Jones started after the dog.

When Rover saw that the farmer was coming he ran up to him and barked, and then ran on again towards the creek. Suddenly Rover disappeared around the trunk of a large gumtree. Then he came out again and barked, and then stood wagging his tail until Jones came up.

The farmer stopped, looked at the dog, and then, stooping down, he looked into the hollow trunk, and started as if he had been shot. "Well, I never see the like, 'pon my word," he exclaimed – for there lay a little nine months' old baby asleep.

"Blest if it' aint Williams's youngster. I wonder how in the world he got here; hanged if I don't believe Rover carried him here out of the fire." Jones lifted the baby out, and all glowing from his rosy sleep the cherub boy he kissed.

Then he tore home at a great pace, Rover quietly following.

"Maria! Maria!" he shouted when near the house, "blest if I ain't got Georgie Williams."

Mrs. Jones ran out in a great state of excitement, and exclaimed when she saw the child, "So it is, the darling little beauty. Oh you little sweet."

"I wonder how he got there, Henry?"

"Blest if I don't believe Rover carried him there; and look here, Maria, I'll bet that was Rover scratching at the door last night, but those wretched curs of ours drove him away."

"Yes, perhaps it was, Henry, but if Rover carried the baby all that way why didn't he bring him to the house?"

"Because he was afraid of our dogs."

"I'm blest if that dog ain't got more sense than a good many men. Rover, good dog, you're worth a bag of money, you are."

"Well, what are you going to do, Henry?"

"Well, I'll put Jess in the cart after breakfast and we'll go to Willunga and find out if Fred Williams was there yesterday. If he was we may be able to catch him."

Accordingly after breakfast Jones and his wife set out for Willunga, taking the baby and Rover with them. Upon their arrival there was great excitement, and Rover was caressed until he began to get savage at all the worry.

Jones found that Williams and his wife had left early in the morning for Adelaide so the landlord of the Bushman's Home insisted upon putting his horse in his Tilbury, and driving Jones, the baby, and Rover into Adelaide.

The rest is soon told. Next morning Williams and his wife were found on board the Royal Duke, and after Boniface had gently broken the news Jones appeared with the baby and Rover.

The story soon got abroad, and those on board will never forget the scene.

Mrs. Williams was hysterical with joy, while her husband hugged the dog as if he were the child.

Rover was the pet of the voyage, and Williams refused a large sum of money for him. "No," said he, "I'll never part with Rover as long as I live."

The day before Christmas Day the vessel reached port, and before parting with Rover the passengers and crew made him a present of a handsome brass collar suitably inscribed.

This all happened many years ago, and Fred Williams has long since finished with this life. Rover, too, has had his day, as every dog will, and what remains of him now occupies a prominent place in George Williams's drawing-room, where he serves as an object lesson to the children as each Christmas their father relates the wonderful story of how Rover saved him from the fire.